the dead of night

true crime junkies
book four

Christy Barritt

chapter
one

ZOE HAMLIN UNZIPPED THE TENT, stepped into the nighttime, and took a moment to breathe in the fresh air around her.

Alaska. Was there any purer, more beautiful place on earth?

Coming here had been on her bucket list since graduating from high school four years ago.

Finally, she'd talked two of her friends into taking the trip with her. Most of their money had gone to airfare. That meant primitive tent camping and meals over the campfire. She wouldn't have it any other way.

Her parents had warned her of the dangers before she came. Said that three twenty-two-year-old women traveling by themselves to the wilds of Alaska wasn't a good idea.

Of course Zoe wouldn't have come here to Salmon-by-the-Sea alone—there was safety in numbers.

She and her friends had taken all the necessary precautions. Besides, from what she'd heard, this was one of the safest towns around. That feeling she'd had earlier . . . the feeling of being watched. That had just been her imagination.

She brushed off the flash of worry that tried to creep into her thoughts.

Their site was at the back edge of the campground—just what she'd wanted. Trees of the Chugach Forest hugged the site, the mountains rising steeply on one side and dropping on the other. If she listened carefully, she could hear Talisman Creek, full of salmon, gurgling in the background before it flowed to the Eagle River and then to Resurrection Bay.

She smiled as she thought about the water.

Earlier today, Zoe had met a guy in town.

He was cute. *Really* cute.

The two of them had flirted a little. She planned on trying to find him again tomorrow.

Maybe a little fling while she was in Alaska could be fun.

Especially with Mr. Blue Eyes.

But right now, nature called.

She'd checked the time on her phone before climbing from her sleeping bag. Three-thirty a.m. The middle of the night, for sure. But she needed to run to the restroom and couldn't wait any longer.

Quietly, she zipped the tent back up. Her tentmates

were heavy sleepers and didn't even stir. She considered waking one of them to go with her but decided against it. She should let them get their rest.

Stretching, she scanned the dark campground, but everything was silent around her. All the other campers had retired from partying and gone to bed, probably in preparation for whatever activities tomorrow held.

For Zoe and her friends, that meant hiking. But a fishing trip just might be in the works. How could they come to a fishing town and not fish?

Before Zoe could head to the bathroom, a stick cracked in the forest behind her.

Her muscles tightened, and she quickly flipped on the flashlight she'd brought with her.

The beam scattered across the ground.

She'd been warned many times since arriving about the dangers of bears and moose in these mountains. There were signs everywhere, plus the campground employees had been sure to mention it.

Was one of those creatures out there right now watching her? Probably not a moose. They weren't hunters. They were mostly dangerous when people stumbled upon them.

But a bear . . .

Zoe's lungs suddenly felt as if they'd been filled with the small pebbles beneath her feet. She took a step back as her mind flitted.

If a wild animal came at her, she could dive into her tent.

But would a tent really do any good? Certainly, a bear with its long claws could slice right through the nylon fabric.

Doing so would also put her friends in danger, as Zoe and her friends were all sharing the one tent.

Zoe took a deep breath as she tried to calm herself. Why would a bear come after them here when salmon filled the riverbed so close by? There was plenty of food to eat around here without dining on people.

Could bears be rabid?

She had no clue—but she definitely needed to look that up.

Another crack sounded.

Zoe's thoughts rushed as she tried to make sense of what was happening.

Then she heard, "Help!"

Her lungs tightened.

Was someone calling for help? Or had she imagined the cry?

The voice had been so faint . . . it was hard to know for sure. Her imagination raced at full speed.

Then she heard it again, a little louder this time.

"Help!"

Zoe's heart pounded harder.

She hadn't imagined that.

The voice had sounded like . . . a little girl.

Was there a child in those woods? Was she wandering out there alone?

She remembered the eight-year-old girl she'd met earlier today. Aleut was here on a camping trip with her family.

When Zoe had run into Aleut, the girl had been racing around the campground with a stick in hand. Her mom and dad were nowhere to be seen.

Free-range parenting. That was what she'd later heard the girl's mom call it.

Zoe had grabbed the girl and pulled her out of the gravel street just as a truck full of rowdy college boys zoomed by. The girl's dark clothing had made her blend into the nighttime.

Was Aleut out there now?

Zoe shone her flashlight into the brush but saw nothing, no one.

Her throat tightened. What should she do?

Her cell phone didn't have a signal out here.

Should she run to the campground office and try to get help? Would anyone even be on duty this time of night?

Maybe she should wake up her friends and tell them what was going on.

But even if she did, what would Caitlin and Winnie do?

They weren't rugged outdoors people. They'd tell her to run to the office—which was a good half mile hike.

By then, this girl could have wandered farther away. With the cliffs in the area, that would be dangerous—especially since it was so dark outside.

"Please . . . help me! I need help now!" The girl's voice pitched higher with panic.

What was going on? What kind of trouble had Aleut found herself in?

Zoe could at least check out the situation. See if she could help the girl.

But Zoe's limbs trembled as she stepped toward the woods.

The mountains around her were vast, something to be both adored and feared.

And it was so dark.

So *terribly* dark. Even with her flashlight, the inky black felt overwhelming.

Around her, everyone remained silent. Asleep probably. She didn't even see any campfire stragglers or late-night partiers.

She swallowed hard before asking, "Where are you?"

Zoe's voice sounded strained, even to her own ears.

"Right here. My foot . . . it got stuck between two rocks. I can't get it out." The girl sniffled.

Aleut didn't sound as if she was far away. Zoe could assess the situation, try to move the rocks, free the girl, and then she would go back to sleep.

After she headed to the bathroom.

Still, fear caused her to hesitate.

Zoe shivered since the temperature had dropped into the forties. As she glanced up at the clear sky above, she sucked in a breath.

A meteor shower.

How beautiful.

But not now. Right now, she couldn't enjoy it.

She frowned and glanced back at the woods. "Tell me where your parents are, and I can go get them."

"No!" The word came out as a half cry. "Don't leave me out here. Please!"

Zoe nibbled on her lip before walking a few steps farther. She looked over her shoulder and still saw the tents. She wasn't in any danger.

A couple more steps wouldn't hurt.

"I'm coming," Zoe said. "Can you say something so I can know where you are?"

"I'm right here."

But why did the girl sound as if she were farther away right now?

Zoe took a few more steps, the beam of her flashlight bouncing in her hands. "I have to be almost to you. Keep talking."

There was no immediate answer.

This seemed more and more like a bad idea all the time.

Zoe simply wanted to help this girl and then go back to her tent. Then she could lie in her sleeping bag and daydream about how she could run into Mr. Perfect again tomorrow.

That was really all she wanted.

To dream about more adventures. Finding love. Experiencing life to the fullest.

She paused, trying to get a sense of where the girl was. "Hello?"

But there was still no answer.

"Where are you?" Zoe called as goosebumps popped up all over her skin. "Can you keep talking to me?"

Again, there was silence.

Had something happened to the girl?

Certainly, Zoe would have heard something if that were the case. Some rustling or the sound of an animal moving in for an attack.

Something.

Chills suddenly went up and down her spine.

She needed to get back to her campsite. She could wake up her friends, and they could decide what to do together.

Because the woods . . . they were closing in on her.

So was the darkness.

Zoe turned, ready to flee back to the tent.

Instead, she collided into something.

No, she collided into *someone.*

She gasped and drew back. As she did, the flashlight dropped from her hands.

She hadn't even heard anyone approach.

Her gaze darted to the person's face.

It wasn't a little girl standing there.

Or one of her friends.

No, it was a man. He wore some kind of wooden mask—it almost looked Native American or Aztec with its straight lines, painted cheeks, and scowling eyes.

Terror ripped through her.

She started to scream when something pricked her skin.

She reached for her neck and pulled out a needle. No, it was more of a dart. A small one.

Where had that come from?

Her head began to spin with wooziness. A rush of adrenaline followed.

Then fear unlike anything she'd ever known burst to life inside her.

Suddenly, the forest came alive around her. The trees were like skeletons, their bones arm-branches reaching for her. The rocks were like an army rising around her. The wind seemed laden with spirits from long ago—spirits bent on haunting her.

She let out a cry as terror consumed her.

"Where's Aleut?" Zoe's voice trembled as she tried to hold on to her senses.

It was no use.

The world around her was spinning.

She closed her eyes, trying to shut out the forest.

"You mean me?" The man's voice changed into that of a girl.

This had been a trick.

A trap.

Aleut was never out here.

Zoe's mind twisted and warped.

What was wrong with her? Why were her senses on overload right now?

She needed to run. To get away from this man.

As she took a step, she stumbled. Dizziness consumed her.

So did the ground. The earth opened beneath her as if a portal to the afterlife.

Yet she didn't sink.

How was that possible?

She looked back at the man.

His image blurred.

Until he pulled off his mask and smiled.

Zoe blanched as she recognized him.

Him? *He* was the one responsible?

No . . . how? Why?

More fear pulsed through her.

He slowly leaned toward her.

Then he whispered in her ear. "You've been chosen."

Chosen? What did that mean?

Was he playing some kind of sick, twisted game?

Zoe didn't know. But she had to try to get away.

She took a step back, ignoring the way the forest twisted.

Had something been in that needle?

The man stood between her and the campsite. That meant getting back to her friends would be nearly impossible.

Still, if she navigated the forest, maybe she could circle back around to the campground office and find help.

If her brain let that happen.

If the forest didn't attack her first.

Suddenly, ants crawled up her legs.

She wiped them away, desperate to get them off.

They bit her, stinging her.

Pain burst on her skin.

"You can run, but the chosen are always found."

Zoe had to get away. Had to move. Had to do something!

She took off through the dark Alaskan forest.

As she did, she prayed she'd survive this.

So she could have more adventures.

So she could find love.

So she could have more experiences . . . but not *this* kind of experience.

Oh, God, no . . . this wasn't the experience she wanted.

chapter
two

IF YOU WANT *answers about your past, come to Salmon-by-the-Sea.*

The message had been sent to Mariella Boucher from an untraceable email address. Attached to the email was an article about twins who had been kidnapped from this town twenty-four years ago.

Twenty-four years . . . that was how old she and her brother were.

Her *twin* brother.

Mariella hadn't shown Matthew the email. Not yet.

Instead, she'd feigned an excuse for coming to the quaint town—for research for a travel podcast.

Her real love was the true crime podcast she was a part of. But she had a decent following on *Take Me Away* also.

She paused as she stood on the docks of the seaside community, which was nestled on Alaska's Kenai Peninsula. The place was picture perfect—and ideal for her travel podcast.

As well as for her quest for answers about her past.

Her throat tightened at the thought.

Salmon-by-the-Sea was just south of Seward, bordered by Resurrection Bay on one side and the Chugach National Forest on the other. In every direction, her eyes feasted—from the sparkling water of the harbor to the snowcapped mountains rising up like a fortress to the almighty glaciers that reminded her of her small mark in the vastness of time.

For this trip, Mariella and Matthew had rented a cabin on the outskirts of town. The place was close enough they could walk to the quaint community, which was nestled on the harbor. Colorful buildings lined the water, and the docks stretched out in front of them like a custom-made Tetris puzzle embellished with boats and other watercraft.

Mariella had ventured out on her own while Matthew stayed in the cabin catching up on some work.

She'd told her brother she needed to take some pictures and find out information about the area. Really, she was searching for answers.

Answers about someone with potentially deep personal ties to her past.

After doing some research, she knew only one person might have the information she needed.

Mariella glanced over at the rows and rows of charter

fishing boats that bobbed in the water. Most of them had silly names—*Seas the Day, Aquaholic,* and *Fishy Business.*

As a moment of self-doubt hit her, she paused near a piling and pulled out her camera. She needed to take a few pictures, and doing so would be a good way to buy some time.

Maybe she shouldn't have this conversation. If she found the person she was looking for, what would she say?

Hello, I heard that twenty-four years ago your newborn twins were kidnapped. Can I ask you some questions about that?

It was brash, and she didn't want to give anyone false hope—including herself.

Just take a picture, Mariella. Pictures always make everything better.

As she tried to frame a shot of the boats, mountains, and water, a family with two teenage boys climbed from a nearby fishing boat and started toward town loaded with coolers, jackets, and exuberant smiles.

Mariella remained where she was, deciding to take a quick selfie as she waited for them to pass.

Turning, she lined up her face in the frame.

As she snapped the shot, the two teenagers burst into a run and raced toward town.

Mariella stepped back, trying to get out of their way.

But as they darted by, one of their shoulders rammed into her—hard.

Mariella sucked in a breath and reached for something to steady herself.

There was nothing.

Instead, she tipped backward, losing her balance.

She grasped at the air, desperate for something to keep her upright.

But it was no use.

Everything happened at once.

She tumbled toward the water.

Her head hit the piling.

Pain shot through her temple.

Then water consumed her.

Numbing cold dissolved her breath.

A curtain of blackness began to close as unconsciousness claimed her.

Jason Somersby paused as he stood on his father's fishing boat with the sun pelting him from high in the sky. Above him, the sound of a helicopter chopped briskly through the air.

He squinted.

That looked like a search and rescue copter. Had another hiker gotten lost? That seemed to happen around here at least once a week in the summer.

He prayed that whatever had happened, everyone was

safe. These mighty mountains and unforgiving landscape were nothing to be messed with.

He continued coiling a rope around his elbow and hand.

Today's charter fishing trip had been a success, but there was still more work to do inside the cabin before he and Pops could call it a day.

He hated to disappear below deck, especially when he could stand outside and admire the woman standing on the pier not far away instead. She'd caught his attention a few minutes ago, and he'd had to drag his eyes away.

She was gorgeous, with wavy blonde hair that flowed well past her shoulders. She wore a pink sweatshirt, jeans, and rainboots as she snapped a selfie.

Honestly, the woman was hard not to notice.

But Jason needed to finish stowing everything away.

Reluctantly, he stepped onto the boat, putting the thought of the woman out of his mind.

Nearly as soon as he looked away, a sound caught his ear.

Had that been a splash?

He looked up and saw the Peterson brothers from the charter fishing trip staring at the water. Those two had been roughhousing all day.

What had they gotten into now?

They stood on the edge of the pier, frozen in place. Their parents were a good ten feet behind them and had paused to stare in confusion.

The frantic motions of the teens made it clear that *something* had happened.

And the beautiful blonde was now nowhere to be seen.

Jason sucked in a breath.

No . . .

He jumped off the boat and sprinted across the boat slip. His gaze searched the water as he raced toward the Petersons.

Ripples spread as if something had fallen in.

"We didn't see her standing there," Billy, the older of the teenagers said, panic in his voice.

The water here was fifteen feet deep. And cold.

If the woman in pink had gone under . . .

Jason tore off his boat shoes and dove into the bay.

Moving quickly, he opened his eyes. The water was clear enough to see several feet in front of him.

He spotted her.

Floating lifelessly in the clear blue of the bay.

Jason propelled himself toward her and wrapped an arm around her waist. Using his other arm, he thrust them toward the surface.

As soon as his head broke the waterline, he sucked in a deep breath.

The two brothers still stood there, along with their parents and Jason's father.

Jason kicked his legs, determined to keep them both

afloat, despite the fact she was dead weight. "Help me haul her in!"

The brothers dropped onto their bellies to help hoist her up while Jason's dad knelt between them.

As the brothers grabbed the woman's arms, his dad lifted her onto the pier.

The woman sprawled against the wooden planks.

Unmoving.

Still lifeless.

Jason held his breath.

The next moment, she flipped to her side and began furiously coughing up water.

Relief filled him.

She should be okay.

But she wasn't out of the woods yet.

He launched himself onto the dock. Water dripping off him, he crawled toward her.

"Someone go get some blankets!" Jason commanded. "There are some on the boat."

"I'll get them!" His dad took off.

Jason knelt over the woman and murmured, "You're going to be okay."

The woman tried to push herself upright but ended up in another coughing fit instead. She dropped back on her elbow and finally drew in a ragged breath.

Jason studied the woman.

She was still lucid. That was a good sign. But she appeared stunned with her pale skin and listless motions.

His dad returned surprisingly fast, two wool blankets in hand.

Jason forgot about the trembles raking through his own body. Instead, he wrapped both blankets around her.

They had to get her warm.

"Should we call 911?" Mrs. Peterson wrung her hands nervously as she watched the scene.

"I'm . . . I'm fine." The woman's voice sounded strained as she said the words. Her hair clung to her face and her clothes to her skin. Her teeth chattered uncontrollably. "I just . . . need to . . . get warm."

"We should take you to the clinic," Jason said.

"No! No doctors." Her words came out harder, more adamant. "I'm fine."

Jason didn't push her.

Instead, he said, "Let's get you into the cabin of *Fishful Thinking*. It's warmer there, and we have some leftover hot chocolate."

"What can we do?" Mr. Peterson stepped closer, his gaze clouded with worry.

"We're good," Jason said. "Pops and I can take over from here."

The Petersons all stared at him a moment before nodding and reluctantly stepping back.

Without asking permission, Jason swept the woman into his arms and carried her to his father's offshore fishing boat. Working quickly, he took her below the deck into the cabin, where he gently set her on her feet.

"I'm going to get you some dry clothes to change into," he explained.

She nodded, still looking dazed and confused.

"I'll grab that hot chocolate," Pops said. "It's still upstairs."

"Thanks."

Jason grabbed a change of clothes he kept on the boat. He always had extra clothing onboard, just in case.

He handed the items to the woman and then pointed to a small stateroom on the other side of the glossy wood door with its rounded edges. "You can change in there. You need to get out of those wet clothes before you get sick."

The woman looked up at him, her crystal-blue eyes uncertain.

"It's okay," Jason reassured her. "You're safe with us."

Then she nodded and slipped into the room.

While she did that, Jason quickly changed out of his own wet clothes.

Performing a rescue was one of the last things he'd expected to do today.

Especially since he'd been trying to rescue himself for the past five years—with no success.

Could he find redemption for something he didn't do?

The more he thought about it, the more certain he was that the answer was no.

chapter
three

MARIELLA STEPPED out of the small stateroom, the sweats and sweatshirt she wore overwhelming her body. But they were warm, dry, and smelled slightly of coconut sunscreen—a pleasing aroma.

She glanced at the man who'd rescued her as he paused near the door. He'd also changed, though he filled out his new clothes much better.

The man had to be close to her age or maybe a few years older.

With his startling blue eyes, thick lashes, and dark hair, she could hardly look away. Instead, the two of them simply stared at each other wordlessly.

Then the other man—the one who looked like an older version of her rescuer—stepped into the cabin with two mugs in his hands.

The spell between her and her rescuer was broken.

As it should be.

Mariella hadn't found herself attracted to anyone since Mark Scott—and *that* had been an utter disaster. He'd used her and then stabbed her in the back for all the world to see.

She shook off the memories of her humiliation.

She'd learned some powerful—and painful—lessons through the experience.

"Drink this." The older man handed her a *1999 Kenai River Classic* coffee mug filled with hot chocolate.

She thanked him before taking a sip. The warm, creamy drink tasted good, comforting.

"That was a close one, huh?" the man who'd saved her murmured.

Mariella quickly looked away, knowing how strange she must appear to be staring at him like she did.

She cleared her throat. "Thank you for jumping in to help me. I don't know what happened. I think I hit my head and went into shock."

"How *is* your head?" He squinted as he studied her face.

She touched her forehead and tried not to flinch at the tenderness. "It's fine. There's barely a knot."

That answer didn't seem to satisfy him as he narrowed his eyes. "You should keep an eye on it. Concussions are nothing to play with."

"No, they're not."

He shifted, appearing as if he wanted to argue, but he didn't. Instead, he said, "I'm Jason, by the way."

"I'm Mariella."

"Well, Mariella, it's nice to meet you." He offered an apologetic smile. "I'm sorry it had to be this way."

"Me too." A smile tugged at the corner of her lips.

"Why don't you sit for a second while you finish drinking?" He nodded toward a small olive-green couch.

Mariella settled onto the stiff cushions, grateful for a place to get warm. Despite the dry clothes, her wet hair made everything feel chillier.

Jason found another blanket and wrapped it around her shoulders as she sipped on her hot chocolate.

She glanced around. The tight but cozy space smelled faintly of fish. It was just big enough for this small couch, a mini fridge, and a two-seater table with a bowl of pistachios on it. But she would bet this room could tell some stories—some big fish stories.

The thought made her want to smile.

"If you've got this handled down here, I'm going to keep cleaning up on the deck," the other man said, nodding above him.

"I've got this, Pops."

The man nodded before disappearing upstairs.

Mariella studied Jason after Pops was gone. "Is that your dad?"

"It is." Jason nodded slowly. "He owns a charter fishing business, and I help him out on his trips."

"That sounds like a nice life."

Something clouded his gaze. "Yeah, I guess you could say that."

Jason wasn't telling the whole truth with those words. Something about his "nice life" made him uncomfortable. Mariella's curiosity swelled.

She didn't know Jason well enough to ask details. Besides, he didn't owe her any explanations. He'd already done enough.

"What brings you to town, Mariella?" He studied her.

Jason was probably talking to her in order to pass time so he could assess her physical state. But for some weird reason, it felt like much more than that. It was strange . . . but Mariella felt as if she'd known this guy much longer.

She cleared her throat again. "I have a podcast that features the best places to travel. I've been focusing on Alaska, so I'm here to cover Salmon-by-the-Sea."

His eyebrows shot up, and a new light danced in his eyes. "You mean the *Take Me Away* podcast?"

Delight filled her, oozing through her blood. "Wait . . . you've listened to it?"

"I was just listening to it this morning before we went out for our charter trip, actually. I really enjoyed your take on Girdwood."

"I'm so glad to hear that. It was a fun town to visit."

"I'm glad you'll live another day to do another travel post on your social media." He offered that movie-star-worthy smile again.

The two of them exchanged a look, and Mariella felt herself blush.

She hadn't blushed since she was a preteen. What was up with that? Maybe she'd never been so instantly attracted to someone either.

Or maybe all her senses were heightened because of the fact she could have died earlier.

That was probably it.

Suddenly unsure what to do with her thoughts and feelings, Mariella cleared her throat, set her mug down on the table, and stood. "Well, I've taken up enough of your time. I should get going."

He stood also. "Don't feel like you have to rush."

She glanced down at the sweats and sweatshirt she wore. "What should I do about these?"

"If you have a chance to return them sometime before you leave town, you know where to find me. I'm usually here on the boat. Otherwise, it's really not a big deal." He grabbed a plastic bag where he'd placed her wet clothes. "Would you mind if I walked you back to land? Just to make sure there are no more runaway teenage boys with a death wish barreling down the pier?"

Mariella's cheeks heated again for no apparent reason.

Except for the fact she liked the idea of spending more time with Jason.

She couldn't let herself get distracted. She'd come here for a reason—to find Bright Armstrong and ask him some questions.

Still, romance seemed a lot more fun.

She smiled softly at him before saying, "Yes, that would be great."

Then she reminded herself that even the most idyllic things—whether it be a town or a person—could have its secrets.

Dark, dirty secrets.

Her throat tightened at the thought.

Something about Mariella intrigued Jason.

He couldn't put his finger on exactly what.

The two of them hadn't exactly had a riveting conversation, though their talk hadn't been a bore either.

But still . . . something about this woman made Jason want to get to know her more. That would be treading dangerous territory. If he was smart, he'd remember the vow he'd made to himself to stay single . . . forever.

It wasn't often he was tempted to forsake that promise.

Mariella, however, was a temptation he hadn't expected.

He stepped off the boat then offered his hand. As her fingers clutched his, a jolt of electricity zapped him.

Jason shoved the feeling down. He wasn't looking for a girlfriend. He didn't want a fleeting summertime fling either.

He wasn't looking for romance at all, for that matter.

That was why his feelings right now caused the start of a headache.

As soon as Mariella stood steady on the dock, he released her hand and began to walk beside her. He watched her to make sure she didn't wobble on the relatively narrow boat slip.

The sun hit Mariella's hair as they strolled across the wood planks. Earlier, she'd been wearing pink—a cheerful color. Now, she wore gray.

Jason liked the pink better on her. It fit her cheery personality.

Overhead, that helicopter still lingered near the mountains.

He frowned. Something bad had definitely happened.

He lifted a quick prayer for the situation.

"I suppose my camera is lost . . ." Mariella glanced at the water and frowned.

He followed her gaze and nodded. "I'm sorry. At this point, I doubt retrieving it is worth it."

"Most definitely not. At least I have a decent camera on my phone." She slowed her steps. "I checked for it when I changed—unbelievably, my cell stayed in my pocket, *and* it still works."

"That's good news, at least."

She slowed her steps a moment and glanced back at another boat before looking at Jason again. "Say . . . weird question, but do you by chance know a man named Bright Armstrong?"

Instantly, Jason felt his gaze darken. "I do. Why are you asking about him?"

Mariella's eyebrows shot up, then she quickly recovered and shrugged. "I thought about interviewing him for the podcast."

"There are far better people you could interview."

She nodded too quickly. "Noted."

Maybe Jason shouldn't have had such a hard reaction. But how could he not?

Bright Armstrong was a terrible man—schmoozy and charming when he wanted to be, but selfish and demeaning when he let his guard down.

The man did whatever he could to make Jason and his dad look bad—all so he could drum up more business for himself. But Jason should have kept his emotions private. After all, Mariella didn't know all those details.

A few moments of silence passed.

"How long are you in town?" Jason knew a change of subject would be good.

"At least a week."

"I hope the rest of your stay goes better than today. I think you're going to find a lot of really amazing things about this place." As Jason said the words, they caught in his throat.

Deep inside, he knew that Salmon-by-the-Sea was great.

But even though he was born here, he was an outcast.

The only people who talked to him anymore were tourists—tourists who didn't know his story.

Most locals pretended as if he didn't exist.

In return, he tried to pretend their attitudes didn't bother him, but they did.

"Any places you might recommend I visit while I'm in town?" Mariella glanced up at him, some of the warmth returning to her gaze.

"Oh, for sure. If you want the best pizza in the state, try The Moose's Caboose. And if you want some decent food with a good atmosphere you'll definitely want to eat at Bottom Feeders. Those are two of the best."

"I should take you to one of those places as my way of saying thanks for saving my life," Mariella said, a flirty yet grateful tone to her voice.

Tempting but . . . "You don't have to do that."

"I'd like to."

Jason shook his head. "It's not necessary."

A frown—one of rejection—tugged at her lips.

He wanted to explain himself, but he resisted. It was better this way. There was no need to lead her on.

They reached the end of the pier, successfully not falling in. But Jason still found himself walking beside Mariella.

She didn't argue. He told himself he wanted to stick close in case she had any ill effects from falling into the water.

But he knew there was more to it than that. It seemed as if there was something more to their chance meeting.

As they walked, he glanced up and saw several locals staring his way.

Like they always did.

He was used to it by now, but that didn't mean he liked it.

Just as they rounded the corner, he spotted a group of tourists gathered near Bottom Feeders. As he and Mariella skirted around them, their conversation caught his ear.

"Another woman is missing from the campground," one of the men said. "Just like five years ago. Happened in the dead of night."

Jason's steps slowed as everything around him faded.

Another woman was missing from the campground? Had he heard correctly?

He knew he had.

That fateful day that had changed his life replayed itself in his mind.

The day that Hannah Bentley, the love of Jason's life, had been camping . . . and was brutally murdered by a maniac who still roamed free.

MARIELLA SUCKED IN A BREATH.

A woman had disappeared from a local campground?

Based on the way the man said the words, there was more to the story.

She started to ask Jason about it.

But when she glanced at him, his face looked strangely pale.

Why the strong reaction? There clearly was more to this story.

The questions circled in her head.

Before she could ask any of them, Jason took her elbow, led her down the store-lined sidewalk, and proclaimed, "We should get you back to wherever you're staying."

She started to argue.

Before she could, a man darted from an alleyway

between two stores. The guy was large with a long beard, plaid flannel shirt, and a scowl.

And he planted himself directly in front of them.

The man glanced at Mariella before glaring at Jason. "If you're smart, walk away from him and never look back."

An ominous tone filled the man's words.

What a strange thing to say.

Mariella waited for Jason to retort. To defend himself.

To explain.

But he didn't.

Instead, he kept a hand on her arm, skirted around the man, and continued walking.

However, a new tension stretched between them now.

Something had shifted.

Jason's steps were more urgent. He scanned everything around them. His breaths came faster and weren't as deep.

All while his face remained pale.

The man who'd given her the warning caught up with them again. Stepped directly in front of Jason, his hands on his hips.

Jason had no choice but to stop.

Mariella's heart raced.

What was happening right now?

The man practically growled as he stood there.

She glanced at Jason. Saw his jaw had hardened. His lips were pinched. His eyes had narrowed.

Then the man demanded, "What did you do with her?"

Mariella's lungs froze.

Was this man talking about the woman missing from the campground?

If so, why would this guy confront Jason about it?

Did he think Jason had something to do with the disappearance?

No, that couldn't be right . . . could it?

A tremble overtook her at the thought.

Jason's blood felt like gasoline that had ignited.

He stared at Crusher Sullivan, not wanting to make a scene.

But it was too late.

Jason already noticed several people on the sidewalk stopping to see what the commotion was about.

Mostly tourists with no idea what was going on.

Then there was Mariella.

Although Jason hardly knew the woman, he hated for this to be part of her first impression of him.

Any chance he had of getting to know her more disappeared like whales in the winter.

Jason drew himself up to full height, all six foot two inches. "I didn't have anything to do with whatever happened to her."

But Crusher, town drunk and troublemaker, remained unmoving, hands still splayed on his hips and his broad chest forming a blockade.

Jason didn't want to deal with this. He'd only wanted to walk with Mariella a little farther. Then he'd planned on going back home to get some rest before the next charter fishing trip tomorrow.

"I said, 'Where is she?'" Crusher growled as he hulked in front of them.

The fire racing through Jason's blood turned to a blaze. "I don't know where she is."

"You're lying." The man punched his finger into Jason's chest.

Jason bristled. He had to use every ounce of his self-control not to snap back.

"I'm not lying. Now, if you'll excuse me." Jason started to walk around Crusher again when the man thrust his shoulder out to block him.

Jason drew in a deep breath to compose himself. Getting into a public brawl wouldn't do anything for his already tarnished image.

Instead, he took Mariella's arm and led her around Crusher.

Thankfully, the man didn't try to stop him again.

He let Jason walk away with Mariella.

But Jason's thoughts raced.

He hated to think that another woman had gone missing from a local campground.

But he had *nothing* to do with it.

However, he wasn't sure anyone here in town would believe him.

"Jason . . . what was that about?" Mariella glanced up at him as they rushed along the sidewalk amid the stares of strangers.

Again, thoughts raced through his mind. Thoughts about what he might tell her to explain what had happened.

But no words could make this situation right or even mildly pleasant.

"It's this way." Mariella pointed to a cluster of rental cabins on the outskirts of town.

She led Jason up to one of them and stopped on the front porch.

Her question haunted his thoughts. *What was that about?*

How did he even answer that?

As soon as he tried to explain, everything about Mariella's countenance would change. He'd never see that same warm look in her eyes again. A look that made him feel hopeful.

Throat burning, he stepped back and shrugged. "It's nothing. But if you want people here in town to give quotes for your travel podcast . . . you should stay far away from me."

Then he turned and walked away.

chapter
five

MARIELLA WATCHED AS JASON DISAPPEARED, wondering if she could call him back.

Wondering what his words meant.

Wondering about . . . everything.

With a frown, she slipped inside her rental and closed the door.

Still stunned, she stood at the entrance a moment. Her thoughts flitted all over the place as she tried to make sense of things.

"Mariella?"

She just then noticed Matthew sitting at the small dining room table, his laptop in front of him, along with some coffee, a bowl of popcorn, and numerous papers.

The two of them shared the same blond hair, blue eyes, and pert features.

But where Mariella was social and extroverted, computer guru Matthew was quieter and introverted. She was the on-air personality while Matthew ran the technical side of things. The two of them made a good team.

When they were fourteen, Matthew had been diagnosed with leukemia. While their parents were both busy with their jet-setting lifestyles, Mariella and her brother had mostly been under the care of nannies from when they were in diapers until their teen years. In many ways, they'd had only each other.

Sure, their parents took them on extravagant vacations once a year. Took pictures on the major holidays. Said glowing things about them as they were showed off at parties.

But that was the extent of their relationship. Mariella and Matthew had been more like a possession their parents had checked off their list of "What a perfect life looked like" than anything else.

Matthew's cancer had made Mariella feel as if she might lose her whole world.

But she hadn't.

After several grueling years, her brother was okay.

But ever since then, she'd hated both hospitals and doctors, and she'd been protective of her younger-by-fifteen-minutes brother. It was one of the reasons she hadn't wanted Jason to take her to the clinic. She told herself her head would be fine.

At the thought, it throbbed.

"Why do you look so shaken?" Matthew looked her up and down as if confused. "And what are you wearing?"

She glanced at her oversized sweatpants and sweat-shirt, catching a glimpse of her damp tendrils as she leaned down. She was sure she was a sight to behold.

"The weirdest thing just happened." She leaned against the door, her thoughts still racing.

Matthew poured her a cup of coffee and handed it to her. Then they sat on the couch a comfortable distance from each other.

Mariella told her brother about getting knocked into the water and being rescued and then about the confrontation the stranger had with Jason as they walked here.

"So let me get this straight." Matthew crossed his arms. "A woman went missing from a local campground last night, and the guy who rescued you was confronted on the street and asked what he did with her? That's disturbing."

Mariella frowned. When he put it that way . . . she supposed it was.

She let out a deep sigh. "I agree. It was disturbing. But the thing is, this guy didn't give me any bad vibes at all . . ."

Matthew gave her a sideways glance. "Just because he didn't give you bad vibes doesn't mean he's a nice guy."

She hugged her cup of coffee with her fingers. When she'd been a beauty podcaster, she'd always started her broadcasts with coffee, what she called nectar of the gods. "I know. But I just can't mesh those two images in my mind. A criminal and a rescuer? Not a normal combination."

"A lot of psychopaths seem nice on the outside. Remember Ted Bundy?" Matthew appeared unconvinced as his lips flickered downward in a frown. "Do you know his last name?"

"No. But his first name is Jason, and his boat is *Fishful Thinking*."

Matthew grabbed his laptop, sat down on the couch with it, and tapped a few things on the keyboard before muttering, "His full name is Jason Somersby."

"That was fast." Mariella's eyebrows shot up in surprise.

She shouldn't be shocked. Matthew could find anything with a computer and the internet. He was amazing like that.

Matthew shrugged and blew on his fingers in mock pride. "What can I say? I'm the web wizard."

No one would argue about that.

"Now, let's see what else I can find out about this guy." He turned back to his computer and pushed his glasses up higher.

He wasn't wearing them as much lately—he'd switched to contacts. Something about him was changing, and Mariella was happy to see her brother coming out of his shell. For the longest time, he'd lived in fear that his cancer would return, even though he'd been in remission for four years now.

Mariella supposed surviving cancer made some people take life by the horns as they got a second chance. But for Matthew, he was constantly waiting for the next shoe to drop.

She held her breath. Part of her didn't want to know the gory details about Jason.

She wanted to believe the man with the beautiful eyes and great smile who'd rescued her today was a hero who'd stepped out of her mind under the "perfect man" folder she had stored there.

But she knew the situation would be entirely more complicated than that.

People were rarely as simple as they seemed.

Including her.

That was why she feared she and her brother had actually been kidnapped from a family here in Salmon-by-the-Sea.

And she was determined to find some answers.

Jason started toward his house but veered off course.

He had left his wallet on the boat, so he wanted to swing by to grab it.

He knew all the back ways through town. They were his preferred method of travel.

He hated feeling like riffraff who needed to sneak around. It wasn't that he feared being seen. Sometimes it was just easier to stay in the shadows. Besides, he didn't need any more confrontations today.

He managed to get back to the dock without being cornered again. That was something to be thankful for.

As he walked toward the boat, his thoughts kept circling back to the fact that a woman was missing from the campground.

When he'd initially heard that helicopter, he'd assumed a visitor had gotten lost. That happened pretty frequently.

But some of the details of this disappearance seemed eerily familiar.

A woman at the campground had gone missing during the dead of night.

His heart thumped harder.

Maybe that was where the similarities between this case and Hannah's ended. Jason didn't know.

Part of him wanted more information.

The other part wanted to stay as far away from this as possible.

He paused on the dock as he saw someone step onto the deck of a nearby boat.

Bright Armstrong.

Jason's gaze narrowed.

The man rubbed him the wrong way.

Sure, he knew the guy had a hard life with multiple tragedies.

But those misfortunes didn't excuse the man's actions.

Why was Mariella asking about Bright? Was she mixed up with him somehow? Jason hadn't asked. Maybe he didn't want to know. But that was just one more reason to stay away from her.

Jason couldn't help but think that there was more to Bright's story.

More to his charter fishing business, for that matter.

The man had recently bought a new house on the water, one double the size of his old house and quadruple the price due to the location.

Was his business really doing *that* well?

Or was there more going on with Bright than he let on?

A few weeks ago, Jason had caught Bright out here on the docks talking to a man wearing all black. Their tones had been hushed, and Jason didn't recognize the guy with him.

Instantly, Jason's suspicions had risen.

These waters were perfect for transporting things without being seen.

Now Jason had to wonder if Bright was up to something.

Jason paused, leaning down to tie his shoes and keeping his head low so he wouldn't be as easily seen.

But Bright remained in his view.

The man glanced around as if looking for anyone who might be watching.

Then he grabbed a black bag from the boat and tossed it overboard.

No, not overboard.

Jason looked closer. A smaller boat had pulled up beside Bright's larger one.

Jason narrowed his eyes as he watched the other boat quickly pull away.

Something suspicious was definitely going on with this guy.

The question was . . . what?

chapter
six

SEVERAL MINUTES PASSED as Matthew researched Jason.

Mariella sipped on her coffee and waited, halfway dreading whatever he might find out.

Couldn't she just keep Jason as the perfect man in her mind for a little while longer?

"Oh, okay . . . here we go." Matthew stared at the screen before letting out a grunt and leaning back in his chair. "You know how to pick them, Sis."

Mariella heard the subtle dig to his words.

Yes, her last boyfriend had been a disaster. Actually, disaster was an understatement. He had been a greedy, malicious pig—and that was putting it nicely.

But Mariella hadn't been in the best place in her life. She'd gotten caught up in a crowd that craved attention and lived to party. She'd thought that was what she wanted for a time too.

She'd turned into someone she wasn't. Matthew was her only anchor to sanity—and her only true friend—during that time.

It had taken Mariella hitting rock bottom before she'd found herself again. The whole process had required leaving California. She'd come to Alaska for part of a travel series she was doing, but she'd ended up finding so much more.

She'd never imagined she would like the cold weather. The short winter days. The total absence of any glitz or glamour like she'd experienced back in California.

But somehow, America's last frontier felt like home.

As did the people she'd met. Even though they'd started out as strangers, they'd come together to form *The Round Table*, a true crime podcast.

So far, they'd solved three cases, which far exceeded her expectations. When they'd started, Mariella had thought they might uncover a few clues to help authorities find answers to the cases they were looking into. But never in her wildest dreams did she think they'd actually catch a killer.

Or three.

Between those larger, more intensive investigations, Mariella covered smaller cold cases for supplemental episodes. It kept her and Matthew occupied and kept the podcast listeners tuned in. Mostly, she brought cases to the public's attention in order to prod people who might know something to come forward.

Mariella wasn't exactly the feet-on-the-ground type of investigator. No, she was more the research-online type.

Which had worked well for her.

Duke McAllister, Andi Slade, and Ranger Garrett were more skilled at the riskier aspects of investigating. The sixth member, Simmy Samuels, worked in more of a support position. She was the glue that held them together with her sweet, nurturing spirit.

Together, they were strong and made a good team.

She and her new friends didn't always see eye to eye on everything. No, they were all vastly different.

But something about the Arctic Circle Murder Club —that was what Mariella had named them—was special. She hoped she wasn't the only one who thought so.

Because sometimes the whole arrangement felt on the verge of collapse.

Mariella wasn't sure if she felt that way because it was reality or if it was because she always felt like good things were on the brink of disappearing.

She supposed the truth was yet to be seen.

She glanced back at her brother again, still unsure if she wanted to hear what else he had to say.

One way or another, she needed to find out what he'd discovered. The way Jason had left things when he walked her to the cabin made it seem as if he wouldn't be reaching out to her again.

As quickly as their bond had formed, it had been broken.

The sooner Mariella accepted that fact, the better.

"So get this. Five years ago, another woman went missing from a campground," Matthew read from the computer. "Two days later, she was found dead."

Mariella sucked in a breath. "How did she die?"

He swallowed hard. "There was an arrow through her heart."

"What?" Mariella's voice came out at a high pitch.

"It's true. She was found at the bottom of a cliff. The theory is that she was being chased, was shot, and then fell."

"That's terrible."

Matthew continued to study the screen. "It is. The police never caught the person responsible, but Jason was the prime suspect."

Mariella's lungs grew even tighter. "Why?"

"The two of them were dating, and they were at the campground together. They had a fight and . . . I guess he made the most sense to people. It's always the boyfriend, right?"

Mariella rubbed her arms, suddenly chilled. "I hope they find this new girl who's missing . . . alive."

"Me too. Do you still think this Jason guy is innocent?" Matthew studied her unapologetically.

She knew her brother earnestly wanted to know what she thought.

But she had no idea how to answer that question.

Before she could think about it longer, a strange noise sounded outside.

She and Matthew looked at each other, wrinkles forming on each of their brows.

What *was* that sound? She'd heard it somewhere before, though she couldn't place it now.

With a touch of hesitation, she paced toward the window.

But she couldn't bring herself to look outside.

Then she heard it again. It almost sounded like . . . someone blowing through a conch shell. She recognized the sound from a trip she'd taken to Hawaii a couple of years ago.

But . . . why would someone be in the woods playing a conch shell?

A shiver raced through her.

Maybe Salmon-by-the-Sea wasn't as safe as she'd assumed.

In fact, this whole town was beginning to feel haunted.

Several minutes passed as Mariella stood by the window listening. She had to remind herself to breathe, to swallow even.

The eerie sound of the conch shell continued to float through the air.

The noise was followed by what sounded like an owl hooting and then screeching.

She shivered, something about the cacophony unsettling . . . and unnatural.

"What should we do?" Concern tugged at Matthew's eyes and lips.

"I have no idea." She stepped back from the window. "I mean, I guess it isn't a crime to make noises outside someone's cabin."

"But it sounds like this person is close—really close."

Mariella rubbed her arms. "Again, spooky but not a crime, right? Maybe someone's doing some type of ritual. Are there Native Americans in this area?"

He shrugged. "Honestly, I don't know."

A few minutes later, the sounds faded.

Mariella glanced out the window one more time, hoping for a glimpse of whatever those noises had been. She wanted an explanation that would make her feel better, that would clarify everything.

But she saw nothing.

Only the beautiful wilderness out her back door.

What had that been about?

Was it something to be concerned with?

She wasn't sure.

But so far, nothing about this trip had worked out the way she wanted.

And her original reason for coming—to talk to Bright Armstrong—wasn't even a blip on the horizon.

chapter
seven

TLATOANI WAS ONE WHO SPEAKS, the ruler and owner of land.

He required sacrifices.

Human sacrifices.

He always made it clear whom he'd chosen for the honor.

Unless those sacrifices were made, great tragedy would befall all those around.

Including me.

And I didn't want any more tragedy in my life.

Hadn't I had enough?

I stood in the woods and placed my instruments back in my backpack.

To anyone watching, I appeared normal. An everyday man out for a short jaunt through the beautiful wilderness.

No one knew how I was one with nature or how the

earth spoke to me. If they knew, they wouldn't understand.

So it was better if I blended in.

Better if I cared for this community behind the scenes.

If I protected this land on my own terms, just as Tlatoani instructed.

My ancestors had been hunters.

They'd lit fires while trappers beat drums, blew conch shells, hissed, and uttered cries. Then the hunted prey would flee in fear—and run right toward my people. Trapped as my ancestors surrounded the prey, tightening their circle.

Then they would kill the prey with arrows.

That was what I did, except I was only one person. Working alone was more difficult.

But I knew Tlatoani—as well as Huītzilōpōchtli—was pleased with my work.

I was honored to be the chosen one.

After my sacrifice last night, maybe this would all be over.

Things would return to normal.

The ransom had been paid.

But then why did I feel unrest? Like Tlatoani wanted more of me?

My chest tightened.

It didn't make sense.

I found a fallen tree in the woods and leaned against it.

After searching through my backpack, I found what I needed and lit some incense.

Then I cried out to Tlatoani.

I asked him for answers, for clear direction.

Nothing.

I asked again.

Then waited.

That was when I felt the slight tremor beneath me.

It was a sign.

Tlatoani's response.

Evil was still descending on this land.

I could feel it in my blood.

And I had to do whatever needed to stop him.

That meant another sacrifice was necessary.

I glanced at the sky. "Show me whom you desire."

As I whispered the words, I began to walk.

I was headed toward the campground, I realized.

It wasn't just the campground.

It was sacred ground, the place where generations before gathered to worship.

I'd do whatever it took to save this land.

Even if people misunderstood my good deeds.

Even if they thought what happened was terrible.

I was doing this for the town's own good . . . even if no one understood.

eight

AS MARIELLA SAT at the table still thinking about Jason and Bright and her to-do list for while she was here, Matthew suddenly sat up straighter across from her.

"Get this. I just checked the town's social media." His voice held a new zing. "They're looking for volunteers for a search party to walk through the woods and look for the missing woman. Her name is Zoe."

"Wait . . . really?" Mariella sucked in a breath. "I want to help."

Matthew's features pinched in clear skepticism. "I'm not sure that's a good idea."

"I know I'm not much of an investigator. But I want to help, and this is the perfect way to do so, to prove myself."

He gave her a pointed look. "You're supposed to be gathering information for your travel podcast."

"I know, and I'll still do that. But why not do this

also?" She gave the look right back to her brother, not backing down. Once she got something in her head, it was usually impossible to change her mind.

Matthew should know that all too well.

He stared at her another moment before nodding slowly. "Sure, if that's what you want. Why not? It's not a trip with my sister without some adventure."

Her pulse kicked up a notch. One obstacle overcome.

She was certain there would be more.

But she'd take them one at a time.

"Wait . . . when are they meeting?" Mariella leaned closer to the computer.

He glanced at his screen. "In twenty minutes."

"Perfect. I'll get changed. You want to come too?"

"Well, I'm not sending you out there alone." Matthew stood and stretched, his thin body and lean muscles extending outward.

"I won't be alone. It's a search party."

Matthew ignored her comment and glanced down at his outfit. "I guess sweats and flip-flops won't work."

"Probably not."

Just as she stepped toward her bedroom, a tremble shook the cabin.

She grabbed the wall.

A tremor? Was this an earthquake?

"We're in an area where there's always seismic activity." Matthew seemed to read her thoughts. "In fact, this state has the most seismic activity of any state, and the earthquake that hit Anchorage back in 1964 was the largest, most devastating in the history of the United States. I think it registered 9.2 on the Richter scale. Do you know how crazy that is?"

"You're not making me feel better . . ."

"You should look up pictures from the area afterward. It was just plain crazy. It took the city years to recover."

"Still not feeling better . . ."

Matthew shrugged. "What you're feeling now is probably nothing to worry about. I've felt tremors up in Fairbanks before also, and nothing happened with them."

She remained frozen.

But her brother was right.

Everything went still, almost as if the earlier shaking hadn't happened.

She was from California. She should be used to tremors.

Still, she felt unnerved.

Her gut told her this trip wasn't going to go as planned. Not by a long shot.

If she were smart, she might leave now.

But she already felt too invested.

Ten minutes later, Mariella and Matthew were out the door—Matthew in sensible jeans, a navy-blue sweatshirt with "California" stretched across the chest, and hiking boots. Mariella had dried her hair and changed out of Jason's clothes into jeans and a lightweight pink shirt.

Everything was better when it was pink.

She knew people called her Malibu Barbie behind her back. And for good reason. She was slender with blonde hair. Her favorite color was pink. She loved all things sparkly.

She'd changed on the inside—but her outside was taking a little bit longer to catch up. However, she *had* cut back on getting her nails done, getting extensions, and all the other high-maintenance habits she'd been so immersed in back in California.

Trauma, on more than one level, had changed her.

"You ready to go?" Matthew glanced at her. "You should grab a jacket."

Even though it was June in Alaska, the air could still feel chilly. The highs today were in the mid-sixties. But with the wind coming off the water and glaciers surrounding the bay, the air felt cooler.

Mariella just so happened to have a pink windbreaker that matched her pink shirt. She grabbed it and slid it on. There would be no camouflaging herself out in the woods. People used to joke that with all her bling, she could be spotted from space.

"Let's go," Matthew said. "But the two of us . . . we need to stick together."

"I agree." Besides, they'd always stuck together. That was what twins did.

She couldn't imagine life any other way.

A rush of nerves swept through Mariella at the prospect of walking in the woods and looking for a missing woman.

Yet she was inexplicably drawn to this as well.

Was it because of her meeting earlier with Jason? Because of her involvement in the true crime podcast world?

Was it a way of delaying finding out answers to questions that might change everything about her past and what she held to be true about herself?

She wasn't sure.

She only knew she had to be a part of this search party.

She'd track down Bright later.

Finding this missing woman—and proving to herself that she was capable—seemed more urgent.

MARIELLA AND MATTHEW drove to the campground, but the parking lot was filled to capacity. The whole community appeared to have shown up.

Instead, they found a spot along the side of the narrow mountain road and hiked nearly a half mile to the Wanderlust Campground.

From what she could tell, the place was fairly primitive, with a guard station and a shower house the only permanent structures. Most of the sites didn't appear to have water or electrical hookups. They were, however, spacious, and each one mashed up against the ethereal forest.

A crowd had already gathered near the shower house.

From the research Mariella had done, there were only two thousand full-time residents here in Salmon-by-the-Sea. But in the summer that number swelled to more than four thousand with seasonal workers coming in. The influx of tourists probably tripled that number.

She wasn't sure if the people here for the search party were all locals or if some visitors—like her and Matthew—had also shown up.

As they joined the crowd, Mariella glanced around.

She told herself she wasn't looking for Jason, but she was.

Him showing up here seemed risky, especially if people were suspicious of him. She could only imagine the scrutiny he'd be under.

Her heart ached at the thought.

Living like that couldn't be easy, especially on an ongoing basis—and much more now that someone else was missing.

Mariella and her brother listened as an Alaskan Search and Rescue leader, a man who looked like Grizzly Adams, gave instructions to everyone gathered.

"Thank you all for volunteering," he started. "We need everyone to check in so we can keep an account of who's out there—we don't want anyone else to get lost. Each group of volunteers will be with a trained leader. Again, we want to avoid anyone getting hurt. Understand?"

He ran through other instructions and then people were split into teams. Their team leader showed them a map of the area they'd be searching. The grids laid out there were specific and detailed to ensure every part of the forest was searched.

Then their leader showed them a picture of the woman.

Zoe Hamlin. Twenty-two. From Kansas. Dark curly hair, a bright smile, and brown eyes. Her skin was olive and her face an oval shape.

She was beautiful, especially with the gleam of adventure in her gaze.

She was last seen at one a.m. when she and her friends extinguished their campfire and went to bed.

Her tentmates—two friends who'd traveled here with her—hadn't heard Zoe leave.

Though Zoe was in shape, she didn't have very much experience with this kind of terrain.

A man around their age stepped toward Mariella and Matthew's team, a rescue bag and walkie-talkie strapped around his waist.

His name was Sean, and he was probably in his mid-twenties. From what she'd heard him say earlier, he was a firefighter in town. He seemed like an outdoorsman with his barely-there beard, flannel shirt, and confident demeanor.

They'd been assigned to his team.

"You guys ready?" he asked.

Mariella nodded, pushing down a surge of anxiety.

She really didn't know what she was doing. She wasn't the "outdoorsy girl" type. She was more comfortable in a shopping mall or emceeing an event. But if she stuck with everyone, she should be okay.

The question was . . . what if Mariella found something she didn't want to find?

Jason walked back to the cabin he shared with his dad.

The place wasn't quite a mile outside of town and on the edge of the Chugach Forest. The next nearest neighbor wasn't within eyesight, which meant plenty of privacy.

It wasn't unusual to see a moose on the property or eagles flying overhead. A short jaunt through the woods led to the creek, where Jason liked to spend time fishing—and clearing his head.

Today might be one of those days he needed that.

His thoughts wouldn't settle.

And it wasn't just because of Bright Armstrong.

He hadn't been able to stop thinking about that other woman who'd gone missing.

Who was she? Was it an out-of-towner? A local?

Did anything about her disappearance match Hannah's disappearance?

He ran his hand through his hair.

Then he wandered outside to find his father.

Just as Jason suspected, Pops was outside the smokehouse prepping some salmon. His father was in his element when it came to anything to do with fishing or the water.

He stood outside now wearing his boots, a vest, and a floppy hat.

People said Jason and his father looked alike. Sometimes Jason could see it, especially in the eyes and build.

Pops was only fifty-four but appeared older with his thinning gray hair and premature wrinkles born from hours in the sun.

Plus, Pops had been through a lot.

Jason's mom had died in an auto accident when Jason was only two. He'd been a single dad since then.

Pops ran a successful fishing business, but it wasn't always easy. Lots of physical labor and long hours.

Then there was everything that had happened with Jason . . .

"What's got you so upset?" His dad looked up from the wooden table where he fileted another large king salmon.

He already had several filets in the smoker that they would eat at a later time.

The scent of the slow cooking fish filled the air—smoky and rich. The aroma represented home to Jason. Usually, it brought him comfort.

But nothing could console him now.

"A girl went missing from the campground." Jason crossed his arms and leaned against the post of their back porch.

His dad paused and stared at him. "Just like Hannah?"

The loaded question hung in the air.

Jason shrugged. "That's how it seems. When I was walking through town, I heard they were setting up search parties to look for her."

"You going to help?" Pops remained frozen as he watched Jason.

"I'm not sure that's a good idea." Jason had considered it. But the situation was complicated.

He'd been well-versed over the years in search and rescue operations. Sometimes he traveled out of town in order to help with rescues.

But never here. Here, no one wanted his help.

His dad's gaze latched onto his. "You didn't have anything to do with Hannah's death."

"We both know that, but most of the other people here in town don't believe I'm innocent."

A frown tugged at his dad's lips. The accusations had been hard on him also. "Sometimes I think it would be better if you went somewhere to start fresh. You know that?"

Jason's jaw tightened. "You need help with your fishing business. I'm not going to leave you. I'm not going to let them run me off."

"It's been a long time since I've seen you happy. I hate that for you. I can find someone else to work for me. Gerald always hires and trains college students from the Lower 48 during the summer. I could do the same."

"But you won't find someone as good as me." Jason cast his father a grin.

Gerald was his father's best friend. The two of them, along with three other men, played cards together every week. They'd been doing so for years.

"That might be true. But your happiness is more important than my own." Pops continued fileting the fish.

"I get that, Pops. But I'm going to be okay."

His dad glanced up, his head still lowered. "I saw the way you looked at that woman earlier, the one you rescued. You like her, don't you?"

Mariella filled his thoughts again. "She *is* intriguing. But that doesn't matter. I walked her home, and Crusher confronted me. Once she realizes what I've been accused of, she won't come near me again."

That had been Jason's experience for the past several years.

He couldn't fully blame anyone for the reaction. Getting caught up with the wrong guy could be dangerous.

The thing was, Jason *wasn't* the wrong guy. But that was his label, and very few people looked beyond it.

"You never know." Pops' blade sliced through a layer of meat. "When you meet the right one, things will be different. It was like that with your mom and me."

His father was probably right. But sometimes Jason felt as if he were living in a cycle impossible to break free from.

"I'm going to go start dinner," Jason announced, wanting a break from this conversation.

He stepped inside the house, his thoughts still racing.

He checked his phone.

The town's Facebook page contained updates.

But as he looked at the newest one, the air left his lungs.

The woman who was missing was Zoe Hamlin.

Zoe Hamlin?

No, no, no . . . no!

Jason pressed his eyes closed.

He'd met Zoe yesterday. Talked to her. Spent time with her.

It had all been innocent. Nothing serious. Nothing but conversation.

But if other people found out the two of them had been together before she went missing . . . he'd end up in the limelight again.

Everyone would jump to conclusions. Those who hadn't already assumed the worst about him would start assuming.

Sweat covered Jason's brow as his heart pumped harder.

Things weren't going to get better, were they?

In fact, Jason had a feeling that things would get a lot worse.

chapter
ten

I **STOOD** in the forest and watched the search parties around me. I'd hiked with my backpack from my ceremonial spot at the edge of the forest. It had taken me an hour, but I'd reached the campground.

I knew the woods like the back of my hand, as the saying went.

I preferred walking through the mountains over taking the sidewalks or roads. There was more privacy this way.

More time for me to commune with Tlatoani.

I held onto the straps of my backpack as I glanced around again.

These people trying to be part of the so-called "search parties" . . .

They were oblivious.

People didn't even know the greatness that was so close.

They saw me but didn't realize my strength. How powerful I was. That I was the protector of this land.

I liked it that way.

I liked being one with nature, and I planned on staying like this for as long as possible.

Whatever the spirits told me to do, I did.

That was why I'd made that sacrifice last night.

As soon as I'd seen that woman gallivanting through town, I'd sensed in my spirit that she was the one. She hadn't been paying attention and had practically run into a woman with a child. Then she'd spilled her coffee and hadn't bothered to clean it up.

Selfish.

That's what she was.

Then Tlatoani had sent me a sign, a confirmation.

Just like five years ago.

Like the wise men following a star, sometimes the gods used nature to speak, guide, and lead.

Several people passed me as they trekked through the woods, and I smiled—not too brightly. Not in this situation.

They returned my glance with a quick one of their own.

Like I said, I blended in. Looked like the rest of humanity.

There was no reason for anyone to suspect me.

I traversed the woods with a search party, though I knew exactly where the sacrifice was located.

I didn't let anyone else know, however. Half the fun was waiting for the discovery.

Guilt flooded me at the thought. That wasn't the way of Tlatoani. There should be no delight in the sacrifice.

Hopefully, he didn't realize how much I enjoyed doing his work.

If he did, I hoped he'd forgive me.

As I glanced ahead, I spotted a woman with blonde hair and bright clothes.

I frowned.

I got a bad sense about her, especially when I heard her talking to some of the people around her about crime and solving cases.

A nearby branch—a small one—fluttered from the treetops, brushing her arm.

Tlatoani didn't like her, I realized.

But why?

I glanced up at the sky through the tree branches as my thoughts wandered.

She must be a threat.

Tlatoani was telling me to keep an eye on her.

She could be trouble.

The spirits guided me and whispered words only I could hear. They'd spoken to my ancestors as well.

This was our way of life.

Not many understood, though. I didn't even try to explain it. It was best if others didn't know about my connection to nature.

They couldn't know my secrets.

Those were mine to keep.

I continued to walk, acting as if I searched for clues.

Instead, my gaze remained on the blonde.

Tlatoani, give me confirmation so I can be sure . . .

I glanced up again.

It was too light outside to see the stars. It was the wrong time of day for him to answer.

He preferred the dark of night to communicate.

But he'd been speaking in strange ways lately. Probably because it was more urgent.

I had to remain diligent. I couldn't miss any signs.

I looked up and saw a twinkle in the sky above.

I froze.

A twinkle.

But it was daylight.

My breath caught. An ermine emerged from the brush. Looked around. Then scrambled away.

Right in front of me.

Unusual behavior.

They usually remained hidden when potential danger was around. But something must have stirred the white, short-tailed weasel out of its nest.

Something important.

It was a sign.

Yes, a sign from Tlatoani.

I knew it was.

But a sign for what?

To act again? To be diligent?

I didn't know.

I glanced at the woman again.

I was drawn to her. That wasn't an accident. And it wasn't because she'd talked about solving crimes. I didn't *fear* her.

Then why did my throat tighten?

It's her.

My breath caught.

The gods were speaking, weren't they?

They'd chosen her.

So soon? I glanced up.

But I knew the answer was yes.

The last sacrifice hadn't been enough.

The gods demanded more.

Apprehension gripped my muscles. I would obey.

But how? And when?

There's no time to waste.

I knew what Tlatoani was telling me.

But this wasn't the way I usually operated.

Besides, she was with too many others right now.

I reached into the pocket of my jacket.

It was broad daylight. I couldn't bring my bow and arrow.

Instead, I had a small wooden blowgun loaded with a tiny dart.

This would do the trick.

I'd laced the tip with Turbina corymbosa. It was a

morning glory plant, one I grew myself since it wasn't native to the area. In the past, it was used to induce visions —or hallucinations. There was just enough of the drug on the tip to cause confusion for a while.

My steps became lighter as my mood brightened.

This would be fun—a challenge.

Tlatoani didn't want me to wait five more years to do his will again.

Maybe after this he would have better things in store for me.

After all, I only wanted to please him.

Too bad death was the only way to do so.

MARIELLA CAREFULLY WALKED through the forest with Matthew beside her. She'd been chatting with the other people on her team for a while, but now she was quiet.

She glanced around.

The place really was beautiful. Based on the research she'd done for her podcast, she knew the forest was comprised of spruce, hemlock, and birch. Boulders dotted the landscape. Steep drop-offs occurred in the blink of an eye.

This wasn't a place anyone should wander at night.

But it *was* breathtaking during the day.

Sometimes, there was a break in the trees and the mountain range would appear in the background, complete with the glacier. From what she'd read, almost forty glaciers flowed from Harding Field down to this area. She wasn't sure which one she was looking at now. In other circumstances, she might ask.

But right now, she needed to focus on finding Zoe.

Ten people were on her team, and they'd spread out. They were instructed to search the forest for anything out of place or any broken branches or footprints.

The task felt overwhelming.

But it also felt good to be doing something helpful, to work as part of a community.

Some of the volunteers on her team were locals, but a couple were from the campground and two others had heard about the search and come down from Seward. As they walked, Mariella heard dogs barking in the distance. She felt the soft reassurance of the wind whispering through the tree branches.

As the terrain began to slope downward, she watched her steps.

"Is it true another woman disappeared from this campground five years ago?" a woman beside her asked Sean.

He hesitated a moment before saying, "Yes, that is true."

"And she turned up dead? Murdered?"

"Also true." The man looked as if he'd rather not talk about this.

Mariella listened carefully, curious about where the conversation would go.

"They never caught her killer?"

Sean frowned. "Everyone knows a man in town is guilty. There's no evidence to prove he did it; otherwise, he'd be behind bars. Maybe even on death row waiting to get fried. But one day, he's going to mess up and get caught."

"You think that man is responsible for this too?"

Sean shrugged. "Can't say for sure. We used to be good friends. Until Hannah died."

Mariella's breath caught.

He talked like judge and jury about Jason.

Anger burned inside her. She wasn't sure why she felt the need to defend Jason—she hardly knew the man. But she didn't think he was guilty.

Sure, maybe she was drawing conclusions too quickly. But still . . .

She paused and glanced down. She stood not far from a rocky outcropping of boulders that shifted at a ninety-degree angle toward Eagle River below her.

Something beneath some underbrush caught her eye.

As the rest of the group continued forward, she remained where she was and brushed the leaves away with her foot.

Her heart pounded harder when she saw pistachio shells there.

Pistachio shells . . . just like she'd seen on Jason's boat.

That had to be a coincidence, right? Other people ate pistachios also.

But if that was true, why did her heart race out of

control? Why was she hesitating to let anyone know what she'd found?

Before she could think about it any longer, a shuffle sounded behind her.

She turned but saw no one.

The hair on her neck rose as an uneasy feeling washed over her.

She should keep moving.

She shifted to catch up with the rest of the group when something pricked her shoulder.

Her head swam.

What was happening?

She staggered forward, trying to brush it off.

Until she lost her balance.

Then she began to fall forward . . . toward the cliff.

Jason had just started making some chili when someone knocked at his door.

He turned and saw his best friend Dustin Spriggs step inside.

Dustin was the one friend who'd stuck by Jason through everything. Still, the two of them preferred to hang out only when away from the scrutiny of others. It was easier that way.

"What's going on?" Dustin raised his hand in a fist bump.

Dustin was the ultimate outdoorsman with thick, sun-streaked hair, a tanned complexion, and a wardrobe that consisted of Carhartt pants and boots.

"Not much but dinner." Jason turned back to the stove and stirred the pot. "You?"

Dustin did ATV tours in the summer and snow machine tours in the winter. He must have finished up early today. He usually didn't pop in to hang out until closer to eight.

He grabbed some pistachios from a bowl on the counter and popped one in his mouth. "Heard the hullabaloo around town about that woman."

Ah . . . the real reason he'd come by.

Jason's muscles tightened. "Crazy, huh?"

"More than crazy. I thought about you. You doing okay?" He popped another nut in his mouth.

Was he doing okay? That was a great question. "I think so."

Come to think of it, Jason really didn't want to talk about it—which meant a subject change was in order.

"Did you take off early?" Jason stepped away from the simmering pot and began to collect the empty cans to put in the recycle bin.

Dustin shrugged as he leaned against the kitchen counter. "Had the day off. Helped out with the search party for a while. Then I decided to stop by to check on you."

Jason's breath hitched at the mention of the search party. "Lots of people out there?"

"Oh, yeah. Tons of people."

That was good news, Jason supposed. Maybe they'd find this woman before it was too late.

The sound of tires crunching on the gravel outside his house caught his ear.

His back muscles pinched.

"Expecting someone?" Dustin straightened.

Jason shook his head. "No, I'm not."

He didn't like unexpected visitors. Not anymore.

He stepped away from the stove, slipped the kitchen towel off his shoulder, and placed it on the counter. Then he walked to the front window. Dustin followed.

Crusher had pulled his jacked-up truck to a stop in front of Jason's house and stared at him, threat in his dark gaze.

"What is he doing here?" Dustin muttered, stopping beside him to watch.

Jason didn't want to know.

But he had a feeling things were about to go south.

chapter
twelve

MARIELLA LUNGED toward the drop-off before she managed to throw her body weight back.

But it was too late.

Her feet began to slide.

And slide.

And slide.

Her arms flailed in panic.

Finally, her hand caught one of the boulders.

She jerked to a stop.

Pain shot through her shoulder.

She ignored it.

She was safe—for now.

But her heart pounded out of control. The distance below her seemed to stretch on for miles. The distance above her appeared unreachable. Every time she blinked, the pitch of the cliff became greater.

She squeezed her eyes shut as her head swam.

What was going on? Why did her mind feel like it was swimming through muck?

She looked up again, still trying to make sense of things.

A Labrador retriever looked down at her.

"Barkley!" A woman peered over the edge and gasped. "Oh, my goodness. Are you okay?"

Mariella glanced at the river as it rushed below her.

Trembles overtook her.

One wrong move, and she might cascade the rest of the way down. Her head spun as wooziness enveloped her. Why did the rocks seem as if they were crawling? As if they wanted her to fall?

Like they wanted to claim another life?

She pressed her eyes closed.

None of that made sense.

What was wrong with her mind right now?

"I've been better." Mariella's voice cracked.

At once, she had visions of what it might be like to die like this. How much pain would she feel? Would she pass out first? Would her body bounce on the rocks as she plunged to her death?

Her throat swelled with terror.

Shuffling sounded above her. She dared to pluck her eyes open.

When she did, she saw six other people had appeared above her—including Matthew.

"It's going to be okay, Mariella," he assured her.

Barkley continued to stare, yapping excitedly almost as if playing a game.

The dog's owner explained to everyone how her dog was friendly, but he'd gotten away from her and . . . she blathered on and on, clearly upset.

She thought her dog had scared Mariella and caused her to fall.

But that wasn't the case at all . . . was it? Was the dog the shuffling she'd heard?

Nothing made sense.

This was twice that Mariella could have died today.

What were the odds? Yet both times truly seemed accidental . . . right?

"I've got you." Above her, Sean lay on his stomach and extended his arm.

Matthew appeared beside him, doing the same. "Can you reach my hand?"

Her first instinct was to say no.

They were too far away.

And if she let go of the rock . . .

Mariella hesitated and looked down once more.

The landscape seemed to move around her. Why did everything keep shifting? Or were her eyes deceiving her?

Drawing in a deep breath, she reached for Sean's and Matthew's hands.

Sean grabbed her arm first and effortlessly pulled her up.

How had he reached her so easily? Had she not fallen as far as she thought?

Why did her thoughts feel so fuzzy?

Finally, she reached the top and nearly hugged the ground as she crouched on her hands and knees. Her limbs shook too badly to stand. Not yet.

Letting out a deep breath, she lifted a quiet "Thank you" to anyone she owed thanks to.

She was on solid ground.

For a moment, she almost felt like she was a character in *Final Destination* and that death was following her . . .

When she was ready, Sean helped her to her feet and held on to her arm while she found her balance. Matthew grabbed her other arm.

"Thank you . . ." she murmured.

"No problem. I'm just glad you're okay." Sean studied her face. "How did you get separated from the rest of the group?"

The reason slammed back into her mind.

Mariella glanced at those pistachio shells, and another tremble raked through her.

She couldn't keep her discovery quiet. Not if it meant potentially saving a woman who could be lost in these woods.

Then she remembered the prick she'd felt in her shoulder.

She reached for the spot, but there was nothing there.

Had she imagined it?

Had an insect stung her right before she lost her balance? Had she subconsciously known that dog was coming for her and moved away?

She wasn't sure. She'd felt so strange afterward. Had it been an allergic reaction?

"Mariella?" Sean stared at her in confusion.

He'd asked how she had gotten behind everyone.

With a shaky hand, Mariella pointed to the ground. "I saw those and wondered if they were significant."

She watched as Sean spotted the shells.

Then something crossed his features.

Realization.

If he'd been friends with Jason, he'd likely know Jason liked pistachios. At least that was Mariella's assumption—that those shells on the boat had been his. She supposed they could belong to his father or someone who'd been on that charter fishing trip. But . . .

Either way, she didn't like the connections her mind formed.

For now, she needed to stay far away from anything that could potentially harm her . . . or *Final Destination* might have its way.

"Maybe we should go back to the cabin so you can rest," Matthew suggested.

It was getting late. Though the sun was still out and fairly bright, it was close to eight p.m.

Maybe some rest was a good idea.

Jason braced himself for more trouble.

He'd grown weary of the fight. Of the constant accusations.

But he wouldn't back down. Not to this guy. Not to anyone else.

He opened the door and stepped out, Dustin beside him.

Crusher stared at them, his snaggle teeth displayed as he sneered at them.

"What are you doing here, Crusher?" Jason stood with his hands on his hips on the wooden porch.

"Someone needs to say it," the man growled.

"Say what?"

"You'd be better off dead!" The next instant, Crusher lifted a bottle with a cloth stuffed into the end.

In two seconds flat, he lit it on fire and threw it toward the house.

The bottle landed on the lawn, and fire ignited across the dry grass.

As Crusher squealed away, Jason ran toward the flames and tried to stomp the blaze out.

Dustin grabbed a hose and sprayed down the area.

It took several minutes, but finally the flames were extinguished.

The remaining charred grass and scent of smoke served as a reminder about what had happened.

Dustin gripped his shoulder. "You okay, man?"

Jason shrugged as he stared at the burned grass, his heart pounding erratically in his ears. "To be honest, sometimes I just don't know anymore."

How much longer could he live like this?

Would he always be a target?

Crusher's words echoed in his mind. *You'd be better off dead.*

What if the man was right?

MARIELLA HAD HARDLY BEEN able to sleep all night.

She couldn't stop thinking about that missing woman.

As far as Mariella knew, the woman still hadn't been found.

Where was she? Was she alone out in that vast wilderness? Had someone taken her? Had she somehow slipped down the cliff into the river—just like Mariella almost had?

After tossing and turning in bed, she finally got up and got dressed.

By the time she stepped into the living room, Matthew was doing burpees. He'd started a new workout routine several weeks ago.

Mariella was proud of him. He'd been putting a lot of time and effort into improving himself lately.

"Morning," she muttered as she paused in front of him.

"Morning. You're already dressed?" He paused and looked her up and down curiously.

"I'm going to walk into town. Maybe work on my podcast for a while." *Find out if we were kidnapped as newborns.*

She still couldn't figure out, if that were true, what her parents' involvement or motives might have been.

They were fairly wealthy and could have adopted legally.

Or what if they'd thought they were adopting legally, but Mariella and Matthew had actually been abducted and sold on the black market?

The possibilities—and horrors—seemed endless.

The truth also remained that her parents had never mentioned them being adopted. However, her mom and dad both were brunettes. They'd said the twins' genes must be recessive.

And their parents were so different than them. Serious, work-oriented, and the bookish types.

Mariella had never quite felt as if she fit in.

But never had she imagined that might be because they weren't actually related by blood.

She had so many questions. She hadn't ventured to ask her parents any of them yet. She needed more information first.

"You sure it's safe for you to go into town?" Matthew tilted his head.

Mariella shrugged. "Considering I don't have to walk through the woods or anywhere isolated to get to town, I think I'll be fine. You want to come?"

She hoped he said no. She needed to do this alone.

She feared Matthew would be devastated if he learned the truth—if it *was* the truth.

Plus, another part of her wanted to find some answers about Zoe. Maybe she wanted to prove to herself that she was capable of investigating.

The other cases the murder club had solved . . . she'd helped with them. But Duke and Andi had been the ones who ultimately tracked down the bad guys. Sometimes, Mariella wanted more. She wanted to be more hands-on.

"I have a video call in a few minutes with an app developer, so I think I'll stick around for now. But maybe later?"

The Round Table wanted to start their own app to make it easier for users to find them. Matthew was trying to figure a few things out first.

This was why she and Matthew worked so well together. He liked to handle things behind the scenes. In the process, he gave her space to explore and do the things she loved.

"Sounds like a plan." Using the mirror near the front door, Mariella quickly put on some pink lip gloss and rubbed her lips together.

Then she grabbed a lightweight jacket and stepped outside into the bright sunlight. She slipped her oversized sunglasses on, glad Duke wasn't here to call her Hollywood.

It was his newest nickname for her.

She knew this time of the year in the area was often cloudy and rainy, so she was grateful for the blue skies.

She started down the narrow gravel road, lined on one side with the forest and on the other with secluded driveways leading to other cabins. A half mile later, she emerged from the residential road and the town came into view. A few minutes later, she found the coffee shop she was looking for.

Perkatory was merely a walk-up window located on the corner of a string of shops. The place was small with no inside seating.

Keri, the woman who owned it, was in her thirties and had bright red hair. Her dog, an Australian shepherd named Louie, worked in the shop with her. He was the first to greet customers, and he enjoyed head rubs while people waited for their orders.

Mariella had spoken to Keri yesterday when she first arrived in town and had enjoyed chatting with her.

After a few minutes of chitchat, she ordered a white mocha and then waited for the drink to be ready. She started to ask Keri some questions about the town and the people who lived here. Before she could, Keri shared that she'd only been here for a year.

She wouldn't be a great source of information, unfortunately. But that was okay. Mariella had a lot of other ideas.

She turned and glanced around the town.

Several tourist groups already headed toward the docks, where they would no doubt take tours of Resurrection Bay or charter fishing trips. Some people drove farther up the mountain, where they could take helicopter tours of the glaciers. Plus, she'd heard others offered jet ski rides or kayak sightseeing tours.

This place was a playground for those who loved the outdoors.

As she continued to wait for her coffee, her gaze zeroed in on someone across the street.

Jason.

Her heart instantly pitter-pattered.

Equally as fast, the air left her lungs in a rush of fear.

Mariella didn't know what to make of him. Her logic and her intuition seemed to collide. At a gut level, she believed the man was innocent. But she'd been too trusting before, and it had cost her dearly.

She nibbled on her lip as she tried to sort her emotions and figure out what to do.

Jason looked up and saw her but quickly looked away.

Something about the motion . . . it seemed to confirm his innocence in her mind. He didn't act guilty—he simply acted accused.

And it wasn't fair.

To take it further, she wasn't going to let Jason pretend she didn't exist—especially if he was doing it as an excuse to protect her.

Thankfully, her mocha was up. She thanked Keri before grabbing her drink and hurrying across the road.

Jason would talk to her whether he wanted to or not.

"Hey, Jason!" He didn't slow down at the familiar voice.

He'd hoped by avoiding eye contact with Mariella that she'd let this go. There was no need to pretend the two of them should even get to know each other.

Because their kindling friendship wouldn't lead anywhere—especially if things continued to unfold as they had so far this week.

It was best if Mariella simply continued on with her stay here and acted as if they'd never met.

But it didn't seem as if it would be that easy.

Because the next instant, Mariella was beside him, slightly out of breath and the coffee in her hands sloshing through the tiny opening in the lid.

"Hey, for a minute I didn't think you heard me." She sucked in several breaths as she fell into step beside him.

Jason kept walking, barely glancing her way. He had a charter trip starting in an hour, and he needed to get ready for it.

He also needed to figure out a way to put distance

between himself and Mariella. As intriguing as she was, the two of them hanging out would be a mistake.

Keeping his voice hard, he said, "I heard you."

"But you didn't stop?"

"It'd be better for you if I didn't."

"I don't think so." Her tone sounded so hopeful—and maybe naive, even though Jason didn't really think of her that way.

At those words, he paused and turned toward her. "Why aren't you running away from me like most people do?"

Mariella studied him a moment before finally shrugging and saying, "Because I don't think you're guilty."

"You don't know me."

"But I know guilt."

Jason stared at her another moment, unsure what to say. What did her words mean? She knew guilt because she'd experienced it? Or because she could identify it?

He wasn't sure.

He let out a breath. "I don't know how to respond to that."

"I want to hear your side of this." A determined look filled her gaze.

That sounded like a terrible idea. He'd tried telling his side of the story. No one had believed him.

No one except Pops and Dustin.

Jason shook his head and took another step. "I've got to get to work."

"So what I'm hearing is that you can't talk now, but later might work. Yes?"

He paused again and turned toward her. "Are you asking so you can do some type of exposé? So you can put it on social media that you went out with a potential killer?"

Her eyes narrowed. "Who do you think I am? A sicko?"

The way she asked the question sounded awfully convincing.

But trusting people came so hard sometimes.

Jason stared at her another moment until he felt himself relent. "If you want to talk, I can meet you tonight. If you haven't been scared off by then."

Something twinkled in her eyes. "It's a date. Where?"

"Bottom Feeders. Six-thirty."

"I'll be there."

Mariella had no idea what she was getting herself into. She might regret this.

And so might Jason.

chapter
fourteen

MARIELLA FELT a rush of nerves as she walked up the dock toward Bright Armstrong's boat several minutes later—after she'd finished her coffee and built up her nerve.

She had started to do this yesterday before things fell apart.

But she couldn't stay in town forever so she might as well get this initial conversation over with.

She knew exactly what his boat's name was and where it was located. She'd done her research.

As she headed toward his boat, she glanced over and saw where *Fishful Thinking* was docked.

Would Jason and his dad be leaving for their charter fishing trip soon? Were they both aboard the boat now?

She didn't know. But she set those thoughts aside.

Just as she reached the boat, *HydroTherapy*, a man stepped out.

She gasped as she observed him a moment.

The man had white hair and wrinkly skin. But his square jawline seemed familiar, as did his eyes.

Could this man really be her father? And if so, how was she going to handle that and proceed?

He stepped off the boat and glanced at her. "Can I help you?"

His voice sounded rougher than she'd expected, more gruff and less friendly.

She swallowed hard before plastering on a smile. "I wanted to inquire about a charter fishing trip."

"When are you looking at?"

"I was hoping within the next few days."

He let out a condescending laugh. "Sorry, sweetheart. I book weeks in advance. I'm sure there are other people around here you can try, though."

Something about his tone rubbed her the wrong way.

"I've heard the best things about you," she said instead.

He began cleaning his boat slip, casting a quick glance at her. "No offense, sweetheart, but you don't look like the charter fishing type. Maybe you'd be better on one of those luxury yachts over there."

Another thought hit her, one that she hadn't considered.

If this man was her dad, she didn't like him.

That was something she wasn't sure how to handle.

"Now if you don't mind, I've got some work to do." Bright glanced at her again, clearly dismissing her.

It didn't appear she'd be getting any answers this way. She'd have to find out the truth by some other means.

She begrudgingly thanked him and stepped away.

But she couldn't ignore the disappointment pressing inside her.

The charter trip had been cancelled.

Jason shouldn't be surprised, he supposed. But he *was* disappointed.

He operated better when he had something to distract him. Working usually did the trick. Plus, he did love being out there on the water.

But apparently rumors were already spreading around town, and he suspected that was why the trip had been cancelled.

As Jason stepped off the boat, he glanced across the docks and his gaze stopped on someone.

Mariella.

He narrowed his eyes.

She hadn't heeded his warning and was talking to Bright Armstrong anyway.

Was she interviewing the man for her travel podcast?

Jason's spine tightened as suspicions pulled taut through his muscles.

Did Mariella somehow know the man? Were they secretly working together in some way? Conspiring to ruin Jason or his father?

He shook his head. The thought was ridiculous. But Bright *was* their biggest competition, a man who'd love nothing more than to see Jason and his father's business shut down.

Plus there was the fact that Bright might be doing something illegal, though Jason hadn't figured out what yet.

He'd considered looking into it. But didn't he have enough problems without adding more to his list?

He ducked back, keeping an eye on Mariella and Bright for another moment.

The two of them talked, but their interaction didn't exactly seem friendly.

In fact, when Mariella turned away from the man, she rolled her eyes.

What was that about?

He almost wished he knew her better so he could ask.

As she started back down the dock, he climbed on the boat again.

He didn't want to answer any more of her questions or see her inquisitive looks.

But he stored that information away at the back of his mind.

Mariella may not be as trustworthy as she wanted to seem.

Jason would be wise to remember that.

Because not everything that looked beautiful actually was.

chapter
fifteen

MARIELLA COULDN'T STOP REPLAYING her conversation with Bright.

The truth was, she wasn't sure if she wanted that man to be her father or not. She didn't get good vibes from him.

Yet at the same time, she craved answers.

So she would need to continue looking.

That was why her next step led her to the library.

Though she'd found some articles online, she knew that many older newspapers hadn't loaded their past articles on the internet for everyone to find.

Besides, libraries were great resources, and she hoped to ask the people working there some questions.

It was only a short walk through town to get there. When she stepped inside, she saw she was the only other patron there, other than a mom with a toddler sitting on a colorful beanbag in the children's section.

A man working behind the front desk smiled pleasantly as if glad to have someone to talk to. "Can I help you?"

Perfect. She hoped this guy was as friendly as he came across. If he was talkative, that would be another bonus.

She approached the desk, one with stickers across the front. Some of the stickers were from various places around the world. Others had bookish sayings on them.

It gave the place personality.

She plastered on her best smile as she looked up at the man. "I'm hoping you can help me. I heard that twenty-four years ago newborn twins were kidnapped from this town. I'm a true crime podcaster, and I was hoping to find out more information."

He clucked his tongue and shook his head. "Oh, yes. Who in town can forget about that? So tragic."

The man—probably in his fifties—was thin with graying hair and wise eyes. His name tag read, "Roy."

He held a stack of flyers in his hands. As Mariella glanced at them, she saw it was for a vigil taking place this afternoon for Zoe. A quick scan showed it was being held in the town square.

If Mariella was able, she would try to attend.

She turned her attention back to the reason she came. "So you were here when the kidnapping happened?"

"I was. Been here thirty years myself. Not continuously, but most of them. Can't seem to get enough of this place. It gets in your blood, you know?"

"I can imagine." Mariella tilted her head. "Is there anything you can tell me—off the record if you prefer—about the kidnapping?"

"I can do you better." He crossed from around the counter and headed to a computer for patrons, set up on a desk in the corner. He motioned for her to be seated while he typed several things on the keyboard.

"We don't have microfiche," he explained. "But we scanned all our old newspapers, and most of them have metadata attached to them. So all you have to do is search. We didn't put this on the web yet. It's been a work in progress. But I'm sure I can find you some articles in here. They can help tell you what my memory may have gotten muddy."

As he began to scroll, trying to find the right references, Mariella wanted to keep him talking. "Even if it is a little muddy, what do you remember about the kidnapping?"

"From what I recall, Bright and Phyllis had just put their two-week-old newborn twins, a boy and a girl, down for a nap. They went outside to do some yard work, and one of their neighbors pulled up. They started chatting for a while. I guess they figured their babies were safe in their cribs. However, when they went back inside, their children were gone."

Mariella's heart beat faster. "Was there any evidence left as to what might have happened?"

He clicked his tongue. "There were footprints by the

back door. But the police never matched them with anybody."

"What's the theory in town about what happened?"

He scrolled some more, not missing a beat as he talked. "There were all kinds of rumors. Let me tell you, people started locking their doors after that. But the truth was, no one knew exactly what happened. Locals thought a stranger had been watching the house and snuck in the back door when they saw the opportunity. Then they grabbed the babies and fled."

"How would that be possible? Wouldn't someone have seen a stranger running through town with newborn babies? I mean, how did they get away?"

"There's another road that runs on the backside of Bright's property. The neighboring house that backed up to their property was empty. It would have made it easy for a quick getaway."

"But no one saw anything?"

He shook his head. "No one saw a thing."

"That seems like a shame."

"It was more than a shame," Roy said. "Phyllis ended up dying three years later. Doctors say it was a heart attack, but everyone around here believes it was heartbreak that did her in. She was never the same after her babies were gone."

Compassion welled in Mariella's throat. "Was she a nice woman?"

Mariella caught herself. She heard the emotion in her

voice and knew if she didn't rein it in quickly that this man would probably get suspicious and know there was more to her story.

"Phyllis was very nice," Roy said. "She'd do anything for anybody, and she always had a smile. On the other hand, Bright has always been a little rough around the edges. Definitely more so after all of this happened."

"I bet."

However, that didn't excuse his behavior today.

Before Mariella could ask any more questions, Roy paused and pointed at an article. "Here are several you can read. I'm not sure if they'll tell you anything that I didn't. But it'd be a great place to start."

She offered a grateful smile. "Thank you."

"No problem. If you have more questions, you know where to find me." He nodded toward the front desk.

As Mariella stared at the newspaper articles, she tried to brace herself for whatever she might discover.

After Mariella disappeared, Jason's father decided to take off for his own fishing trip. He invited Jason to go along, and maybe Jason should have said yes.

Being out on the water was a good excuse to get away from the people in town.

But Jason said no instead. He had too many other things on his mind.

As he started back down the boat slip, he paused again.

Bright Armstrong was still here. He was surprised no one had shown up for a charter fishing trip with him yet. It was getting late to be leaving.

Then he saw a small fishing boat with two men in it beside Bright's larger one.

That same boat that was here before.

His back muscles tightened.

As the boat pulled away, Jason made a split-second decision.

He knew he might regret this.

But maybe he wouldn't.

His own fishing boat was docked beside his father's.

Working quickly, he jumped aboard, started his engine, and took off.

He glided across the bay, reminding himself to stay a safe distance behind the other boat.

But he wanted to see where these guys were going. See if he could figure out some answers about what Bright was up to.

The water was beautiful, a green blue and as clear as ever today.

Numerous boats were out as well as a few larger vessels on marine life viewing tours.

As he continued to glide across the bay, he spotted some sea lions gathered on a large rock near the shore.

Higher on the cliffs, mountain goats roamed, minding their own business.

Tourists were going to have a field day once they saw that.

He slowed as the other boat went around a bend in the shoreline.

As he got closer to the mouth of the bay, the swells grew so large that his boat rocked dangerously.

This area of the water wasn't ideal for a small vessel like his.

He'd give it another few minutes before he turned around.

Then he saw the other boat pull onto a rocky, secluded shore.

He grabbed a ball cap and pulled it on low over his eyes. Then he remained out of sight, watching what happened.

The two men climbed off their boat and grabbed the bag they'd brought.

After muttering a few things to each other, they began walking toward the mountain that jutted at an eighty-degree angle from the shoreline. Jason knew there was a crack between the rocks that allowed people to climb at an easier incline up the mountain.

He needed to make another split-second decision.

Should he follow them?

Or should he mind his own business, leave this alone, and get back to town?

chapter
sixteen

I **STOOD** in the crowd and watched the ceremony.

They didn't call it a ceremony, but I did.

In ancient days, my ancestors met near the temple, where they offered tributes of their labor to those in charge. Gold. Animals. Sometimes even children.

The way it should be.

Life required sacrifice. That was what community was about. People so easily forgot that. They only thought of themselves.

So selfish.

That would be the downfall of society—not knowing our places.

As I stood there, a few people called hello. I nodded and said hello back.

People had gathered to raise awareness about the missing woman. I heard her name was Zoe.

I preferred to call her my sacrifice.

Names were inconsequential to me. Only a person's spirit mattered.

Tlatoani had chosen my last sacrifice. I wasn't sure why he'd picked who he had. I only knew he had spoken.

I was given a gift—I could sense people's essence. Could sense if they were kind or evil, giving or stingy, loving or hateful.

My first sacrifice had been careless. My second had been selfish.

I still wasn't sure about this new sacrifice. But my initial sense was that she was trouble.

As I scanned the crowd with their candles, I saw the other one again.

The newest chosen one.

The blonde with long hair that fell halfway down her back. She had big eyes, an easy smile, and loved pink. Pink —a color that screamed, "Look at me! I'm special!"

I'd attempted to do away with her yesterday in an easier manner than the others, but she'd survived my efforts.

The threat hadn't been eliminated as I'd planned.

I frowned.

That was a problem.

Especially as a new urgency pressed on me.

Others may not feel it, but I sensed the tremors around me. Tremors that would become dangerous if the gods were not appeased, especially Huītzilōpōchtli.

That meant I didn't have much time.

But this wasn't the place to act . . . was it?

My jaw tightened.

I couldn't get caught up in routines. Couldn't get caught up in the thought pattern of "this is the way things have always been" or "this is the way I've always done things." Tlatoani spoke in different ways at different times.

His methods were sometimes unexpected, but I needed to be open to listening and obeying.

So maybe finding my prey at night wasn't the solution. Not the only solution at least. Other methods could be employed.

Still, I would need to be careful as I waited for the right opportunity.

I couldn't be caught.

If I was, who would carry out the master's plans? No one.

Because no one else believed like I did. No, they might believe in Jesus or Muhammad. They might even believe in themselves or in politicians.

But I knew the true source of power.

I was at one with the earth around me in a way most of these people couldn't begin to understand. They claimed to admire the beauty around them, but they couldn't appreciate the intricacy of this landscape. To most people, it was simply a photographic opportunity.

Because they were shallow and out of touch.

I looked at the sky, and my heart pumped harder.

Tlatoani, I need another sign. Another confirmation.

As I waited, someone stepped before the crowd and began to talk about the importance of finding Zoe. I tuned the man out.

I didn't need to hear this. It didn't matter.

Instead, I looked at the sky again.

A sign from the heavens . . . that was what I needed.

I'd asked Tlatoani, so now I waited.

I sucked in a breath when I saw an eagle flying overhead.

Was that it? The confirmation this was all legit?

My heart soared.

It was.

Earlier, I'd been upset when the sacrifice hadn't died.

Now I saw this as a challenge.

My new sacrifice would be different than the others.

I glanced at her again as she stood there so innocently. She stared at the speaker on the stage. Then she glanced around.

A growl rumbled inside me.

There was that curiosity again.

Curiosity that could mess up everything.

But that was okay.

Her time was coming.

Coming quickly.

I'd need to keep an eye on her as I planned my next move.

Timing was everything.
I cracked my knuckles.
Should the timing be right now?

JASON MADE HIS DECISION. He pulled his boat ashore and moored it to a nearby rock.

Remaining hidden, he peered around some boulders to see what those men were doing.

They still had that large black bag with them. But they started climbing up the cut-through.

This area was part of Caines Head State Recreation Area. During World War II, Fort MacGilvray was built as a command center at the top of the cliffs. Though long closed, there had once been searchlight stations, artillery, and radar installations through the bay as part of the Seward Harbor Defense System.

During the war, the Japanese had occupied two of the Aleutian Islands. Fearing future attacks, the US military had rushed to make Seward a heavily fortified town.

Five hundred soldiers had been stationed here at one

time, and the remains of their brief stay could still be found hidden on—and in—these cliffs.

The question was: what were these two men doing here today? Their actions contained an air of secrecy.

These guys didn't appear to be tourists looking for adventure.

They had a definite purpose. They weren't even dressed to hike. Not really. Not in their black utility pants, black T-shirts, and military-style boots.

Jason had a feeling they were bad news.

Once they disappeared from sight, he followed them.

He'd been out here before. Before he was a town outcast, he and his classmates frequented the location for bonfires on weekends.

The area really was beautiful, and this cove in particular was secluded.

He stayed light on his feet as he scrambled up the rocks, trying to see where these men were going. The path here was narrow and rather straight, so he needed to be careful if he wanted to remain unseen.

His thoughts continued to race.

Were there drugs in that bag?

But if those guys were smuggling drugs, why carry them up the side of the mountain? It made more sense for them to take them out to sea, where they could distribute them to other places.

He couldn't figure out why they might head in this direction.

Did it have anything to do with the old military base?

As Jason continued forward, his thoughts drifted toward all the times he and Hannah had hiked this trail. They'd had some really good times together. He'd been certain they would grow old with one another.

But that dream had died right along with her.

Along with many other dreams in the process.

Sometimes it all still seemed like a nightmare he'd wake up from.

But he'd never awoken from it. This was his reality.

If Mariella knew what was best for her, she'd stay far away. Jason had tried to tell her that, but she hadn't listened.

He needed to try again.

He didn't want to be mean to her. Or rude.

But he needed to think of a way to get through to her.

Because Mariella might think Jason was innocent now. But once she found out all the details of his past . . . she'd quickly change her mind.

The thought of disappointing her stung a little too much. The realization was strange. He didn't know her well.

But that didn't change how he felt.

He paused when the men ahead of him stopped at a section of the trail.

A moment later, they veered into the woods.

Jason remained where he was.

Had those men seen him? Was that why they'd changed course?

Should he return to his boat or keep following them?

He wasn't sure.

But he needed to be very careful.

Mariella stood among the crowd at the vigil being held for Zoe.

She'd left the library thirty minutes ago—it had closed so everyone could be at the vigil—and she'd come to the town square, joining the crowd already gathered.

As she stood there, her thoughts still swirled over what she'd learned from those newspaper reports.

In one of the articles, an FBI agent had been interviewed about what it would have taken to get the twins out of the state.

Unfortunately, it was easier than it seemed due to the proximity of the water as well as all the small airports in the region.

Though the feds questioned local pilots, and no one claimed to have seen anything, the most likely theory was that the babies had been taken to a private airplane and then transported from this area. No one here had seen them since. There had been no leads.

Someone somewhere had to know something.

But in all these years, no one had come forward.

Mariella pushed down her discouragement and glanced around.

She couldn't believe the number of people who had come out for the vigil. Even though it was the middle of the day, everyone held candles. Several city leaders stood on a makeshift stage at the front of the crowd and gave inspiring speeches about coming together and not losing hope.

A man and woman stood to the side of the others, probably in their late forties or early fifties. Based on the grief and worry in their gaze, they had to be Zoe's parents. The man was beefy and tough-looking, wearing a T-shirt that read Hamlin Welding. The woman was smaller, blonde, and almost fragile in appearance.

Mariella had started at the back of the crowd, but as more people filled in she'd been thrust into the center of the throng. Her position didn't give her the opportunity to watch everyone around her, which was what she wanted.

She was trying to get a feel for the people in this town —and not just for her travel podcast. It was because she wanted answers.

And . . . she couldn't help but think about how killers sometimes showed up to be a part of these things—for some sick reason she'd never understand. Was the killer here now?

As Mariella stood there, a woman wearing a turban and hippie-style skirt caught her eye. She'd seen the woman earlier. The gal had set up a table on the street corner where she offered to read people's palms or give them a tarot reading.

Mariella wasn't into that kind of stuff. At all. Never had been, even in her partying days.

But several people had approached the woman, who went by Bianca, for a reading. Mariella had overheard someone ask Bianca if Zoe would be found.

Bianca had told them in a hushed voice that, yes, she would be found.

What Bianca didn't say was whether or not Zoe would be found alive.

Staying vague made her answers seem genuine.

Right now, Bianca mixed with the crowd. But her hand was raised in the air as if she tried to get a signal from another world to give her answers about the situation.

Mariella used to think that anyone who practiced any type of religion was a kook—whether that be the occult or Muslims or Christians.

But since being in Fairbanks, Duke had invited her to go to church with him, and she'd found herself enjoying it. The services weren't like she thought they'd be. They'd made her wonder if maybe there was more to religion—or relationship as Duke called it—than she'd ever assumed. If nothing else, she was curious—and more open-minded.

Her gaze drifted from Bianca across the crowd to Sean, the man who'd led the search and rescue yesterday.

He spoke with a police officer, but the conversation

looked personal—maybe even secretive. Interesting . . .

Before she could theorize on what they were talking about, an eerie feeling came over her. The hair on her arms rose, and she glanced around.

Why did she feel as if someone was watching her?

She scanned the crowd, but no one caught her eye. Most people were either staring up front as the mayor spoke or they whispered to the people with them.

Beyond the crowds, the mountains rose. They were close enough that anyone could be standing among the trees at their base watching without being seen.

Was that what was going on?

Before Mariella could think about it much longer, someone appeared beside her and asked, "How are you feeling today?"

Sean stood there. He must have wrapped up his conversation with the officer.

She touched her palms, which were still sore from being scraped, and shrugged. "Doing okay."

"I'm glad."

"How did the rest of the search go? Any luck?"

He grimaced and shook his head. "Unfortunately, we didn't find any leads."

"I'm sorry to hear that."

He paused as if formulating something else he wanted to say. "I heard you were talking to Jason Somersby."

At once, her lungs tightened. *This* was why he'd come over—not for a friendly chat.

She nudged her chin higher. "I did meet him, if that's what you mean."

"You should stay far away from him." His voice came out lower, almost more . . . threatening.

"That's what people keep saying."

"And for good reason." Sean's nostrils suddenly flared. "He never deserved Hannah. She was too good for him."

Mariella's eyebrows shot up. Bitterness stained the man's words.

There had to be a story there.

But before she could ask him any questions, a new sound split the air.

Gunfire.

Panic filled the square as the crowd began to scatter.

Mariella's mind whirled.

A gun? What was going on?

As the tide of people scrambled toward safety, someone grabbed her arm.

Not casually.

But tightly.

So tight that she flinched.

The offender tugged at her, almost as if trying to pull her away.

Before she could figure out what was going on, the person holding her arm jerked her.

She stumbled sideways through the crowd as someone dragged her away.

At once, Mariella knew she was in serious trouble.

chapter
eighteen

JASON REMAINED WHERE HE WAS, waiting to see what those men were up to as they veered off on a side trail.

Then he heard voices.

Not from the men.

The voices were feminine.

Wait . . . were there other hikers out here?

He ducked behind a tree, wishing he could disappear.

The last thing he wanted was for those two men to hear him talking to someone.

But the women must have seen or heard him.

They paused and stared his way, fear in their eyes.

Jason could run into the woods, but that would only look more suspicious. Still, maybe they hadn't seen his face. Maybe they would think he was a random weirdo they couldn't identify.

But that could creep them out even more.

His stomach tightened.

As they cautiously started walking again, he realized they would see him.

Then they might start screaming.

For that reason, he raised his hands and stepped out of the woods, ready to explain himself. That seemed the best route to go.

"Hey, how's it going?" he started. "I didn't mean to scare you."

The two women gasped and huddled together, acting as if he were a mass murderer about to kill them.

"I just stepped aside to wait for you guys to pass by," Jason continued. "I didn't intend to frighten you."

"You were watching us." One of the women stared at him with accusation in her eyes.

"No, I wasn't. I was just up here taking a hike."

"Then why did you hide behind a tree?"

"I wasn't hiding. I just didn't want to startle you." He reminded himself to keep his voice casual, but his anxiety was ratcheting, making his words come out faster than he intended.

They still stared at him as if trying to form their judgment.

Then the second woman's eyes widened. "Wait . . . you're that guy. The one they think abducted that camper."

The blood drained from Jason's face as his heart

pounded harder against his rib cage. "No, you're wrong. That wasn't me."

"Please, don't hurt us." The first woman's voice shook with fear. "We'll do whatever you want."

More tension spread through him.

"I don't want anything. I'm not going to hurt you." Jason took a step back. "In fact, I'm just going to leave you alone. I didn't mean for any of this . . ."

"No, it's too late, you creep!" the first woman said. "I'm calling the police!"

The tension in him turned to panic. "You don't need to do that. I was just hiking."

"You were hiding in the woods watching us!" the first woman continued. "You were going to try to snatch one of us. Or both of us!"

She grabbed something from her belt.

Bear spray.

If that woman doused him . . .

Jason had tried to explain. To do the right thing.

Now the only thing that made sense was for him to get out of here before he got hurt.

He turned just as the woman hit the cannister nozzle. The scent of chemicals and hot peppers filled the air.

Before the spray reached him, Jason darted back down the steep trail.

Following those two men had been a bad idea.

But not for the reasons Jason had suspected.

He hadn't been caught by those men.

However, this was even worse.

These women represented a whole new level of danger.

Mariella felt the grip around her bicep tighten.

A yelp escaped.

Whoever had hold of her . . . he was hurting her.

She was certain it was a man based on the strength of his grip.

But who? Why?

She glanced around, but it was total chaos.

She couldn't see who the guy was.

Had the gunshot been meant as a distraction? To scare the crowd so this person could get to her?

Then, all at once, whoever had grabbed her let go.

Mariella froze where she was and glanced around.

But everything blurred.

Her head throbbed.

There were too many people. Too many people going in different directions.

She had no idea which of those people might have grabbed her. Or why he let her go.

Sean was here, not far away. So was the officer he'd been chatting with.

Had it been one of them? Had they been trying to pull her to safety?

She wanted to believe that, but she didn't.

The man's grip had been too tight. Too forceful.

But why her?

What sense did that make?

She had to be overreacting.

She was simply immersed too deeply in violence and crime. So much so that she saw danger everywhere.

That had to be it.

Mariella's heart throbbed in her ears as she tried to make sense of things.

But it was useless. Nothing about this made sense.

She couldn't help but feel she was in danger.

Yet she didn't know from whom or why.

chapter
nineteen

MARIELLA SHOWED up at Bottom Feeders a few minutes before six-thirty to grab a table.

But she felt unsettled.

When she got back to the cabin earlier, she and Matthew had decided to head back to the campground area.

Something was bugging her about yesterday.

She was certain she'd felt that prick in her neck before her mind had gone wonky.

She knew it was literally like looking for a needle in the proverbial haystack.

But they'd gone back to the site and searched the ground. Matthew had brought a large magnet with him he'd purchased at the hardware store on the way out.

It had taken the two of them twenty minutes, but they'd found a small dart in the area where Mariella had fallen. Seeing it had given her a sense of victory.

And fear.

But at least maybe she wasn't losing her mind.

They'd taken it to the police station. The officer she spoke with didn't look crazy about the idea of testing it—in fact, he acted as if nothing would come from it.

But he'd promised to see what he could do.

At least it was *something*.

Mariella hoped the officer truly did follow through.

For now, she found a table near a window overlooking the water and settled back to wait for Jason to arrive.

She was still shaken from everything.

From what she'd heard, the gunfire earlier was from a weapon that had been accidentally discharged by someone in a nearby cabin. She wasn't sure if the person had been arrested or not—rumor was it hadn't been malicious but an accident.

No one had been hurt. That was the good news.

But her arm was still tender where that faceless man had grabbed her. In fact, she had a bruise there. She knew she hadn't imagined the whole thing.

Just like she hadn't imagined feeling that dart.

She wanted to believe someone had been trying to save her from the chaos of the crowd, to pull her away from danger.

But she didn't feel confident in that.

Pushing those thoughts aside, she glanced around. The restaurant was crowded, but the scent of seafood and spices tantalized her. Ordinarily, this would be a fun dinner out.

But not considering everything that had happened.

As she sat there, she froze.

The hair on her arms rose again.

Was someone watching her?

She was getting that feeling all too often lately.

She glanced around but didn't see anyone.

So why the feeling?

She had no idea. She tried to put it out of her thoughts.

Matthew had insisted on coming with her, but he'd found a seat at the bar. Truthfully, Mariella felt better having someone here watching her back—especially in light of everything that had happened.

She glanced around the room and wondered if Jason would actually show up or if he'd simply said he'd come to appease her. The jury was still out.

She'd heard more people talking about Jason—just like earlier on the search and rescue. He'd been judged and sentenced in these people's minds.

Small towns could be great places . . . until they weren't. Until they were a place where you couldn't escape the rumors. Until they became a biome of lies and gossip.

Until you were an outcast.

Mariella lowered her menu and glanced at the time.

It was six-forty.

Jason wasn't here.

He'd stood her up.

Matthew glanced back at her from the bar. His look made it clear he was thinking the same thing.

She'd give Jason five more minutes. Then she'd assume he wasn't coming.

But Mariella felt surprisingly disappointed at that thought.

Jason stood outside the restaurant, just around the corner where he couldn't be seen.

Part of him was ready to call it quits for the day.

After the confrontation with the two women on the trail, he knew he had no hope of finding those unknown men with the black bag.

Instead, he'd quickly made his way back down to his boat and came back to Salmon-by-the-Sea. He halfway expected those women to report him and for Chief Dunne to find him at any minute.

He'd been tempted to go home and forget about his dinner plans.

But something had led him to Bottom Feeders.

He wasn't the type to stand anyone up.

And Mariella . . . the thought of leaving her wondering where he was . . . it was unsettling for some reason.

After a few minutes of hesitation, he peered inside.

Sure enough, Mariella was there.

Sitting at a table.

She had actually come.

The woman had nerve—he'd give her that.

But he still wasn't so sure he wanted to meet with her.

Not because he was *afraid* of meeting with her. He wasn't even afraid of her judgment. He'd already faced enough of that.

He was afraid of messing up someone's life again.

Besides, why add another complication to things?

Plus, there was still something about the woman he didn't trust.

Like why had she been meeting with Bright?

Jason knew Mariella was a podcaster. She'd told him that.

Was all this just so she could get more information from him? He'd been tempted to look her up, to find out more about her.

But he didn't. He knew the information available online about a person wasn't always true. Whether it was information someone had put out there themselves that made them look like perfect people living perfect lives . . . or false information added by others that bordered on slander.

Either way, neither was real.

Jason sucked in a breath, deciding he *would* go inside. He'd just get this over with.

Mariella would be leaving town at the end of the week. Then he'd never see her again. She'd carry on with her life, and he'd carry on with his.

With that thought, he spotted Mariella as she glanced at someone sitting at the bar.

A man with blond hair.

They were here together, weren't they?

The muscles between Jason's shoulders tightened.

Mariella had brought someone with her? Was that guy her boyfriend? Were they going to corner him and teach him a lesson?

Life had taught him to be cautious—and to expect the worst.

He glanced at the man but didn't see any cameras or anything else suspicious.

Still, he remained cautious.

He took a step back, about to leave.

Then he stopped.

Jason had always told himself that running away was not the solution. It was why he'd stayed here in town.

So why run away from this?

If things got too hairy inside, he could always leave.

But for now, Mariella wanted to talk. She hadn't ghosted him as soon as she learned what had happened here in town.

Maybe this was worth a try.

He swallowed hard and hoped he didn't regret this.

Then he pulled open the door and stepped inside the restaurant.

He ignored sideways glances from a few locals. Instead, he steered between the tables to Mariella, pulled out the chair across from her, and sat without any fanfare.

The menu slipped from her fingers as she looked at him, seemingly startled at his presence.

Then she tilted her head. "You came."

"Sorry I'm late."

"I didn't think you were going to show up."

He shrugged. "I try to be a man of my word."

"I like people who keep their word."

Jason stared at her, his thoughts still racing. She was surprisingly confident and calm right now.

When he'd first seen her, he'd assumed based on her looks that she was shallow and materialistic.

But so far she seemed to be nothing like that.

He locked eyes with her. "You don't care what people think, do you?"

Something raced through her gaze, maybe regret. "It depends on the circumstances."

"I get that." His gaze zeroed in on her hands and the scrapes there. They hadn't been there earlier. He was sure of it. Concern pulsed through him. "What happened?"

She glanced at her palms and shrugged. "Just a little accident."

His eyebrows shot up. "Another one?"

"I guess I'm a magnet for trouble."

Maybe she was . . .

Mariella scanned everything around them before looking back at him. "You're quite the celebrity around town."

"I don't think I'd call myself a celebrity. I'm infamous if anything." He shifted in his seat. "I know I said this last night, but it bears repeating again. People aren't going to trust you if you're seen with me."

She shrugged, unbothered. "I have a lot of the information I need. I'm not too worried."

"Then why did you bring that guy along with you?" Jason nodded behind him.

Her cheeks flashed red. "I told Matthew I would come alone, but he insisted that was a bad idea."

Jason waited for her to explain.

"I'm sorry," Mariella continued with the shake of her head. "That's my twin brother. Sometimes he can be a little overprotective of me."

Jason glanced back at the guy, who gave him a hard look.

Now that she mentioned it, Jason could see the resemblance.

Things began to make a little more sense.

His shoulders softened some.

"I can appreciate that." He turned to the menu and tried to set his mind at ease. "Their burgers are excellent here, by the way."

"I don't generally eat beef. Besides, I'm in a seafood town. I feel like I should eat some of the fresh catch."

"You can never go wrong with seafood here."

The waitress—a woman he'd never seen before—came and took their orders. Jason got that burger he'd mentioned, and Mariella got a salad with salmon.

That part was over. Now the fun part came.

Small talk.

Before that could start, his gaze drifted toward the door.

Bright Armstrong stepped inside.

Jason glanced at Mariella and saw her eyes widen.

He remembered the meeting between the two he'd seen earlier today.

Something about it still didn't sit well with him.

"Did you get what you needed from Bright yet?" Jason said, cutting to the chase.

Her startled gaze met his. "W-what do you mean?"

"You were going to interview him for your podcast, right?"

"Oh, that's right." She let out an almost nervous laugh. "No, I didn't. You warned me away from him, remember?"

He tried not to show his distrust, but something wasn't adding up.

If she hadn't interviewed Bright, what had they been talking about?

Had she been lying about her whole reason for being here?

What was she trying to hide?

Jason wasn't sure.

Could he trust Mariella? Or would he be a fool to do so?

chapter
twenty

MARIELLA TURNED her gaze away from Bright as he met with some other people and sat on the opposite side of the restaurant.

She hadn't meant to stare at him. Hadn't meant to give anything away to Jason.

Yet he seemed to know something was going on.

Maybe she shouldn't have asked Jason if he knew Bright to begin with.

But she hadn't known Jason would react the way he had.

So she'd lied about wanting to interview Bright for her podcast.

She didn't want people here to know the real reason she'd come to this town.

Not yet.

She stared at Jason as he sat across the table from her.

So ruggedly handsome in a boy-next-door type of way.

Funny . . . she'd never seen herself as the type to be attracted to an outdoorsman. No, it had always been businessmen or other influencers or entertainers.

Jason was so different from them.

Yet she was so incredibly curious about him.

"Why don't you just say whatever is on your mind?" He leaned back in his seat and waited.

Mariella touched the bright yellow straw in her glass of ice water and began to swirl it, the motion matching her thoughts.

Why beat around the bush anymore?

"I know what I've heard around town." She stole a glance up at him. "But I've never been one to trust gossip. I want to know your side of the story."

He glanced down as if contemplating how to respond. Then he slowly nodded. "Okay then. What do you want to know?"

"I want to know about what happened five years ago and why people think you're guilty."

He drew in a deep breath, one that appeared heavy and burdened at the same time.

Would he tell her his story? She wasn't sure if he trusted her enough to do so.

But she hoped he would.

She waited as Jason studied her, seemingly trying to figure out how much to say.

Part of her was certain he'd change his mind and switch subjects.

Then he said, "The truth is that I grew up here in this town. When I was eighteen years old, I began dating a girl named Hannah Bentley. I had been crushing on her since I was fifteen. It took me that long to build up the nerve to ask her out."

Mariella smiled at the mental image—especially since it was hard to imagine Jason being scared of anything. "That's sweet."

Jason nodded, but grief now filled his eyes. "Once the two of us started dating, we were inseparable. I was head over heels in love with her. We dated for the next three years. She decided to go to college up in Anchorage to study education. But she came home that May to work for the summer like usual. She had a weekend off, so we decided to go camping with some friends of ours."

Mariella held her breath. She knew where this was going, and she dreaded the rest of the story—especially since Jason still seemed so dreamy when he said Hannah's name.

That was what Mariella wanted for herself also. She wanted a man who looked as if his heart and mind went into a different stratosphere whenever he talked about her. She wanted someone who only had eyes for her, who thought she was the perfect person for him.

Was she a hopeless romantic? Maybe. But she'd rather be that way than to settle for someone or have someone settle for her.

Mariella waited to hear what else Jason had to say. But before he could continue, their food was delivered.

The plates in front of them smelled tantalizing.

But Mariella was more interested in hearing and learning more about Jason than eating.

He lowered his head a moment as if lifting a prayer before picking up a fry. He didn't seem to have much interest in eating either, however.

His voice sounded heavier, deeper as he continued. "That night we were all sitting around the campfire having a good time. Until Hannah and I got into a fight. It was probably only the third fight we'd had since we started dating."

"What was it about?" Mariella might as well get the full scoop. She lifted her fork and poked around the lettuce, pretending to be interested in her meal.

Jason let out a long, burdened sigh. "It was stupid. There was this other guy at the campground, staying probably four sites over. I thought he was flirting with Hannah and that she was flirting back. I asked her to stay away from him. She insisted they weren't flirting, and I was being overbearing. Maybe I was. I'm not sure anymore. I just didn't like the way he looked at her."

Mariella could see it all playing out in her mind's eye. "What happened then?"

"We'd all been drinking that night. It was late anyway,

so I decided to go to bed and sleep it off. To be honest, I haven't touched alcohol again since that night. *A lot* has changed in my life since then."

Mariella heard the emotion in his voice, and she nodded. "I bet."

"I asked Hannah to turn in for the night too. Told her we'd talk things out in the morning. But Hannah refused. She stayed outside to cool off. Said she needed some space. The next thing I knew, I was asleep. I'm not proud of that fact. But it was a mixture of exhaustion, alcohol, and the cool mountain air, I suppose. When I woke up the next morning, she wasn't in the tent with me."

Mariella could hardly breathe. "What happened next?"

"I figured maybe she was so angry with me that she'd camped out with one of her friends. So I woke up everyone, trying to find her. But she wasn't with them either."

"I can only imagine you were beside yourself."

He ran a hand over his mouth as if concealing a frown. "I was getting worried, but it wasn't full-blown yet. Then I realized she could have just gone back to her parents' house. I mean, it would have been a long walk in the dark, but she could have done it. Or she could have called a friend for a ride even."

"But she didn't," Mariella added.

Jason glanced at the table again unable to disguise the grief in his eyes. "No, she didn't. I called her parents, and they hadn't heard from her. They started calling some of her friends in town. None of them had heard from her either. By that point, it was about ten a.m. The last time I'd seen her was about two-thirty a.m. There was no telling where she was by then."

"So what did you do?" Mariella took a long sip of her water, the chatter of patrons around her fading. Even Taylor Swift crooning from the overhead speakers became merely a background noise.

"We told the camp office, and they called in park rangers. They in turn called the police, and the local police called the state police. Until they got there, my friends and I, along with a few other campers who'd heard what was going on, had begun to search the woods hoping that maybe Hannah had just wandered off and gotten lost."

As he wiped a tear from the corner of his eye, compassion spread through Mariella.

That was true grief.

And to Mariella it proved again that Jason wasn't guilty.

chapter
twenty-one

"WAS Hannah the type to go off alone in the woods?" Mariella asked as her conversation with Jason continued.

"At night? No." Jason thought about it a moment before shrugging. "I mean, she grew up around here. Her dad is a bush pilot. She was pretty self-sufficient and familiar with this area. But at night things can get confusing, even for seasoned hikers."

Mariella shivered as she imagined how Hannah must have felt out in those woods alone and lost.

"Things just exploded from there." Jason let out a shaky breath before running a hand through his hair. He glanced outside at the water in the distance as he seemed to collect himself. "We searched but didn't find her. Volunteers searched but didn't find her. We looked for three days without finding anything."

He paused, and Mariella waited for him to finish, sensing he needed time.

"On the fourth day, we found her sweatshirt caught on a branch about a mile from our campsite. It was in the woods near a drop-off by the river."

Mariella swallowed hard. She thought she knew where Jason was going with this, but she hated to think about that.

"Her body was found at the bottom of the cliff," he finished.

Mariella narrowed her eyes. "Wait . . . so it was an accident?"

"That's what they thought at first. But . . . when rescuers reached her body, they discovered an arrow had been shot through her heart."

His words hung in the air with enough finality that Mariella shivered.

What a horrible way to die.

And for Jason, what a horrible reality to live with.

Jason stared at Mariella, waiting for her reaction.

He knew his story was a lot to take in. He didn't like to talk about it.

Besides, there weren't that many people to talk about it with, except maybe his dad and Dustin. He had a couple other friends who still stuck by him. Even then, Jason couldn't help but notice they kept their distance.

But for some reason, it had felt good to tell Mariella his side.

Even though she still hadn't reacted.

A moment later, she finally did.

"I can only imagine how hard that would have been to go through." Her voice sounded soft with compassion. "And I'm sorry. I'm sorry that her killer still hasn't been found and that people are still looking at you."

A burst of warmth spread through his chest at the kindness of her words. "Thank you."

She shifted, and Jason knew she was about to say something uncomfortable.

He braced himself.

"Look . . . I know this is going to sound funny." Mariella leaned toward him with her elbows on the table. "And I had no intention of saying this before I came into town or even before I met you tonight for dinner. But you opened up to me so . . ."

He took a bite of his fry and waited for her to continue, truly curious about where she was going with this.

"My own story is a little strange," Mariella continued. "Because I started out going to college to study communications. I wanted to be an entertainment reporter on one of those TV shows like *Entertainment Tonight*. In fact, one of my parent's friends worked as a producer on the show and basically told me I was a shoo-in."

"So what happened?"

"Before I graduated, I started making these videos for my socials. Long story short, I became a beauty influencer with more than a million followers. But that all blew up, and I started searching for something else to do that I was good at—and that I enjoyed. That's when I became a travel podcaster. But it's not my main thing."

Jason picked up another fry. "What *is* your main thing?"

Another moment of hesitation crossed her features.

What was she so scared of saying?

Her gaze flickered back up to his. "I promise I didn't track you down for this reason. I didn't track you down *at all*. I had no idea when we met what your story was. I need you to understand that."

"You're making me a little nervous, but okay."

She let out a long breath. "It's a long story how it all came together, but some people I know . . . we all started this true crime podcast. In fact, we've successfully solved three cases so far, and we've brought attention to a lot of other cases."

Jason stiffened. True crime? That couldn't be a coincidence.

At once, his guard went up.

He studied her, searching for the truth in Mariella's eyes. "You're saying that's not why you came here?"

Mariella nodded. "You can ask my brother. We first came to Alaska a few months ago. I had no intentions of staying, but I fell in love with the state. Now I'm trying to see as much of it as I can in between working on my other projects. That was why we came here. If that other woman hadn't gone missing, I probably would have never known at all what happened five years ago."

"So where are you going with this?" Jason's voice contained an edge of caution.

She leveled her gaze with him. "Why don't you let us take on this case?"

Alarm instantly went through him. Something like that would bring more attention to him. That was the *last* thing he wanted. "I don't think that's a good idea."

"I'm not going to push you into anything, of course. But the people on my team . . . one's a lawyer and another one is a former investigator with the Army CID. Another one is a survivalist who works for the park service."

"And your role?"

Mariella blew out a breath. "I'm the one that puts it all together. I narrate. I find the stories and set things up. I'm basically the face of the podcast. The rest of the people in the group . . . they're not so much in front of the camera people. But I am."

"I can see that." He glanced behind him. "And your brother?"

"He's our tech guy. He does research for us, and he produces the show. Then there's Simmy . . . she's great with people and brings a nice calm balance to all of it."

This was the last thing Jason had expected to hear. "That's all very interesting."

"So does that mean you want us to help?"

He thought about it a moment, but he remained unsure. "I don't know . . ."

"It couldn't hurt to have us look into it, especially since you're innocent. We can help prove that."

Mariella sounded awfully sure of that fact. "I've been searching for answers for five years, and I haven't found anything."

"I can imagine that that's frustrating. And I'm not saying we know some type of magic formula that will guarantee we'll find answers. But if all of us come together and try to find the truth, at least it's *something*."

He considered it a moment. "I've never been one to turn down help. But you don't know what you might be digging up . . . There's a killer out there who got away with this five years ago, and he's not going to like someone trying to hunt him down."

"That might not make a difference. Because now this other woman has disappeared. If it's the same guy, he doesn't seem to be shying away from the spotlight."

Jason twisted his neck. "No, I suppose you're spot on."

Mariella stared at him. "So what do you say?"

He thought about it another moment as he contemplated his response.

chapter
twenty-two

MARIELLA HELD her breath as she waited for Jason to reply.

Would he be offended by the offer and think she'd simply tracked him down, hoping to capitalize off his heartache? Or would he realize the truth—that she really did want to help?

She saw the thoughts racing through Jason's gaze as he contemplated what to say.

She should probably distract herself with her salad to give him space as he considered her offer. She'd barely touched her food.

But she couldn't bring herself to eat.

Finally, Jason shifted, and Mariella knew an answer was coming.

"Okay," he finally said with a quick nod. "I'll work with you guys. What do I need to do?"

Relief—and delight—shot through her. "Let me call

them and see when they can be here. Then I can get back with you, and we can go from there. Do you work every day?"

"In the busy season, my father and I usually work seven days a week. But in general, we're back from the charter fishing trips by about five. So I have the evenings."

"That sounds like a tough way to live. No time to enjoy life?"

"Sometimes I think it's better for me if I stay busy. However, it's only like this in the summer. In the winter we don't really take the boats out to go fishing very much."

That made sense . . .

Mariella finally stabbed a bite of her salad as she thought things through.

But it was getting late, and Matthew was sending her impatient glances.

Jason had already finished his burger, so she called the waitress over and asked for a to-go box. Then she took the check.

But Jason slipped it from her grasp. "I'll pay."

"You don't have to do that . . ."

"And neither do you."

"But I owe you. You saved my life."

His gaze burned into hers. "You don't owe me anything, and never think you do."

The seriousness of his tone made her lungs freeze.

He didn't want her to be indebted to him. She supposed she could appreciate that.

"Besides, my dad taught me I should always pay for a woman's dinner if we were eating alone. And . . . if I recall correctly, you did call this a date." Jason flashed a smile as if trying to lighten the mood.

"I guess I did, didn't I? Thank you."

He left some cash on the table, and they stood. As they did, Matthew wandered over, and Mariella introduced them. They shook hands stiffly, each man eyeing the other.

He didn't blame Matthew for being cautious. Anyone would be in this situation.

When the three of them stepped outside, it was still bright even though it was already eight.

No sooner had they stepped onto the sidewalk than a man charged down the street right toward them.

Mariella froze and grabbed Jason's arm as alarm rushed through her. "Who is that guy?"

"I have no idea," Jason muttered, his muscles bristling as he edged in front of her.

Apparently, the man knew exactly who Jason was.

The guy reached them and grabbed Jason's shirt. In one quick motion, he shoved Jason against the brick wall and got in his face.

Wait . . . she did recognize him. From the vigil earlier. He was—

"What did you do with my daughter?" the man

demanded, rage dripping from his words. "I swear I'll kill you if you don't tell me."

Jason's heartbeat ratcheted.

This must be the father of the woman who'd just gone missing.

Zoe.

Jason's throat tightened as he stared at the man, one with crazy, grief-stricken eyes.

"I didn't do anything to her." Jason was careful to keep his voice calm.

In some circumstances, Jason would fight back. He had some self-defense skills.

But in situations like these, fighting back would only make him look worse in the eyes of those around him.

He also tried to practice turning the other cheek. It was a struggle at times, but doing so was wise.

So for now, he let this man pin him.

"Where is she?" Zoe's dad demanded again, thrusting Jason against the brick.

"Hey!" Mariella grabbed the man's arm, fire igniting in her gaze. "Put him down before you hurt him. He doesn't have your daughter."

The man whipped around so quickly that Jason feared Mariella might be injured in the line of fire. Thankfully, she wasn't.

"Who are you?" the man growled at Mariella.

"It doesn't matter who I am." Mariella kept her chin raised. "What matters is that you're accusing an innocent man."

He turned back toward Jason, sneering with malevolence. "I know *exactly* who he is. He killed that other girl, and now he has my daughter. I'm not going to let you get away with this."

Just then, a police officer pushed through the crowd.

Yes, a crowd had gathered.

Jason hadn't noticed in the flurry of things.

Some of the onlookers even had their phones raised.

Officer Longwood—an old classmate of Jason's—put his hand on the man's chest and pushed him away. "I know you're upset, Mr. Hamlin, but this isn't the way to go about doing things."

The man remained grounded where he was, still scowling at Jason. If looks could kill, Jason would be dead.

"He's just walking around like nothing happened." Hamlin sneered again.

"Confronting him like this isn't doing anyone any favors. He's not worth going to jail for." Officer Longwood definitely wasn't a fan of Jason. He didn't bother to hide the judgment in his gaze.

Hamlin stared at Jason another moment before dropping him to the ground.

Jason's lungs eased as the man backed off.

But he didn't dare lower his guard.

Especially because Hamlin still shot daggers at Jason with his eyes.

Jason stood still, bracing himself for whatever might happen next.

Because there were no guarantees this man would walk away before enacting his own form of justice.

chapter
twenty-three

MARIELLA WATCHED everything unfolding and wished she could step in and help.

Thankfully, Officer Longwood had shown up when he did.

Finally, Hamlin took another step back. But his entire body still looked tense.

"Go back to your cabin, and I'll be in touch with any updates," Officer Longwood told him. "I promise."

The man let out another grunt, practically appearing barbaric with his sweaty brow, bulging veins, and blood-shot eyes.

But he took a step back.

Then he glanced at Mariella. "I'd stay away from him unless you want to end up missing also."

The man's words felt like a slap across the face.

But even more so, this wasn't fair to Jason.

Matthew lightly touched her arm to let her know he

was there. She'd nearly forgotten in the flurry of things.

Zoe's father stormed away, leaving the rest of them standing there in shock.

And it wasn't just them.

The crowd that had gathered also seemed stunned.

Officer Longwood looked at Jason, an aloof look in his eyes. "Are you okay?"

Jason smoothed his shirt and nodded. "I'm fine."

But based on the scowl the officer gave Jason, the man doubted his innocence.

"If there's nothing else, I'll be on my way." Jason raised his chin and nodded down the sidewalk.

Longwood's gaze continued to sear into him. "You're free to go."

Jason took Mariella's arm, glanced back to make sure Matthew was following, and then pushed through the crowd. "Where are you parked?"

"Over there." She pointed to her vehicle.

He walked her and Matthew to the sedan and paused. "Are you still sure you want to do this?"

Mariella didn't even have to think about it. "I'm positive."

His shoulders softened with relief. "Okay then. We can catch up later. But for now, it's better if you go back."

"Can I give you a ride?" She nodded at her car.

He glanced back at the crowd, several of whom still stood on the sidewalk gawking at him. Then he shook his head. "No. I'll be fine. Just take care of yourself."

But Mariella had to imagine he was anything but fine. That confrontation had shaken *her* up. Had given her a glimpse into what Jason's life must have been like over the past several years.

She frowned at the thought.

It must have been pure agony.

Back at her rental, Mariella made calls to the murder club.

To her delight, Duke and Andi said they were available to come this weekend—a week earlier than what they'd originally planned. And the weekend started tomorrow.

The cabin she'd rented was plenty big enough for them to stay there.

Meanwhile, Simmy and Ranger couldn't make it right away because of Simmy's job. She had a hard time getting off work at the trading post sometimes.

But they'd also sounded willing to take on the case and said they'd do whatever they needed to do to make it down to the Kenai Peninsula as soon as they could.

She tried to fall asleep that night, but she couldn't.

She had too many thoughts racing through her head.

Instead, she sat up and reached for the feather she'd left on her nightstand.

She'd found it on the welcome mat when she got back tonight. A bird—a big one—must have lost it in flight somehow.

Weren't feathers good luck?

She wasn't sure. She wanted to believe that.

Either way, it looked beautiful and soft and full of promise.

Setting it back down, she threw the covers off and paced toward her window.

She stared at the mountains outside. As she did, she remembered hearing the sound of that conch shell yesterday.

She shivered.

What had that been about?

She wasn't sure. Maybe it was nothing, just an innocent bystander having some fun and being one with nature.

The sound had just been so eerie . . .

Her thoughts turned to Zoe, and Mariella imagined again being out there alone.

The woman still hadn't been found, and it was going on almost forty-eight hours.

Even if the woman had just gotten lost, the amount of time she'd been missing was reaching a critical point.

Mariella knew what it was like to be scared out of your mind.

A few months ago, she'd been abducted by a man called the Ice Fairy Killer. He'd been ready to dump her in the river where her body would freeze. Then he planned to pull her body out and use her as a model for an ice sculpture.

Thankfully, her friends had found her in time.

She never spoke to others about how that experience had changed her. She didn't want people's sympathy.

But she was terrified. She didn't like going certain places—isolated places—alone anymore. She looked at strangers with a new wariness.

She'd started seeing a counselor online, and that had helped some.

But Mariella knew she still had a long way to go before she could properly heal.

As she stood by the window, movement in the trees caught her eye.

She blinked.

Were her eyes deceiving her?

She couldn't be sure. But there was definitely movement, and it wasn't a branch swaying with the breeze.

No, whatever it was, it had caught her eye.

Mariella dropped the curtain and shrank away from the window.

But she immediately gravitated back toward it.

This time, she stood at the edge and only nudged the curtain a little.

It could have been a wild animal.

Or it could have been a person.

Her throat tightened.

Was someone outside her house right now?

Her heart sped as she considered what to do.

chapter
twenty-four

MARIELLA CONTINUED TO WATCH, transfixed by whatever was moving outside.

Part of her wanted to call the police.

The other part thought that would be an overreaction —especially until she knew more.

Maybe the events of earlier today were messing with her mind, twisting everything into something scary and dangerous.

That was probably it.

But that reassurance didn't calm the tremble raking through her muscles.

She continued to watch. She hadn't seen any more movement.

Maybe whatever had been there was now gone.

But just as the thought entered her mind, a shadow moved.

Not a shadow.

A man.

He stepped from the brush.

Mariella's heart pounded harder as she watched, wondering what he would do.

He skulked toward the cottage, his motions tight and brooding.

As he got closer, an overhead light hit his face and his features came into view.

Panic raced through her.

It was the man she'd seen earlier. The one who'd confronted Jason.

Zoe's father.

Based on his bristled shoulders, flared nostrils, and fisted hands, he was angry.

What was he doing here? Had he followed her?

Maybe he thought Mariella knew something about Zoe because he'd seen her with Jason.

She shrank back, leaving the curtain cracked only an inch so she could see a little.

The man stormed toward the window and pressed his face into the glass as if trying to see inside.

Mariella stumbled backward.

As she did, she bumped the nightstand.

The lamp atop it clattered to the floor with a loud crash.

She glanced back at the window, fear pulsing through her. She'd made too much noise.

Now Hamlin knew without a doubt that she was inside.

Hiding was no longer an option.

"I know you're in there!" Hamlin yelled. "We need to talk!"

Talk? He didn't look like he wanted to just talk.

He looked ready to kill.

Suddenly, the walls seemed too thin. The doors too flimsy. The distance between her and this vigilante too small.

She took another step back but stumbled, sprawling on the floor. Her breathing felt labored as she realized how vulnerable she was.

This man was so angry . . . she had no doubt he could break down the door, find her, and pin her against the wall just as he had done to Jason earlier.

The question was: would he take things that far?

Jason needed to blow off some steam.

He had too many thoughts running through his head.

Too many regrets—regrets over things he wasn't even responsible for.

Right now, he regretted that Mariella had to witness that scene earlier. Moments like those had become an ugly reality of his life.

Though he still wasn't sure if he completely trusted

the woman, he didn't want to see any harm come to her either.

Now it appeared he'd pulled Mariella into danger.

She didn't deserve this.

To be fair, he didn't either.

Sometimes he dreamed about what it would be like to get away from this town. To start fresh somewhere. To be treated as a normal guy. But something always held him back.

Despite everything, this place was still home.

He had grown up on the water. From the time he was old enough to walk, Jason had gone along with his father on fishing expeditions.

In fact, when Pops was younger, he'd won several fishing championships. He'd developed quite the name for himself. But he'd settled down once Jason was born. After Jason's mom died and he became a single dad, he'd focused solely on charter trips.

It was dark outside as Jason wandered down to the docks toward *Fishful Thinking*. His father's boat was one of Jason's favorite places to escape to when he needed to clear his head. Usually at this time of night, the marina was private, except for a few people with houseboats.

Something about the water always calmed his soul. He liked to think that water was the place Jesus went when he needed to reflect also.

He'd become a Christian after Hannah's death, even

though he didn't attend church every Sunday. He preferred to read his Bible on his own.

It wasn't ideal, but there were only a couple of churches in town, and though the people there probably had good hearts, he'd never felt truly welcome.

Jason tucked his hands into his pockets as he strolled down the pier, looking at the waves bobbing in the bay like they didn't have a worry in the world. The water didn't fret about incoming storms. It simply went with the flow, knowing everything would work out in the end.

There was no place like this town . . . unless you got on the wrong side of things.

Was there even a chance for him to be redeemed?

He didn't think so.

He found comfort in knowing that even Jesus wasn't welcome in his hometown. This wasn't a burden Jason carried alone or one that others couldn't understand.

He turned onto the slip where his father's boat was docked and paused.

He sucked in a breath when he saw a word had been spray-painted in red on the hull.

Killer.

His heart pounded harder.

He glanced around, looking for the culprit.

But whoever had done this was long gone.

A flash of anger burst inside him.

Jason didn't deserve to be targeted like this. But his dad *definitely* didn't deserve to be targeted at all.

His dad already had enough on his mind, especially since he'd recently been diagnosed with rheumatoid arthritis. The disease had made it far more difficult to run the charter fishing business, especially when he had flare-ups.

In fact, if this whole ordeal continued on like it had been, his father could end up losing customers.

Without customers, they couldn't pay their bills.

They could lose their business.

Their home.

Everything.

Jason stared at the stark word one more time before shaking his head. He needed to grab some supplies and wash this off before his father, or anyone else, saw it.

chapter
twenty-five

AFTER JASON GRABBED some cleaning supplies they kept inside the boat, he got to work scrubbing the side of the vessel until the word disappeared. Then he cleaned up his mess, ready to turn in.

What a night.

What a day, for that matter.

He was certain this wouldn't be the last of the threats or vandalisms that happened.

Before he could start back to town, Chief Dunne walked down the dock.

Headed toward . . . him?

Based on her gait, that was how it appeared.

He paused and waited.

She stopped in front of him.

Dunne was Hannah's aunt. The woman had it out for him ever since Hannah had been found.

Hannah's family had never really liked him. And they made that clear after their daughter's death.

He hadn't been good enough for her while she was alive. And now that she was dead, he was scum.

The woman was in her fifties with tanned skin and dark hair scattered with a few grays. She was petite but on the stout side with a square face and unsmiling lips.

"Chief . . ." Jason nodded at her.

"Jason." She nodded curtly. "Do you have a minute?"

"Of course. Would you like to go on the boat?"

"Right here is fine." Her voice sounded hard and determined. "You been in the forest near the campground lately?"

"Wanderlust?"

"That's the one."

"I haven't been there in years. Why?"

"Some pistachio shells were found near the site where Zoe Hamlin disappeared."

His breath caught, but he tried not to show it. "Really? That's interesting. But what does that have to do with me?"

"I know how fond you are of pistachios."

"I do like them. But . . . I haven't been to the campground. And, even if I did go, I wouldn't leave anything behind. Is that what you're accusing me of?"

Her gaze remained hard. "We sent the shells out for testing. We should be able to see if anyone's DNA is on them. If it's yours, you should know I'm coming for you."

The blood drained from his face. "Noted."

"Don't leave the area."

"Hadn't planned on it."

"Don't." She turned and walked away.

But his heart still stammered out of control.

He hadn't left those pistachio shells. Had someone left them there to set him up?

He didn't know.

But he didn't like the sound of this.

Suddenly, all he could think about was getting back home.

Jason started back toward the town but paused. He couldn't handle running into more people who might throw hateful scowls or messages at him. Instead, he veered away from the shops and toward one of the paths cutting through the woods.

Maybe some quiet time in nature would help ease his tension.

But as soon as he stepped between the trees, the truth began to haunt him.

He'd met Zoe.

If people found out . . .

No . . . there was no way anyone should find out. He should be okay.

But what if people here in town did somehow discover that fact? If they made assumptions?

A flash of fear swept through him.

Everything would fall apart.

Mariella would definitely go running. Anyone in their right mind would.

If Jason wasn't careful, he would either spend the rest of his life in prison or someone would kill him in the ultimate act of self-proclaimed justice.

Mariella continued to stare at the window from her position on the floor.

She couldn't see the man, but she heard him. Heard how angry he was.

Just then, her bedroom door flung open.

Matthew.

"I called the police." His gaze veered from Mariella to the window. "What's going on?"

"It's the guy we saw earlier today. He's here." She pointed to the front of the cabin. "At the window."

Matthew scowled before bracing himself. "He thinks we have something to do with this because of your association with Jason."

The way he said Jason's name dripped with derision.

Her muscles tightened defensively. "Jason didn't take the girl."

"You don't even know him." His voice remained tight and almost accusatory.

Mariella started to rebuke his statement when the man outside banged on the window.

"I know you're in there," Hamlin yelled. "Tell me where my daughter is. I'm not gonna stop until I find her. Nothing will stand in my way."

Her blood turned cold.

She believed him.

He was desperate to know what happened to his daughter. She could understand that. Part of her even respected it.

At the same time, she knew nothing. Telling this man she knew nothing probably wouldn't get her very far. He didn't seem to be in an exactly rational frame of mind.

"We just need to wait it out until the police get here." Matthew remained by the door, his phone in his hands and a pensive expression on his face.

He didn't like this any more than she did, but he was surprisingly calm.

And he was probably right. They just needed to wait this out. The police would be here soon, and they would take this man away. Then Mariella and Matthew could get some sleep.

As that thought filled her mind, a new sound filled the air.

Glass shattering.

As wind swept through the room, she realized Hamlin had broken the window.

She stared at the rippling curtains. At the shards of glass now on the floor.

There was nothing to keep this man out.

Fear rippled through her.

Then she saw a leg and arm penetrate her room.

Hamlin was climbing inside, she realized.

twenty-six

AS MARIELLA SAW the guy climbing through the broken window, Matthew grabbed her hand, and she scrambled back to her feet.

They had to get out of here.

She and Matthew ran from the room.

But the man was surprisingly fast as he lunged toward them.

Just as they reached the hallway and she tried to close the door behind her, Hamlin grabbed her arm.

"I need to talk to you." He ground out the words, his sweat reeking of desperation.

"Get your hands off her!" Matthew stepped forward and shoved the man back.

His words ignited another firestorm inside Hamlin.

The guy grabbed her brother's shoulder. Then his fist collided with Matthew's jaw, and Matthew staggered backwards and hit the wall.

"Matthew!" Mariella reached for her brother.

But the man already stormed toward him again.

What would he do now?

Mariella didn't have time to think.

She just needed to act.

She grabbed her brother's arm and pulled him back.

She needed to put space between them.

She glanced around.

Saw the bookcase against the wall.

Quickly, she grabbed it and tipped it over trying to block the man.

The knickknacks and books on the shelves clattered onto the floor before the wooden shelves landed on top.

That only slowed up the man a moment.

He grunted and stepped over it.

Mariella kept her grip on Matthew as they backed away together.

Run! That was what they needed to do.

So why was she having so much trouble turning around and doing just that?

She glanced at Hamlin again and saw the anger saturating his eyes.

This guy was willing to beat them half to death if it meant trying to find answers, wasn't he?

Another shot of fear raced through her.

Movement sounded just outside the cabin, and her spine pinched with more fear.

Had this guy brought backup?

Were she and Matthew cornered?

No, please . . .

The prayer escaped her before she realized what she was doing.

These moments . . . they'd been happening more and more lately.

Who was here?

She couldn't bring herself to take her eyes off Hamlin as she waited for whatever was about to happen next.

The next instant, someone yelled, "Police!"

Then something crashed.

Officers flooded inside and took charge of the situation.

Mariella's shoulders drooped with relief.

Maybe they were safe.

Mariella watched as the police handcuffed Lucas Hamlin.

He'd been obstinate with the police. He yelled that he wanted answers. That Mariella knew what had happened to his daughter.

All because Mariella had been spotted having dinner with Jason in town.

As Hamlin was escorted outside, Police Chief Suki Dunne approached them. She'd introduced herself a few moments earlier.

Paramedics had already treated Matthew and given

him a cold compress to put on his jaw, which was swollen and bruised. Thankfully, it didn't appear to be broken.

Really, all of this could have been much worse.

"Are you two okay?" Chief Dunne glanced back and forth between them.

Mariella wound her arms together in front of her and nodded, even though she felt anything but okay. "I guess. Just shaken."

"I'm sorry that happened to you." The chief's lips drew downward in a compassionate grimace. "I can only imagine how frightening it was."

Mariella glanced beyond her at the police lights flashing through the open front door. "Is he going to jail?"

Chief Dunne followed her gaze, and her frown deepened. "We'll probably keep him there tonight at least. Do you want to press charges?"

Mariella glanced at her brother, trying to read his thoughts.

Part of her wanted to do just that.

To put this guy away so he couldn't hurt anyone else.

To get justice for the injustice she'd received tonight.

She also remembered that Hamlin was a grieving father and practically out of his mind with worry.

How could she fault him for that?

"I don't know," Mariella finally whispered honestly.

Chief Dunne's jaw twitched. "You have some time to think about it. I know this is a tough situation."

"To say the least." Mariella glanced behind her. "He broke the window."

"I know you guys are here visiting and that this place is a rental. I'll have one of my guys come to fix the door and cover the window, so you'll be safe tonight. That is, if you still want to stay here." The chief gave them a look, almost as if she were trying to feel them out.

Mariella nodded. "We do."

But part of her wondered if it was foolish to do that.

However, she'd backed down to bullies before. She didn't want to do it again.

"If there's anything else you need or that we can do for you, please let us know." Chief Dunne took a step back then paused.

Mariella knew the woman had something else on her mind.

She waited for the police chief to continue.

The chief's gaze locked with hers, and she lowered her voice before saying, "Jason Somersby is someone you don't want to be hanging out with."

Mariella's pulse ratcheted. "Why is that? Innocent until proven guilty, right?"

Chief Dunne didn't even blink. "Everyone around here thinks he killed Hannah and got away with it."

Mariella shook her head, abhorring the certainty in the chief's words. "I just don't understand why. What evidence is there that he did it?"

"He was the last one seen with her, and they were

arguing. He was also the one who ultimately found her body." She raised an eyebrow. "Coincidence? Or was it because he knew exactly where to look?"

Mariella's heart pounded in her ears.

Did those facts change anything about the situation? About how she felt about Jason?

Mariella wasn't sure.

Maybe she simply had great intuition.

Or maybe she was simply an idiot . . .

twenty-seven

I PAUSED IN THE WOODS.

Today hadn't worked out the way I thought.

I'd tried to grab the threat at the vigil, but there had been too much confusion.

I'd sensed it was better if I let her go.

So I did.

But now, I needed to think of a way to get her without calling attention to it.

I'd been watching her—even at the restaurant.

But she hadn't been alone.

So now I stood in the woods.

I'd followed her home.

Had considered making my move there.

But I didn't.

That man had been there.

He'd been totally unaware of my presence.

But I'd watched him.

He'd crouched in the woods observing the cabin for the longest time.

I could see by the way he fisted his hands that he was angry, that he was building up his nerve to make some kind of move.

I didn't stop him.

Instead, I watched.

My pulse raced when I saw him break in.

The man was coming unraveled.

Part of me hoped he'd make the sacrifice for me.

But then it might not count.

I'd considered stepping in to stop him.

But I couldn't do that.

Instead, I trusted Tlatoani that he would provide.

Several minutes later, the cops had come.

Tlatoani *had* provided.

But that also meant I needed to wait.

But how much longer?

I could feel the change in the air, in the earth.

I knew I didn't have much time.

For now, I slipped between the trees.

Tomorrow was another day.

chapter
twenty-eight

MARIELLA HARDLY GOT any rest that night.

She hadn't been able to sleep in her room. Not after what happened. Every time she looked at her window and saw the wood covering it, bad memories claimed her thoughts and imagination.

Instead, she'd grabbed a blanket and a pillow and slept on the couch. Though there were other bedrooms, the couch somehow felt safer.

She'd also worried about Matthew. He'd said his jaw was okay, but she saw his discomfort when he thought she wasn't looking.

Finally, at nine a.m., Mariella threw the blanket off and got up to fix herself something to drink.

As she made the coffee, she noticed that Matthew still hadn't emerged from his room.

Hopefully, he'd gotten some rest last night. Sleep would help him heal after being socked in the jaw.

When the coffee was done, she drank her mug slowly, letting her thoughts percolate.

What would this day hold?

Hopefully, no more danger. Would it hold answers about Bright Armstrong?

She wasn't sure. Part of her wanted to forget about him.

But she knew that wasn't possible.

Still, what was her next step? Should she try to be forthcoming with him?

Mariella didn't know.

She took another sip of her coffee.

She knew Andi and Duke were slated to arrive sometime today. She needed to check her phone and see if there were any updates from them.

Until they got here, Mariella would probably play with her travel podcast on this area and try to put together a script.

She had several other small items she needed to work on for her business.

She also wanted to research Hannah Bentley's death.

Maybe she shouldn't.

But she knew she wouldn't be able to stop herself. She wanted more information.

As her phone buzzed, she glanced at the screen and saw a text from Alpine.

Alpine Grist was an investor who'd agreed to cover their expenses as well as offer them a hefty payment for them to create more podcasts. He'd come to Mariella with the idea, and she'd convinced the rest of the team to go along.

Andi thought the man was hiding something, and she could be right.

There was something about the way Alpine looked at Mariella that made her uncomfortable, that made her think maybe there was more to his motives than he let on.

She just wasn't sure what.

But she really hoped that partnering with him didn't turn out to be a mistake. If so, it could ruin their true crime podcast, and she knew that. The team might not ever trust her again.

Mariella tried to stay positive while remaining cautious.

She hesitated a moment before clicking on the text. She never knew exactly what Alpine would say, and sometimes his texts sent her emotions into a tailspin.

Her gaze skimmed the words.

> Thinking about you. Hope your cases are going well. You should come visit me down in LA sometime so we can hang out and talk business.

She set the phone down and frowned.

Hang out and talk business?

Mariella had a feeling those were code words for something else.

She wanted to believe the best in the man, but she was jaded from her time in LA.

Maybe that was why she felt so attracted to Jason. He was so different from every other guy she'd met. The last thing he wanted was attention—and, in some ways, that was like a breath of fresh air.

He didn't care about style—though he had plenty—and he liked living the simple life. Plus, he was loyal to his father.

There were so many intriguing things about him.

Then she remembered the accusations against him and frowned.

She took another sip of her coffee, letting the warmth fill her.

Setting it down, her fingers lingered over the keyboard in a moment of hesitation. Then she typed Hannah's name into the search engine and waited for the results.

With another fishing charter canceled again today, Jason needed something to do.

He thought about going back out toward the fort to look for more evidence, but he decided against it.

For now.

He needed to keep his nose clean.

Instead, he decided to chop some firewood.

Burning off some stress would be good for him.

He stepped out the backdoor and headed to the wood pile.

He placed a log atop another log and then raised his ax.

As the tool hit the wood, it split with a crisp slice into two perfect pieces.

He smiled.

Back before he was the town outcast, Jason used to enter the lumberjack contest Salmon-by-the-Sea held every year in September. He'd won every competition he entered.

It was all about the method—one his dad had taught him. Other than losing his mom, the first two decades of his life had been idyllic with fishing, being outdoors, having lots of friends, and dating Hannah.

He worked awhile longer, piling up wood beside him before lowering the ax.

He needed to come back and gather the wood and place it in a stack against the outbuilding.

Right now, he wanted some water.

He took his gloves off and stepped into the house.

As he did, his gaze stopped at something on the table.

His heart pounded harder.

A bow and arrow lay there.

He'd never seen them before.

Slowly, cautiously, he stepped closer and examined them.

He couldn't be sure, but he'd bet these were the same

type that had been used to kill Hannah. Wooden. Hand-made. Rugged.

Maybe even the same bow.

Had someone left these here to send a message?

Or had they left them here to frame him? Was this evidence that had been planted?

Panic raced through Jason.

Someone was determined to make him pay for a crime he didn't commit.

He stared at the bow and arrow another moment, trying to figure out what to do.

Then he grabbed them and stormed outside.

No way was he taking the fall for something he didn't do.

He broke them in half as he walked.

Then he grabbed some of that freshly cut wood.

He would make a fire and burn this before anyone saw it.

The sooner, the better.

chapter
twenty-nine

MARIELLA STARED at her computer as pages and pages of articles appeared.

Though Salmon-by-the-Sea was a small town, Hannah's murder had gotten lots of attention.

Mariella stared at a picture of the woman. She was gorgeous in a homegrown kind of way, with honey-blonde hair and a bright smile. She looked like the kind of woman every guy would fall for and want to settle down with.

The opposite of Mariella, really. Mariella had a reputation of being high-maintenance and liking attention. Plus, there was that scandal back in California with Mark . . .

Her cheeks heated.

Sometimes, she still had trouble trying to figure out how to move on from that.

Her gaze stopped when she read Jason's name in one of the articles.

There he was, named as a person of interest.

Even Hannah's family members had been quoted—all saying they suspected Jason.

Mariella let that thought settle.

Why would Hannah's family suspect him? They should have known him. Certainly, they didn't think he could be violent like that. It didn't match the image she had of this man.

Just then, a pounding sounded outside her house.

No, on her front door.

Mariella's muscles instantly tightened.

What if someone else had come to give Mariella a piece of their mind? To teach her a lesson or to demand answers?

After last night's incident, she needed to be cautious.

She stared at the door, her heart pounding furiously as she considered what to do.

Jason stared at the fire.

Enough time had passed that his thoughts had settled, and logic had begun to creep its way in.

Maybe burning the bow and arrow hadn't been the best choice. But he'd panicked. He knew how being seen with them would look.

But what if there had been evidence on them? Evidence that could have cleared his name?

As he stared at the fire, he realized it didn't matter.

It was too late.

This just kept getting worse and worse.

As he continued to stare into the flames his lungs felt tight, as if he couldn't breathe.

It was one thing when people assumed he was the one behind Hannah's death.

But it was an entirely different thing if somebody was setting him up to take the fall.

Was that what was happening?

His dad hadn't left that bow and arrow out. Right?

He shook his head. No. He couldn't have. His dad wasn't the bow and arrow type.

But his dad had left early this morning—before Jason had gone outside.

So if someone had placed the bow and arrow there, it would have had to be during the time while Jason was out chopping wood.

That had probably been an hour.

So how had someone gone inside his house without him noticing?

They would have had to park far away where Jason couldn't hear the car. Then they would have had to sneak inside to leave the items there, and then sneak away all without being seen or heard.

That seemed unlikely.

But maybe they'd hiked in.

If Jason had to guess, his dad probably had left the front door unlocked.

Usually, this town was so safe that the locals didn't always bother to check to see if they locked up behind themselves.

People who lived here would know this.

Did that mean that the person who'd done this was a local? That they'd known that the house was probably unlocked, and this would be a great time to plant some evidence?

Certainly this person had heard him chopping wood. Had seen him outside.

Had the person who left it even stood at the window and watched him chop wood for a while, secretly delighting in what was about to transpire?

Had they left the bow and arrow to taunt Jason? Or were they sending the police over later so it could be discovered, and he could look even more guilty in everybody's eyes?

He didn't have any of those answers. But he caught himself glancing over his shoulder looking for flashing police lights.

There were none. Not yet.

He needed to search the rest of the house. Look for footprints. Maybe even search the woods.

And he would—as soon as this evidence was burned.

He took a fire poker and moved some of the wood.

All evidence of the bow and arrow was now gone, except for the aluminum tip. Jason would fish that out of the ashes later once it cooled.

If he was smart, he would pretend like he had never seen the weapon there in the first place. He would deny it if anyone asked.

Then another thought hit him.

To prove his innocence, he needed to find the real person who'd done this. Mariella's true crime podcast would work on the case. But he needed to be proactive also.

He'd sat back for so long, assuming it was someone from out of town who killed Hannah.

But now that this killer had struck again, he had to wonder if it was someone local. Someone who knew he could walk into a house without worrying about a door being locked.

Who could that be? Who'd want to do this to him?

A lot of people had made their hatred toward him clear.

Crusher.

Sean.

Officer Longwood.

Chief Dunne.

Even Bright Armstrong.

Would any of them really take things this far?

He wasn't sure. He couldn't afford to be too trusting.

His thoughts shifted. Would the killer really target him right now?

On second thought, maybe not.

In fact, what if . . . what if the killer himself hadn't left the bow and arrow? What if it was someone who was sure Jason was guilty. Who obsessed over the fact that he was still walking as a free man. Who wanted to make him pay for Hannah's death.

Most likely, it was someone who cared deeply about Hannah.

If it *was* someone local, Jason needed to find him before this person succeeded in framing him.

MARIELLA CONTINUED to stare at the door, uncertainty gripping her until she could hardly breathe.

Had Hamlin been released from police custody? Had he come back to finish what he started?

Memories of seeing his bulky frame climb through her window flooded her mind, and she pressed her eyes closed. Fear pummeled her.

Then she heard, "Mariella? It's me. Duke. Andi too."

Relief flooded her.

They were here already.

Not a crazy person wanting to teach her a lesson or cause her harm.

A burst of excitement flared in Mariella's chest.

Seeing her friends was just what she needed.

She threw the door open and saw the two of them standing on the porch with bags at their sides.

Andi, with her white-blonde hair, blue eyes, petite frame, and rebel demeanor.

Duke with his barely there beard, towering six-foot-plus frame, and broad shoulders.

The two of them formed a somewhat intimidating pair.

Plus, Mariella had noticed the way they looked at each other. They clearly liked each other. But she knew it was complicated since Duke's fiancée was missing—and had been for more than two years now.

He seemed like the noble type who'd wait for resolution rather than risk cheating. And Andi was smart and respectful.

Mariella threw her arms around both of them at the same time. "I'm so glad you could come."

"We're glad we could be here," Andi murmured.

She ushered them inside before shutting the door and turning toward them. "I wasn't expecting you guys to be able to get here so soon."

"Alpine arranged a flight for us and a rental car," Andi said.

Mariella flushed at the mention of the man.

As a step sounded behind Mariella, Duke's gaze wandered over her shoulder.

His eyes narrowed. "Matthew? What happened to you?"

Mariella turned to see her brother had emerged from

his bedroom. He still wore the flannel bottom pajamas he'd slept in and a black T-shirt.

But his jaw looked just as bruised and swollen as it had before—if not worse.

Poor Matthew . . .

He rubbed his jaw a moment before shaking his head. "Long story. And I'm not the only one." Matthew nodded at Mariella.

She touched the bump on her forehead—with her scraped hand. "He's right—it is a long story."

Andi crossed her arms, looking like the former no-nonsense trial lawyer she was. "We have time."

Matthew exchanged a glance with her.

"How about if Matthew and I get changed, and then we can head out for lunch and talk?" Mariella suggested.

"That sounds like a plan to me." Andi touched her stomach. "It just so happens that I'm starving."

An hour later, Mariella, Matthew, Andi, and Duke were taking in the sights of Salmon-by-the-Sea.

They stopped by a food truck that sold fish tacos and each ordered different varieties. Andi chose Cajun inspired, Duke got extra meat, Matthew picked the classic, and Mariella had tried grilled fish with pineapple and guacamole.

Since the sun was out and the temperature in the low

sixties, it seemed the perfect opportunity to eat outside. As they sat at a picnic table with the spicy and savory scents of their tacos floating through the air and birds singing overhead, Mariella spotted Bianca again.

The psychic had set up a table on the sidewalk and tried to attract customers. Just as before, she had people stopping to talk to her.

It was strange to Mariella.

But she turned her thoughts away from the woman.

The four of them caught up for several minutes. Andi told them that she was now doing odd jobs since she'd recently been fired from her job cleaning a business complex. She did a few things for Duke's tour group on the side.

No one brought up Celeste, Duke's missing fiancée, which led Mariella to believe there were no updates on that situation either. For the longest time, Duke thought she'd been abducted by a serial killer stalking the Dalton Highway up north.

But the killer had been captured, and Celeste hadn't been one of his victims.

After catching up, Mariella and Matthew filled Andi and Duke in on everything that had happened here in Salmon-by-the-Sea.

"You're leaving out one little detail," Matthew said when Mariella finished.

Tension grew in her gut. She knew exactly what he was getting at.

Despite that, she kept her cool and asked, "What's that?"

"Mariella and this guy hit it off." Matthew said the words dryly and with a half eye roll. "You should see the way they look at each other."

Andi and Duke both turned to look at her, waiting for confirmation.

"I don't know if I would say we hit it off." Mariella shrugged and lifted her taco, which lost half its topping in one fell swoop. "But I guess, yes, we connected. He's a nice guy, and I don't think he's hurt anyone. I think it's just bad luck."

Andi nodded slowly as if reserving judgment. "I suppose I need to keep an open mind."

"Always a good idea."

"So where do we start?" Duke wiped his mouth with a napkin and balled it up. "Good taco, by the way."

But before Mariella could answer, someone across the street caught her eye.

Jason.

He paused on the corner near some shops and looked around as if something were wrong.

"Speaking of Jason . . ." Mariella turned back to her crew. "Excuse me a minute."

Then she hurried across the street toward him.

chapter
thirty-one

AS I LINGERED IN TOWN, I saw my sacrifice.

She'd run across the street to talk to Jason Somersby.

I'd still been waiting for the right opportunity to grab her.

The other women had been easier since they'd been camping. I had simply waited for the right moment, lured them out, and then done what I needed to do.

I preferred to use the ritual grounds whenever I could.

I felt at one with my ancestors when I did.

But this new one . . .

I frowned as I leaned against one of the buildings in town.

She seemed to always be with people. In fact, people seemed drawn to her and her bubbly personality.

I drew my gaze away and glanced at the sky.

Are you sure she's the one?

But I felt it in my soul. She was.

Tlatoani wanted this woman. And I needed to deliver.

I felt the rumble again.

The danger was getting closer.

I was running out of time.

When would the opportunity present itself?

I had to trust Tlatoani. That he would provide.

I needed that opportunity to come soon, however.

My pulse kicked into gear at the thought of it. I tried to tell myself I wasn't excited. But I was.

I only wished I could do what my ancestors had done.

That I could collect the skulls. Line them up like trophies.

But then people really might find me. As protector of this land, I couldn't let that happen.

So I would play by these rules, set by mere mortals.

That didn't mean I'd like it.

I glanced across the street again.

But maybe for this one I'd make an exception.

Maybe I could arrange it so I could keep a memento of my success . . . I didn't know.

I knew it wasn't wise to add a trophy.

But I'd have to think about a way I might be able to make it work.

chapter
thirty-two

JASON SAW Mariella heading toward him, and a surprising burst of pleasure warmed his veins.

She paused in front of him, looking adorable in her rainboots, an olive-green jacket, and pink camo shirt. Her blonde curls were big and somehow happy looking as they framed her lovely face.

"I'm surprised to see you here." She looked up at him with those big blue eyes of hers. "I figured you'd be out on a fishing trip."

Some of his good mood vanished. "The people scheduled to go with us this morning canceled."

Mariella narrowed her gaze as if she'd heard the underlying message in his tone. "Why is that?"

"They said it was because one of them wasn't feeling well." Jason shrugged. "But my guess is that they heard I'd be a part of this trip, and they didn't want to risk going out on the water with me."

She frowned and nibbled on her bottom lip. "I'm sorry. I can only imagine that's not easy."

"I worry more about my dad than I do myself." His gaze wandered beyond her, and he spotted Mariella's brother sitting with two other people. "Friends of yours?"

She followed his gaze. "Yes. They're the ones I was telling you about. Andi and Duke. I called them and asked them to come as soon as they could. They left from Fairbanks and arrived this morning."

A surge of envy washed through him, but he quickly put it back in its place. "That's nice that you have friends who will drop everything to come and help you out."

Mariella's cheeks reddened just slightly. "Yes, I guess it is, isn't it? Would you like to meet them?"

Jason hesitated a moment.

Since they'd come all this way to help, he knew the correct answer was yes.

Yet another part of him still held back, felt like remaining private was the best option.

Before he could answer, he heard footsteps hurrying toward him.

He braced himself for another confrontation.

Who would it be this time? A concerned citizen?

A friend of Zoe's?

But instead of a confrontation, his dad rounded the corner.

Jason would have been relieved, but something was clearly wrong.

His father—looking out of breath and frazzled—stopped beside him. "I was just in the hardware store when I heard the news."

"What news is that?"

"The body of that missing camper was found . . . in the same place where you discovered Hannah's body."

Mariella saw the despair wash over Jason's face as he lowered his eyelids and his shoulders slumped.

His father warned Jason to be extra cautious as the news spread around town. Then Pops headed toward his fishing boat.

Jason glanced around, probably waiting for the mob to come after him and run him out of town.

People were already starting to stop and stare.

Before anyone could react, Mariella took his arm. "Let's go somewhere where we can talk. Privately."

"Are you sure you want to be seen leaving with me?"

"After what happened last night, it really doesn't matter anymore."

He froze and stared at her, a knot of confusion forming on his brow. "What happened last night?"

Mariella's cheeks flushed. She forgot she hadn't told him.

"Oh . . . never mind. It's nothing." She waved her hand in the air as if brushing it off.

He shook his head, determined to hear an explanation. "Clearly, it's not nothing. What happened?"

"Zoe's dad happened. He must have followed me back to my cabin after that confrontation with you outside the restaurant. He broke in through the window and demanded Matthew and I tell him what we knew about his daughter. Then he punched Matthew. Thankfully, the guy didn't break my brother's jaw."

Jason raked a hand through his hair as if the despair he felt was too much to bear. "I'm so sorry. It's all my fault."

"But it's not your fault. You had nothing to do with this."

"He came for you because you were seen with me."

"I chose to be seen with you even after I knew what happened." Mariella crossed her arms, not backing down. "Don't shoulder the blame for this."

He stared at her another moment, and she waited for his response.

"If something happens to you I don't know how I'd forgive myself." So many people's lives had already been negatively affected because of him. His father was certainly feeling the brunt of it right now. Others who'd tried to stick by him had also ended up being threatened as outcasts.

This was his burden to carry, not other people's.

"Then let's just make sure nothing happens to me." Mariella stared up at him. "I'm going to tell my friends I need a moment. Then you and I can talk."

Jason said nothing.

Mariella quickly hurried back over to the picnic table and told the gang she needed a few minutes, but they should go explore the town and she'd meet back up with them soon.

She saw the reservation on their faces but ignored it. She had to make these decisions for herself.

And she'd already made up her mind.

But she did hesitate a moment before adding one more thing. "Wait . . . the missing camper? Her body was found today in the same place where Hannah's body was found."

"What?" Matthew looked dumbfounded as he shook his head. "You can't be serious."

"Oh, I'm serious. Maybe you guys could ask around town and find out more information." Mariella took another step away. "I won't be long!"

Then she hurried back toward Jason.

When she reached him, she paused in front of him, her heart racing from the quick walk over. That was what she told herself, at least.

She licked her dry lips, suddenly all too aware of her close proximity to Jason. "Where can we go to talk?"

He glanced around. "Nowhere here in town."

"Then where do you suggest?"

His gaze settled on the woods in the distance. "I know just the spot."

Mariella glanced at the forest and repressed a shudder.

She trusted Jason. She really did.

But another part of her felt apprehensive at the thought of spending time alone with him in a place so remote.

She had no reason to feel that way, she reminded herself.

Because Jason was innocent.

Mariella would have to trust her gut on this . . . and she prayed she didn't regret it.

chapter
thirty-three

JASON DIDN'T LOOK at anyone as they walked through town. Instead, he kept his head held high and his pace brisk.

He wasn't sure if Mariella was wise to come with him or not. He knew he wouldn't hurt her. In fact, he'd protect her if anyone bothered her.

The fact Zoe's dad came after her last night unsettled him, to say the least.

But he could use someone to talk with away from the scrutiny of locals, and he would personally look after her while they were together. He decided to take her to his favorite spot, the same area where he'd gone yesterday to clear his head.

Maybe he'd tell her now that he'd met Zoe. Maybe he should just get it all out in the open. Even if it meant turning one of the few people who believed in his innocence against him.

They reached the edge of town and walked through a small gravel parking lot before cutting up a narrow trail on the side of the mountain.

"By the way, what's the deal with you and Sean?" Mariella asked as they walked.

He flinched at the man's name. "How do you know Sean?"

"He headed up the search party team I was on. He warned me to stay away from you, and he seemed really bitter."

"We were best friends for a while," Jason explained as they began to descend toward the water.

"Really? Wow."

"He liked Hannah also, but she wasn't interested in him. When I asked Hannah out, he was upset—as he should have been. Looking back, I should have talked to him first, but I didn't. Needless to say, he cut me out of his life. He's always said if I hadn't dated Hannah, she'd probably still be alive."

"Ouch. That's rough."

That was an understatement.

He led Mariella down an embankment and around a cluster of trees.

A secluded beach waited on the other side.

As they settled down on the sand, a couple of police boats caught his eye.

They were headed toward the river.

A helicopter also pulsed the air in the distance.

Rescuers were probably going to retrieve Zoe's body.

A moment of silence passed as they watched the rescue vehicles around them.

Mariella seemed to be kind and trusting.

But if she knew he'd met Zoe, she might never trust him.

And he hated that. Hated that because he knew where this new friendship would ultimately lead—nowhere.

He cleared his throat. "Listen, I'm sorry Hamlin broke in last night."

Sorry didn't seem sufficient, but Jason couldn't think of how else to express his utter sorrow over what had happened.

"He was beside himself with grief and worry. I can only imagine what he's feeling now that Zoe's body has been found."

"Did you press charges last night?"

Mariella shook her head, an uncertain look in her eyes. "Matthew and I decided not to. We'd want someone to have some grace with us if we were in his position. So we decided to show some grace to him also."

"That's nice of you."

She shrugged. "I don't know if it's nice. It makes me feel more human."

A couple of moments of silence passed as they looked across the water. If circumstances were different, he'd point out an orca in the distance. He might tell her about the glaciers in the area. Mention the puffins he'd seen just down the shore earlier this week.

But now none of that seemed important at the moment.

"Have you ever heard how Resurrection Bay got its name?" Jason asked.

"No. But I'd love to know."

"Back in the late 1700s, a Russian fur trader and explorer named Alexander Baranov was sailing from Kodiak to Canada when a storm arose. He found these waters as a safe harbor. Since it was Easter when it happened, he named it Resurrection Bay."

"Cool story."

"I think so."

A few minutes of silence passed.

Mariella lifted her head to the breeze and continued looking at the water. "I'm sorry about the tourists cancelling on you. I can only imagine how frustrating that might be."

"I worry more for my dad than I do for myself. He's been through a lot."

"So have you." Mariella turned to study him. "Why do you stay in this town? Wouldn't it be easier just to find someplace new to start over? Somewhere no one knows who you are?"

He nodded slowly. "I'll admit it's tempting. I've thought about it many, many times. But I can't leave my dad. I'm all he has."

"And he wouldn't go with you, maybe?"

"The land where my house is has been in our family for decades, and my dad loves this area. He loves fishing. For him, maybe it's a matter of pride or just stubbornness. But he doesn't want to leave."

"Are you saying he couldn't find anyone to help him if you left?"

"I'm sure he could find someone. But you know how the saying goes—good help is hard to find."

"I do. I just hate to think that you feel like you're stuck here."

Jason's gaze caught hers. "Why do you care so much? You hardly know me."

She shrugged and pressed her lips together as if the answer wasn't simple or easy to explain. "I know. But I feel as if I've known you much longer than I actually have. That probably sounds weird. Probably because it is weird. But it's true."

"I feel the same way," he told her.

Her cheeks reddened. "Wait . . . you do?"

"How is it that I may have just met the right girl but at the wrong time?"

"Life is complicated like that sometimes, isn't it? But honestly, there's a lot you don't know about me."

"I don't feel like there's anything that you could tell me about yourself that would make me feel even a smidgen of disappointment."

"You might be surprised."

"Well, I know this. You've gone out of your way to help me, and you've stood by me when other people have turned their backs. That means a lot to me."

She shrugged. "Well, you did save me from the icy waters of Resurrection Bay."

A slight smile feathered across his lips. "There is that."

"What would you do if you weren't working here?" she asked him. "If you didn't have other obligations?"

A frown tugged at his lips before he shrugged. "I would do search and rescue."

"Really?"

He nodded slowly. "I want to do something where I feel like I'm making a difference."

"I get that."

A few moments of silence fell until Jason cleared his throat. "Mariella, there's something I wanted to mention to you."

"What's that?"

Before he could say anything else, a footstep sounded behind him.

He froze as he waited to see who else was here.

Mariella swung her head around as she heard someone approaching.

Her eyes widened when she saw Chief Dunne heading their way along with another officer.

Based on the way she was walking, she was definitely here for a purpose.

"Oh no . . ." Jason muttered.

"What is it?" Mariella rushed.

"It's the chief. She doesn't like me."

"I gathered that. But why not?"

"Because Hannah's her niece. Chief Dunne never thought I was good enough for her. Neither did the rest of her family. They were the first to accuse me when she went missing." His voice sounded strained.

Mariella's heart beat harder.

Chief Dunne paused in front of them. "Jason . . . someone said I could find you here."

"You were looking for me?" Surprise lilted Jason's voice.

"You need to come down to the station with me."

Alarm filled Mariella. "What? Why?"

But the police chief either didn't hear her or ignored her.

"We can do this the easy way or the hard way," she said instead.

"I don't understand . . ." Jason shook his head, making no attempt to stand or move.

"You really want to talk about this here?" Chief Dunne briefly glanced at Mariella before looking back at Jason.

"I want to know what's happening before I go with you. Am I being arrested?"

"Not yet."

Mariella sucked in a breath. Not yet? What did that mean? "You don't have to go! You don't have to answer any questions either. My friend Andi is a lawyer. I can go get her. She can—"

Jason almost didn't seem to hear her. Instead, his gaze was on the police chief. "What's this about?"

Chief Dunne scowled. "If you insist . . . we have a credible witness who says she saw you with Zoe Hamlin on the night before she disappeared."

Mariella's heart throbbed in her ears.

Wait . . . that couldn't be right.

Jason had never said he knew the missing woman.

Surely, he would have told her that.

Mariella waited for Jason to deny it.

He said nothing.

The breath left her lungs.

It was true, wasn't it? Jason *had* been seen with Zoe. Otherwise, he would have denied it.

"Jason?" She stared at him waiting for him to explain.

He frowned, his eyes suddenly hollow and listless. "I'm sorry, Mariella."

His statement was all the confirmation she needed.

What the chief said was true.

Had Mariella gone to bat for a murderer?

Her thoughts wound and twisted inside her, trying to head down various roads all at one time only to collide.

Before she could ask more questions, Chief Dunne

took Jason's arm and pulled him to his feet. "I won't cuff you. But you need to promise to walk beside me and not make a big fuss."

Jason nodded. As he walked away he looked over his shoulder and called, "It's not what you think. I can explain."

But part of Mariella thought it was too late for an explanation.

chapter
thirty-four

JASON SAT across from Chief Dunne in the interrogation room at the small station.

He felt his blood pressure surging under the weight of accusation.

Unfortunately, this situation felt all too familiar.

"You need to tell us the whole truth." Chief Dunne narrowed her gaze as she stared at Jason.

She didn't even bother to sit. Instead, she stood in front of him with her arms crossed. A stance made to intimidate.

Her judgment was clearly already made.

"What do you want to know?" He kept his voice calm and even.

"How did you know Zoe Hamlin?"

"I didn't really know her. We met when we were in line getting ice cream in town, and then we took a quick hike on one of the trails as we ate." No one else had been on the trail—which had made it perfect. And Zoe had insisted she was up for an adventure.

But Jason never thought *this* would happen.

Chief Dunne's eyes narrowed even more. "Why didn't you come forward and tell us this information earlier?"

"Because I knew how it would sound. I knew the conclusions you'd draw. If I thought the fact I talked with Zoe would help you somehow find her, I would have mentioned it. But really, the two of us just had casual conversation. Nothing that was a big deal."

"You want to tell us about the arrowhead found in the firepit outside your house?"

The pit in his stomach grew deeper. "It's not what you think."

"And where were you on Wednesday night when she went missing? Between 1:00 and 2:00 a.m.?"

His cheeks heated because he knew how his words would sound. "I was at home."

"Can anyone offer you an alibi?"

His throat tightened even more. "No. My dad was out playing cards with some of his friends. I was home alone."

"And your cabin backs up to the Chugach Forest?"

His blood grew hotter and hotter. "You know it does."

Chief Dunne tapped her foot on the floor as she stared him down.

Jason glanced up at her. "Am I being charged with anything?"

The police chief remained silent as she seemed to contemplate her answer.

After Jason was hauled away by the police, Mariella stood there in stunned silence for a moment. What had just happened?

Finally, she shook herself out of her stupor and climbed the bank from the beach to the narrow trail leading back to town.

As she walked along it, it suddenly felt isolated.

Creepy.

The hair on her arms rose again, just as it had several times since she'd arrived in town.

She glanced at the trees surrounding her but saw no one and nothing.

She had no reason to believe she should be in danger.

Yet she felt as if she were.

Her lungs tightened as she glanced around.

Someone could easily be between the trees watching her.

She couldn't be clueless.

Her heart thrummed in her ears.

She should have called one of her friends and asked them to meet her.

Suddenly, she burst into a run.

She needed to get to somewhere she'd be more visible.

Now.

Footsteps pounded behind her in the woods. Branches snapped. Rocks tumbled.

Was it him?

The killer?

She waited to feel pain. To feel something.

She turned to look back when she collided with someone.

Mariella braced herself for whatever would happen next.

chapter
thirty-five

MARIELLA GLANCED UP, dread filling her.

The breath left her lungs when she spotted Duke standing there.

"We saw the police cars and got worried," he explained. "We came to check on you."

Andi and Matthew appeared beside him, their faces lined with concern as well.

Mariella glanced back.

All was silent.

Had she just imagined those footsteps?

Maybe.

All she knew was that she was glad her friends were here.

"Let's go back into town," she murmured.

She didn't relax until they reached Main Street. They paused in front of the candy shop that smelled like chocolate fudge and taffy, and they examined her as if they knew something was wrong by the look on her face.

She turned toward everyone, finally ready to explain. "Jason was just taken to the police station."

The words sounded unbelievable, even to Mariella's own ears.

"What?" Andi gasped. "What happened? Is he under arrest?"

Mariella shook her head, still in shock. "Not yet. But the police chief didn't give him a choice but to go with her." She paused and pressed her lips together. "She said something about Jason being seen with the most recent victim on the night before she disappeared."

"What?" Matthew shook his head, his jaw tightening fast enough to buckle. "I knew that guy was bad news."

"Just because he was seen with the woman doesn't mean he's guilty." Mariella wasn't sure exactly why she was defending him.

"But it doesn't mean he's innocent either," Matthew reminded her.

She rubbed her temples, feeling a headache come on. "I don't know what to think right now."

"I know it's got to be a lot for you." Andi looped her arm through Mariella's. "We can talk more about this later. We also discovered something that I thought you should know."

She would love nothing more than to hear something

that would distract her from this whole Jason situation. "What's that?"

"We went into this gift shop and talked to the woman behind the counter," Andi started. "Zoe has been the talk of the town, as you can imagine. Anyway, it turns out Zoe came into the shop the day before she went missing."

Mariella's eyes widened. "Is that right? Did the clerk say anything specific about her being there? Did she talk to Zoe?"

"She didn't really say much to her other than the perfunctory hello, how are you?" Duke said. "But she did say something interesting. Apparently, the whole time Zoe was in the shop, she was looking over her shoulder, almost as if she was nervous."

Mariella went still as she processed that. "Did she say what time she came in?"

Really what she wanted to know was: was it before or after her ice cream outing with Jason?

"It was around seven, right before closing," Andi said.

So most likely, that was after the ice cream.

"The clerk asked her if anything was wrong," Andi continued. "Zoe said she was fine, but she kept looking over her shoulder. She even dropped her purse. That's how nervous she was acting."

"I wonder what got her spooked . . ." Mariella didn't want to think it had anything to do with Jason.

"There was one other thing she said that I found interesting," Andi continued. "She said when she went to close up that evening, she found pistachio shells on the sidewalk. She wondered if Zoe was being followed . . . and if the person doing so was eating those pistachios because the shells weren't there earlier. The clerk had just been outside tidying up before Zoe—her last customer of the day—came in."

Pistachio shells?

Mariella's heart pounded harder.

She hadn't gotten up the nerve to ask Jason about those yet. She wanted to rationalize that it was a coincidence.

But now they'd come up again.

Were they even Jason's? She hadn't even considered the idea that maybe they were his father's instead.

Her heart thudded into her chest at the thought.

No . . . neither of them was guilty.

It was a coincidence.

That was all.

As Mariella let those words sink in, a familiar face across the street caught her eye.

Bright Armstrong.

In the midst of everything else, she'd nearly forgotten about the man.

But he was the whole reason she'd even come here. She

couldn't allow herself to get so distracted that she didn't find out the answers she needed from him.

Maybe the time was now.

"Excuse me a minute," she murmured to her friends.

Then she hurried across the street.

"Mr. Armstrong!" she called.

Bright stopped on the corner and narrowed his eyes as he turned toward her. "Yes?"

"I was wondering if any charter fishing trips opened up." She glanced back at Duke, Andi, and Matthew. "My friends and I still want to go."

His gaze darkened. "I told you I was booked for several weeks out."

She shrugged. "I just wondered if there were any cancellations."

"No." He started to turn and walk away.

"By the way, are you the man whose twins disappeared?"

He stilled, his gaze darkening as he glared at her. "What about it?"

"I can only imagine how hard that must have been."

He stared at her another moment, something unreadable in his gaze.

Then he started to turn again.

"I'm a twin, you know," she blurted.

He paused, body still tense. "Is there something you want from me?"

Tell him, an internal voice urged.

But the words wouldn't leave her mouth.

Mariella licked her lips as she considered how to proceed.

When she said nothing, Bright dismissed her. This time, he walked away.

She didn't try to stop him.

How would she even suggest she might be his daughter?

She didn't know. But she felt as if she was running out of time . . . and hope.

chapter
thirty-six

JASON WASN'T sure how long he'd been at the police station. It felt like hours. In reality, it could have only been mere moments.

Time seemed to take on a mind of its own to the point where it didn't make sense anymore.

Was today his last day of freedom? Would today have been the last time he sat on his favorite beach and looked out over the bay? That he smelled the fragrant forest around him? That he spotted whales in the water and eagles flying overhead?

Would this be the last time he got to talk to Mariella?

Because certainly she would never speak to him again.

Jason looked up as he heard a flurry of activity outside the interrogation room. The chief had gone out at least ten minutes ago, leaving him alone with his thoughts.

He was pretty sure it was an interrogation tactic.

See if he'd crack under the pressure.

Was she standing on the other side of that one-sided glass, watching him and hoping to see a sign of his guilt?

Or had he simply watched too many cop shows? Did that even happen in real life?

As the sounds just outside the door faded, Jason's thoughts went to Mariella again.

He remembered seeing the shock on her face when she heard about his connection to Zoe.

He hated that. Hated that he hadn't told her.

But how exactly was he supposed to bring the subject up?

The admission would have made him look like a player —and possibly a killer.

So the day before I met you I happened to meet another girl. The same one who disappeared. Just like my previous girlfriend disappeared.

It wouldn't have sounded good.

Besides, he and Zoe had met, had ice cream together, and then flirted a little. But Jason didn't want any more than that—not a fling, not a romantic date, and certainly not a future together. So when they parted ways that night, he hadn't had any intentions of seeing her again. It had just been a friendly moment in passing. They hadn't even exchanged phone numbers.

Still, Zoe had seemed nice enough. He hated to think about what she may have been through.

For years, he'd had nightmares about Hannah and the terror she must have felt in the moments before she died.

It just wasn't right.

But now, would he spend the rest of his life in prison for a crime he didn't commit while the real killer was free to strike again? Who would be next?

Those were the questions haunting him.

And what about Pops? How would he feel when he heard his son was being accused yet again?

The news would devastate him.

And possibly devastate his business in the process.

Jason let out a long sigh. He hated all of this. Hated that he was in this position. Hated that he somehow felt responsible even though he hadn't done anything.

How was he to know when he talked to Zoe a couple of nights ago that this would happen?

He leaned back in his chair, fighting a feeling of hopelessness.

Then the door opened, and the chief stepped inside.

A sick feeling roiled in his stomach.

This was the moment where he learned whether or not he would be arrested and charged with murder.

"What was that about?" Matthew asked when Mariella returned to them.

They still stood in front of the candy shop.

Mariella shrugged. "Nothing. I was trying to get a quote from him for the travel podcast."

Duke's jaw tightened. "He didn't look interested . . . or even especially happy, for that matter."

"He's not," Mariella said quickly, hoping for a subject change. "So what do we do now?" Mariella looked at the group around her. "As per usual, it's not like we have all the time in the world just to stay here and drag our feet. We've got to be proactive and find answers."

Duke placed his hands on his hips, what Andi often called his GI Joe pose.

Usually, when Andi said that it made Mariella giggle.

But she could find no amusement in anything right now.

"I agree," Duke said. "If I was still an investigator with the CID there is one thing I'd do first."

Mariella held her breath as she waited to hear what he'd say. "What's that?"

"I think we should go to the campground." Duke glanced at each of them. "I'd like to get a feel for where these women disappeared. It would be nice also to talk to some of the people there and to learn what they heard."

"Don't you think they already talked to the police?" Andi asked. "Besides, the people who were here two days ago when she went missing could very well be gone right now."

"You're right," Duke conceded. "But there might be some who are still there. Those are the people I want to talk to."

Mariella nodded. "That makes sense. I'm all in favor of that."

Duke studied her another moment as if trying to ascertain whether or not she was strong enough emotionally to do this.

"I've taken on the Ice Fairy Killer and lived to tell about it," Mariella pointed out. "I think I can handle talking to a few campers."

Then he nodded. "Okay then. I can drive us there."

They all piled into his Expedition, and Matthew rattled off directions.

A quiver of nerves rushed through Mariella. Would this prove to be fruitful?

And the even bigger question for her right now: what if she learned something she wasn't prepared to accept?

What if she learned Jason actually was guilty?

DUKE PULLED his SUV up to the campground and found a spot in the lot near the gate.

Mariella was surprised any parking spaces were open.

She didn't know much about camping. In fact, really she'd only gone glamping before—nothing rugged for her.

But she'd heard in the summertime that places around here were jampacked. In fact, the only reason she'd been able to rent the cabin where she was staying was because Alpine had pulled some strings for her.

She hadn't mentioned that to the rest of the team, who had some hard feelings toward the man. No need to stir the pot for no good reason. She'd gone to bat for Alpine, and now she felt the pressure of that decision.

She glanced at the campground again.

Had news of Zoe's death caused people to cancel their plans here?

Most likely.

Andi and Duke took the lead, and Mariella and Matthew followed behind them. That was fine with Mariella. Sometimes she learned more by observing than talking—though her first impulse was to talk. But she'd save those extroverted skills for when she was behind the microphone rather than in the field.

Besides, Andi and Duke were much more experienced at these things than she was. Mariella was perfectly happy to go along right now and watch them in action.

In different circumstances, she'd try to record them. Videos like that were gold when it came to social media and as supplements to her podcast.

But this felt too personal—even though, in reality, it wasn't personal at all. Mariella had only known Jason less than forty-eight hours. It seemed silly to be so loyal to him.

But she was, though she felt uncertain as to why.

It was hard to explain her mix of emotions.

Once the group made it through a narrow path, they all four began to walk side by side.

Just as she had thought, numerous vacant spaces made the place feel almost abandoned—definitely not like it was the height of tourist season.

An older gentleman wearing a uniform and driving a golf cart pulled to a stop beside them. "Can I help you?"

"We were thinking about camping here," Duke started. "Didn't think you'd have any spots open, but it looks like you might. We wanted to check it out first."

The man eyed them a moment as if uncertain if he believed him.

No doubt a lot of people had probably come up here trying to get information.

Mariella could understand his caution.

"We do have some sites that opened up. Had some people clear away from here recently." His gaze became hooded as if he'd remembered a burden he carried. "There's no need to beat around the bush. If you've been in town for any amount of time then I'm sure you've heard about what happened."

"About the woman who went missing?" Andi kept her voice light but solemn.

He took his hat off and scratched his head before replacing it again. "That's right. They found her remains today. Not sure what happened to her, but it wasn't good."

Mariella's heart jumped into her throat at the thought of it. The whole situation . . . it was just so terrible.

"I'm really sorry to hear that," Duke said. "But I'm assuming that was an isolated incident."

"Well, let's just say tragedy sometimes strikes in the same place twice." The man opened his mouth as if to say more but then shut it again. "Needless to say, we do have some sites open so feel free to check it out. If you guys still want to stay here, find me at the front desk, and I'll squeeze you in."

Duke nodded. "That sounds great. Thank you for your help."

Mariella glanced around as they began walking again. The campground was probably a fun place for the outdoorsy types. The surroundings were certainly beautiful, so she could see why people would enjoy staying here.

She imagined Jason here with Hannah and her friends. This seemed right up his alley.

But now this place would be forever marred with tragedy for him.

"I wonder how many of these people were here the night Zoe went missing," Duke murmured as they walked.

"Good question." Andi tucked her hands into the front pockets of her jeans as she glanced around. "I guess there's really no way of knowing without asking them."

"Or I could hack into the computer accounts for the campground and see," Matthew offered as if sneaking into the accounts of random businesses was an everyday occurrence.

Duke pulled his lips together skeptically. "A place like this . . . I bet they don't have a ton of computer records. I'd guess most of their files are handwritten."

Matthew frowned. "You're probably right. It's really a pretty smart idea in some scenarios. In others, not so much."

Then Duke nodded to a group of five twentysomethings who, based on their backpacks and walking sticks, were getting ready to go out on a hike.

Their camping supplies were strewn around their tents and everyone's hair was greasy, making it look as if they'd been here awhile. They clearly didn't just arrive bright-eyed and bushy-tailed.

"Maybe we should start by chatting with them," Duke suggested. "What do you guys think?"

"I think it's as good a place as any to start," Mariella said.

But she couldn't ignore the nerves thrumming through her.

Mariella watched as Duke approached the group, a picture of confidence. She almost felt envious.

Though people assumed she was confident, she questioned herself more than she'd like. Maybe it came from living under the scrutiny of others. Maybe it was because of her ex's betrayal and the humiliation that followed.

Regardless, it was annoying.

"Excuse me," Duke called.

The group of campers turned to him, not seeming to think it was strange that he'd approached.

It didn't hurt that Duke was good-looking either.

Good-looking people *did* have certain advantages. Anyone who denied it was lying.

One of the guys stepped away from the rest of the group and toward him. "Can we help you?"

Mariella waited, curious if Duke would use a cover story or if he'd jump in with the truth.

"We're podcasters looking into the camper who went missing a couple of nights ago," Duke started. "Would you mind answering a few questions?"

The man thought about it a few seconds before nodding. "Don't see why not."

"Were you here when she disappeared?"

"Yeah, we were here the night she went missing." The guy nodded. "The girls at that site were loud, sounded like they were having a lot of fun. When I heard one of them was missing, I just assumed she was drunk and had wandered off and gotten lost or something. But then they found her . . ." His voice cracked. "Now I'm hearing rumors that maybe someone killed her."

"Yet you're still here." Andi edged closer, acting as if she'd done this a million times before. "That didn't scare you off?"

The guy shrugged. "We talked about leaving. But we figured the odds of it happening twice were low."

Mariella started to speak up. Tell them it *had* already happened twice. But before she could warn them, another of the campers spoke up.

"I was in favor of leaving." A woman with dark hair raised her hand. "I'm still kind of freaked out by being here."

"We just all agreed that we wouldn't go anywhere by ourselves and that we'd be extra careful," the man acting as spokesperson for the group said. "Besides, I heard the guy police suspect of doing this is in custody."

Mariella's heart beat harder. Word got around fast.

So did rumors and lies.

"What about the two women she was with?" Andi asked. "Are they still here or did they leave?"

"I heard they wanted to leave, but the chief asked them to stay nearby," the woman said. "They weren't up for staying at the campground anymore. Someone said they found a place to stay in town, and that's where they'll be until the police clear them to leave."

"Thanks for that," Duke said. "Anything else you can remember that seems significant? Or maybe even that seems insignificant?"

The group glanced at each other.

Finally, another woman spoke. "This is probably nothing . . . but I ran into a man in the woods when I got up early to watch the sunrise. He was alone, and he had a map in his hands. He looked startled when he saw me and mumbled something about mapping out the area. It seemed weird to me."

"What did this guy look like?" Andi asked.

"I couldn't see his hair color—he was wearing a knit hat. But he was a white guy, probably in his late twenties. I think he had a medium build, but he was also wearing a puffy jacket that made it hard to tell." She shrugged. "I know that's not much. But just in case it's helpful . . ."

"No, thanks for sharing," Duke said. "You never know what might end up being important."

A white guy in his twenties mapping out the area? Mariella marveled. That could be so many people. And there wasn't anything instinctively suspicious about it.

But given the circumstances . . . maybe he was worth looking into.

thirty-eight

THE GANG STEPPED AWAY to regroup after talking to people at the campground.

"What now?" Mariella started, glancing at each person as they stood by Duke's SUV. "I say we go find Zoe's friends and talk to them."

Duke nodded. "That's what I was thinking also. We just need to figure out how to find them."

"I read in one of the articles about them that they rented an orange VW van for the trip," Matthew said. "I bet it wouldn't be hard to find that around here."

Andi stood straighter and nodded. "Excellent idea."

Ten minutes into their search, they spotted the van parked outside some condos close to downtown. A thrum of nerves swept through Mariella.

What if Zoe's dad was there? There was a good chance he'd be with them, that they'd all been drawn together in the face of this tragedy.

She had no desire to see the man again—not after he'd broken in and punched Matthew. They hadn't pressed charges, but that didn't mean she was comfortable with the man either.

Yet they needed to make some progress with this case. Otherwise, Jason would go to prison and a killer would walk free.

The rest of the gang opened their doors—but not Mariella.

Duke leaned back in. "You're not coming?"

Mariella grabbed Matthew's arm before he could climb out. "I think it's better if Matthew and I sit this one out, especially if Zoe's family is inside."

Duke paused before nodding. "Makes sense. You guys sit tight, and we'll be right back."

Mariella sighed and leaned back as she waited.

More than anything, she wanted to be there in real time as Duke and Andi questioned the women.

Who knew if Zoe's friends would even talk?

Silence stretched in the SUV as she watched Duke and Andi walk toward the door.

This would be the perfect opportunity for her to tell Matthew about the real reason she'd come here. About that email she'd received. About the possibility that they'd been kidnapped as children.

But how did one even bring that up in casual conversation?

"You okay?" Matthew's voice pulled her from her thoughts.

Not really. We may have been kidnapped as children. Our parents may have been a part of it. Or maybe they were clueless about the crime behind our abduction. But even if so, we may have possibly been adopted.

Maybe that explains the lack of warmth they showed us.

Yet if we'd been adopted, wouldn't they have been happy to have us? Wouldn't that have meant they wanted children?

Nothing made sense.

Her theories sounded surreal. Even to her.

She needed something solid before telling Matthew.

But she was no closer to finding answers.

Mariella shrugged as she glanced at her brother. "I guess I'm okay. This investigation . . . it feels personal."

"Because you like this Jason guy?" Matthew raised his eyebrows.

She shrugged again. "Maybe. I mean . . . I'm *intrigued* by him. *Attracted* to him. I want to know him more."

"You need to be careful." His voice tightened with brotherly concern.

"I will be. I promise."

Mariella stared out the window, suddenly not wanting to talk anymore.

Not about Jason, at least.

She still had her podcasts to think about. She needed to stay on schedule with them, which meant she couldn't take a break. So many things had distracted her: Bright. Jason. Hannah. Zoe.

She shoved those thoughts to the back of her mind and stared at the condo.

What was going on inside?

Yes, inside.

She'd seen a woman answer the door. Duke and Andi had talked to her for several minutes. Then they'd gone inside.

That seemed like a good sign.

Maybe Duke and Andi would get some answers.

If anyone could do so, it was those two.

Though Mariella had been determined to prove herself—and she was still working on it—right now, the clock was ticking.

As she stared out the window again, she saw the front door open.

Mr. Hamlin stepped outside.

Her heart began to beat harder.

He glanced at the SUV.

At her?

Mariella slid down in her seat, tugging Matthew with her.

She wasn't sure if Hamlin knew she was there or not.

But Mariella suddenly felt exposed . . . and terrified.

～

The police didn't have enough evidence to hold Jason. He'd told Dunne about the arrow, but she hadn't acted as if she believed him. Instead, she'd warned him to stay in town.

He knew what that meant: he was still their number one suspect and an arrest was probably imminent.

Invisible weights pressed on him as he left the police station. He left out the back, not wanting anyone to see him or to stir up more drama.

Instead, he pulled up the hood on his jacket, trying to obscure his face.

What was he going to do?

What if he did run? Got away from the lies people were telling about him? Started fresh somewhere far away?

But he'd always have the guilt on him of leaving. Pops would be stuck here picking up the pieces of Jason's mess.

That wouldn't be fair either.

He was beginning to feel hopeless.

How could he fix it?

Hannah . . . it wasn't supposed to be like this.

It had been Jason's idea to go camping that fateful night. Hannah hadn't even wanted to go. If only he hadn't pushed so hard.

If they hadn't gone, everything would have been so different.

But regretting the past wouldn't change it. He had to remind himself of that.

As he walked up to his house fifteen minutes later, a

voice drifted from an open window. His dad must be on the phone.

"What do you mean I can't rent a boat slip from you anymore?" His dad's voice rose. "You're the only one I can rent from here in town."

What? Was Walter Tulane reneging on his contract?

That was what it sounded like.

"I'm not going to let you do this!" A slam sounded, as if Pops had pounded his fist on the table.

Then there was silence.

Instead of going inside, Jason peered in the window. Pops sat at the kitchen table, his head lowered and a hand over his face.

An ache cracked through Jason's chest.

Without a place to dock his boat, Jason and his father wouldn't be able to stay in business here in Salmon-by-the-Sea.

It was bad enough that people targeted Jason. Now they had to go after his father also.

He took a step back.

He wasn't sure where he was going. But not inside.

He needed to cool off first.

chapter
thirty-nine

"GET DOWN!" Mariella tugged at Matthew.

He saw Mr. Hamlin and ducked low in the seat also.

Would the man confront them again? Make good on his threats?

She wasn't sure.

She only wanted to disappear.

The man paused near the SUV. Mariella saw his shadow fall over the window.

Was he looking in at them? Considering how he could make them suffer?

She held her breath. He could break this window. Reach in and grab her.

Take out all his anger on her.

She squeezed her eyes shut as fear froze her.

How long would he stay there?

But when she opened her eyes again, the shadow was gone.

Silence stretched for a moment.

Then a car door slammed in the distance, an engine started, and tires kicked up gravel.

He'd left.

She released the air from her lungs and slowly crept up —just to be sure.

But the truck parked near the house was now gone.

"That was too close," Matthew muttered.

"Yes, it was." Her gaze went to the front door again. She saw Duke and Andi step out of the condo.

The whole exchange looked friendly enough as they said goodbye.

Then they were back in the SUV.

"Well?" Mariella asked.

Duke and Andi both turned toward the backseat.

"Two interesting things," Andi started. "First, Zoe felt like someone was watching her the day before she disappeared. She tried to brush it off, and she never really saw anyone. It was just a feeling."

Mariella knew that feeling well. She'd felt it also. "The store owner you talked to said the same thing. That Zoe seemed scared."

"That's right. Second thing," Duke said. "There was a feather outside their tent one morning while they were camping—before Zoe disappeared. They said they didn't think much of it, but it almost looked as if it had been placed there."

Mariella felt the blood drain from her face. A feather? No . . .

"Mariella?" Andi studied her. "What is it? Do you know if Hannah had one of those also?"

"I . . . I don't know," she murmured.

"Then why the strange reaction?" Matthew asked.

"Because yesterday . . . I found a feather by the front door of the cabin."

The gang picked up a pizza and went back to the rental house.

Part of Mariella wanted to get back to town so they could listen to the scuttlebutt by locals. So she could try to run into Bright again and find some answers.

But the other part of her wanted to go somewhere private with no listening ears.

The team had a lot to talk about.

The pizza, topped with pepperoni and reindeer sausage, was delicious.

"So this is what we know so far." Duke sat at the table and leaned back, a half-eaten piece of pizza in hand. "Whoever is behind this crime was in this area five years ago and is also in the area now. It could be someone who travels to this area from time to time, or it could be a local."

Mariella put a mental check mark in the box for Jason being guilty.

"I've seen pictures of the victims, and they don't really share any physical traits other than the fact they're pretty and in their early twenties," Andi added, plucking off a piece of pepperoni and popping it in her mouth.

"What else do we know?" Duke asked before taking another bite of his pizza.

Matthew raised his hand and began to count off evidence on his fingers. "Those other campers saw someone mapping out the woods. Zoe felt she was being watched. Pistachio shells were found near where the initial abduction may have taken place. And a feather was found outside the tent."

"Suspects?" Andi asked.

Mariella sighed and shook her head. She'd been thinking about that all day, but no one rose to the top.

She pushed her plate away before saying, "I wish I had some. Sean—he's one of the guys on the search and rescue team—had a thing for Hannah in high school, but Hannah chose Jason instead. Sean still seems bitter—but bitter enough to kill Hannah in one of those 'If I can't have you no one can' type of plots? Seems unlikely. Other than him . . . I really have no idea."

As they ruminated on those details, a knock sounded at the door.

Mariella stiffened at the sound.

Who was here now?

Zoe's dad again?

Someone else coming to intimidate them for socializing with the enemy?

She glanced at Matthew, who rubbed his jaw.

He was clearly thinking the same thing.

Then Duke rose and strode toward the door. "I've got it."

But Mariella could hardly breathe as she waited to see who was on the other side.

chapter
forty

JASON WASN'T EXPECTING to run into a surly mountain man outside Mariella's cabin.

The man clearly wasn't expecting to run into him either. He grabbed Jason by the shirt collar and practically growled.

Jason tried to explain that he was here to see Mariella.

But the giant would hear nothing of it.

He just growled again, mumbled something under his breath, and then pounded on the door.

Hopefully, in a minute, Jason would see Mariella, and she'd explain everything.

At least the woman on the other side of the hulk seemed calm, like the type who might step in if things got too hairy.

A moment later, the door flew open, and a man stood there.

The guy looked behind Jason, and his expression softened. "Ranger? Simmy? You're here early."

Then his gaze went to Jason, and his eyes narrowed. He didn't say anything.

"We were able to catch an earlier flight and get here," the man—his name must be Ranger—said. "We found this guy outside."

Mariella appeared behind Duke.

"That's Jason," Mariella said. "He's okay. Let him go."

Ranger looked at him one more time and grunted before releasing him.

Jason straightened his shoulders.

He didn't like being manhandled.

But he would pick and choose his fights wisely.

Besides, he needed these people's help.

"Why don't we all come inside and make some introductions?" Duke suggested.

But as soon as Jason stepped inside, Mariella was there beside him. She stared up into his face with such sincerity that he felt the ice around his heart begin to crack and melt.

"They didn't arrest you?" she asked.

"Arrest him?" Ranger grumbled.

But Mariella ignored him.

Jason shook his head. "They didn't have enough to hold me on. Doesn't mean they won't file charges. But right now, they were just questioning me."

She squeezed his arm. "I'm so sorry. I can't imagine

everything that you're going through."

"Does somebody want to fill me in?" Ranger said behind them.

The rest of the group exchanged glances. Then Mariella stepped forward.

"It's going to take a while. But everybody, this is Jason Somersby. Locals think he killed his girlfriend as well as a woman here visiting. But he didn't. In order to prove that, we need to find the real killer."

Jason glanced around the group, trying to gauge their reactions to her blunt words.

He saw curiosity. Skepticism. Wariness.

All things he expected.

He was okay with that.

"Why don't we all sit down?" Duke pointed to the two couches and two chairs that formed a square in the living room. "We were just about to start making our murder board. Maybe Jason has some details that he can add to it."

Murder board? These guys really were the real deal.

Jason had listened to the true crime podcast after Mariella told him about it, and he appreciated the work they'd done. This group was dedicated and thorough, and they put themselves in the line of fire.

But now came the tough part.

The part where Jason tried to earn their trust.

Mariella had never been so glad to see someone.

She had been seriously worried Jason would be locked up and never see the light of day again.

She had a feeling he feared the same thing.

But the fact was, it was still a possibility. He was living on borrowed time right now.

As they sat down, they shared everything they knew. Mariella pulled out some paper and pens and began to tape sheets with the handwritten information to the mantel.

It wasn't ideal for a murder board, but it would work for now.

"I know this isn't the case that we came here to discuss," Andi said. "But with the time element . . . sometimes you just have to consider that things happen as they're meant to. Maybe we should look into this."

"Definitely," Duke said. "If Jason's not guilty, then there's another killer out there."

"I can assure you, there's another killer out there." Jason said the words as if he just needed to make that clear.

Ranger crossed his arms, his gaze still intense. "Any chance a feather was found outside Hannah's tent before she went missing?"

Jason squinted as if confused. "Actually, there was. But why do you ask?"

"A feather was found outside Zoe's tent also," Duke announced.

"What?" Jason shook his head. "I mean, I found the

feather, but I didn't think anything of it. Figured it was nothing more than a large bird that had come through and lost one of them. But now you're saying that isn't a coincidence?"

Mariella looked at Duke and knew that if she didn't say something then Duke would.

She cleared her throat. "And I found a feather outside my front door when I got home yesterday. I didn't think much of it. Not until today."

"What?" Jason's voice climbed with surprise.

"And . . ." Mariella continued. "When I fell halfway down that cliff . . . I thought I felt something prick my neck. Matthew and I went back, and we found a dart. I gave it to the police to be tested, but I haven't heard from them yet."

Jason shook his head and blinked. "Did someone poison you or something?"

Mariella frowned. "I have no idea. It's all very strange."

Jason ran a hand through his hair. "I don't like any of this. Between the dart and the feather . . . does that mean this guy is going to target you next?"

Mariella shrugged. "I don't know. I'm not sure how long it will take the police to test the dart. And as far as the feather . . . I mean, people *do* find feathers randomly."

"Do you still have this feather?" Ranger asked.

"It's on my nightstand. I'll go get it." She quickly

retrieved it and set it on the coffee table in front of everyone as if it were sacred.

"That . . . it looks similar to the one outside of Hannah's tent." Jason rubbed his throat as he stared at it. "Same size and coloring."

Ranger picked the feather up to examine it.

Mariella held her breath as she watched. He held it to the light. Twirled it between his fingers. Brought it close to his nose.

"It's from an owl," he finally announced.

"Is that significant?" Andi leaned back and tapped her pen against her chin as if lost in intense thought.

Ranger remained stoic as he said, "In some cultures, an owl feather is placed in the hands of a person who is about to die."

Mariella shivered.

A person who was about to die? Was that her?

Did someone leave that feather as a sign?

Her heart pounded harder.

"Is that Native American folklore?" Andi asked.

"It traces back to several civilizations." Ranger twirled the feather in his hand, examining it one more moment before placing it back on the table. His cheek twitched as he glanced around the group. "But I don't like the sound of this."

Neither did Mariella.

"Now that we know that, can we assume this guy is Native American?" Duke asked.

"It seems like a good possibility," Ranger said.

Before they could talk more, a noise drifted in from outside. It was a tapping sound, followed by what sounded like a bird cawing with the breeze.

They all froze.

What was that? A wild animal?

Yet it didn't seem quite like an animal. It almost seemed like . . . a human.

She remembered hearing the conch when she'd first arrived.

This felt similar . . . only scarier.

Suddenly, grunts and whistles moved around the building. Plus, there were strange drumming noises.

Followed by . . . an owl hooting.

Maybe not an actual owl.

Maybe someone imitating an owl.

She remembered that feather.

Remembered how it meant someone was about to die.

It didn't make any sense.

Ranger rose. Duke as well.

"Everyone stay low," Duke muttered.

Mariella could hardly breathe.

What if it was the killer? What if he was outside?

Then Duke and Ranger split up, each going to opposite sides of the house.

But the sounds continued, lending an eeriness to the air.

Exactly what was out there?

chapter
forty-one

THINGS WERE DIFFERENT THIS TIME.

This wasn't the way I usually operated.

But it was what Tlatoani directed me to do.

So I listened.

Now here I was.

I needed to place a curse on my next sacrifice.

But if I wasn't quick, I'd be caught.

I couldn't let that happen.

Instead, I performed my ceremony. I channeled the spirits of the wolf, of the bear, of the owl. I swayed as the wind directed and drummed on the trees with sticks nature provided for me.

I was at one with the world around me.

I lifted omens borne of superstition—that was what people would say.

I lingered dangerously close to the house, but I knew Tlatoani would protect me.

When I finished, I glanced at the cabin where my sacrifice stayed.

Everything had gone still. On the other side of those lit windows there was no movement.

That was okay.

I was done now.

I took a bow toward the darkness and then stepped more deeply into the woods.

As I turned from the shadows, I saw the front door open. A man peered out.

He glanced around as if looking for me.

But he wouldn't find me.

The man looked bigger than me. Stronger.

However, it wasn't my physical strength that made me powerful.

It was Tlatoani.

And Tlatoani would protect me . . .

Time was running out, and I would need to execute my steps very carefully.

forty-two

JASON STOOD NEAR MARIELLA, ready to act if necessary.

A killer had already destroyed his life once.

He wasn't going to let this guy hurt Mariella also.

Not if he had anything to do about it.

But really, he wanted to be outside. He wanted to check things out.

Finally, Duke and Ranger came back to the living room. Neither looked happy with their tight shoulders and hard jawlines.

Duke paused in front of the group with his hands on his hips. "I didn't see anything out front."

"I didn't see anything out back either." Ranger crossed his arms, his voice equally as hard as Duke's. "We can go outside and search the woods."

"Not a good idea." Andi sliced a hand through the air as if to nip that idea in the bud. "It's dark and these mountains are tricky—even in the daylight. Am I right? You know I am."

"I agree," Mariella said. "I can't handle any more tragedies. We should play it safe."

"Then we'll just wait it out here." Duke stared at everyone in the room. He didn't appear happy with his statement, but he didn't argue with Mariella either.

Jason stepped forward and ran a hand through his hair, unable to hide his inner turmoil. "I should go. I feel like I'm the one who's bringing this on."

Panic raced through Mariella's gaze. "You don't have to do that."

"I should. I don't want to put any of you in danger."

No one else argued.

He took that as a sign. Maybe the rest of the group wanted him to leave.

Maybe they needed to talk without him listening.

Ranger studied him. "I didn't see your car out there."

"That's because I walked," Jason explained. "It's not that far."

"But it's dark." Mariella's voice cracked with fear. "What if that person is still out there?"

"I've been walking this town for a long time," Jason tried to reassure her. "I think I'll be okay."

She opened her mouth as if to argue but then closed it again. "If that's what you want."

Was this what he wanted? Not really.

He wanted things to be back to normal. But that wasn't the way life had worked out.

"I should go check on my dad." He nodded toward the door. "This has been hard on both of us."

He didn't mention the conversation he'd overheard. There was no need to burden them with his problems. In reality, he barely knew these people anyway.

Mariella still appeared unconvinced that him leaving was a good idea.

"I'll be okay." Jason glanced back at the rest of the group and nodded. "Thank you in advance for your help. I can't tell you how much I appreciate it. If there's anything I can do . . ."

"We'll let you know," Andi said.

With one last glance at them, he stepped outside. Mariella followed him—after first promising everyone she wouldn't stray far—and then they paused on the porch.

"Be careful walking back," she said.

"I will be." He stared down at her, desperately wishing things were different. Wishing he could be carefree and lean down to kiss her. He most definitely wanted to.

But the timing was all wrong.

It would be a mistake.

Instead, he reached down and pushed a hair behind her ear. "I want you to be careful. I don't like what's going on here. I really don't like that someone left a feather here —or that dart you found."

Emotion glimmered in her gaze. "I don't either. But

I've got the gang inside. We're pretty good at watching out for each other."

There was clearly a story lingering in her gaze. She opened her mouth as if she wanted to share more. But she didn't.

Maybe she would tell him another time.

He took a step back. "Good night, Mariella."

She offered a soft smile. "Good night, Jason. Wait . . . call me when you get home?"

He nodded. "Will do."

With one more glance at her, he turned and walked down the dark, quiet road leading away from her cabin.

He didn't know what tomorrow would hold—or the day after that.

Or the rest of his life, for that matter.

In fact, his future wasn't looking bright.

He shoved his hands in his pockets as he walked, his thoughts rolling around inside him.

As he passed by an area of the woods, he heard a footstep from deep in the shadows.

He froze and glanced at the darkness between the trees. "Who's there?"

No answer.

He stared another moment, but no one emerged.

It wasn't worth it to stay and goad someone to come out. The best thing he could do was to head home.

He took a few more steps when he heard more footsteps. This time they quickened, hurrying toward him.

He braced himself.

But before he could turn, someone tackled him to the ground.

He couldn't see this person's face.

But his voice was loud and clear. "I'm going to make you suffer just like you made those girls suffer."

Then something hard hit his head, and everything went black.

As soon as Jason left, Mariella stepped back inside and turned toward the group. "What do you think about him?"

She felt like she was talking to her family about a new guy she'd brought home, wanting their approval. But it wasn't like that.

Yet she really did want to know.

"He seems sincere," Andi said. "I'm usually pretty good at reading people."

Duke nodded also. "He seems like a likable enough guy. I'm not ready to jump in and put my 100 percent support behind him, but he could be the scapegoat in all of this. There's nobody else to blame, so everybody here in town is pouring out all their hatred on him. And if that's the case, I actually feel sorry for the guy."

"So do I," Andi agreed.

Mariella began to pace. "So what do we do now? We have all this information. But where do we go with it?"

"That's a good question." Ranger crossed his arms over his chest. "I'm tempted to get out there and see the woods for myself."

"Maybe you can tomorrow," Matthew said.

"What else can we do besides look in the woods?" Mariella asked. "We need more suspects."

"We should probably tell the police about the feather," Ranger said.

Mariella shivered at the reminder.

Did that feather mean she would be the next victim?

"I can take the feather to the station in the morning," she promised. "I don't think doing so tonight will make the investigation move along any faster."

Everyone looked back at the murder board, studying the clues and what they knew so far.

But it didn't matter. There wasn't a clear suspect—other than Jason.

What if this was just some random guy doing this? What if there was no real connection? Or if this was a copycat crime?

As they contemplated the evidence, Simmy rose to fix everyone some drinks and snacks. One of her love languages was taking care of people.

And sometimes this group needed to be taken care of, for sure.

Mariella would do everything in her power to stay

safe. While she didn't want to lock herself away, she could still take steps to ensure that she was unharmed.

She glanced at her phone. Jason still hadn't called like he'd promised he would do when he got home.

She wasn't exactly sure how far the walk was between her cabin and his house, but she thought she remembered him saying something about it taking fifteen minutes.

It had already been ten so there was still some time.

"What's wrong?" Andi asked.

"I'm just worried about Jason walking back," Mariella said. "He's supposed to call me when he gets home. Maybe I should have volunteered to drive him."

"Give him a few more minutes."

She nodded but still felt unsettled.

It was like she could feel it in the air. Feel that something bad would happen. And then she remembered the sounds they had heard earlier. What had those been about? What exactly was going on here?

If she was smart, she would head out of this town.

Forget about the email that brought her here in the first place.

But apparently she wasn't that intelligent. Because she wasn't going anywhere.

She sipped more of her tea and then glanced at her phone again.

It had been fifteen minutes. She didn't want to rush into things right away by calling him. Still, worry pounded at her.

Finally, twenty minutes had passed.

"I'm calling Jason," Mariella announced.

She dialed his number, but no one answered.

Then she dialed again.

Still no answer.

She turned to the rest of the group. "I think something's wrong. What are we going to do?"

Matthew grabbed his computer. "I'll find his address if that would make you feel better."

Mariella nodded. "It's a start. But I won't feel better until I know he's safe."

chapter
forty-three

DUKE DROVE Mariella to Jason's house while the rest of the gang stayed behind at the cabin.

It was better that way. They didn't all need to go over to his house. That would be alarming for Pops to see so many people show up.

But Mariella's thoughts continued to race.

Was Jason not answering because he was upset with her? Because he wanted to write her off?

Or had something happened?

Usually, when she was stressed, she talked too much. This anxiety felt different.

She hardly said anything on the drive over.

Finally, she and Duke pulled up to a modest house on the opposite side of town. Similar to her rental, it was nestled in the woods on the edge of the mountains.

A truck was in the driveway, and a light shone inside.

Before she opened the door to exit the SUV, Duke turned to her. "You sure you want to do this?"

She didn't even have to think about her answer. "Of course, I do."

He studied her another moment, hesitation marring his features.

Then he nodded.

They climbed out, walked up the wooden steps to the front door, and knocked.

A moment later, Pops answered.

It took a few seconds before his eyes lit with recognition. "Mariella, right?"

She swallowed hard before nodding. "That's me. I'm sorry to stop by so late, but I was looking for Jason."

Lines drew across his brow. "He's not here. Is everything okay?"

"Probably," Mariella started, desperate to reassure him—and herself. But the odds felt against her. "I mean, I'm sure it is. He just told me he'd call me when he got home, and it's been about thirty minutes now. Still no call, and Jason isn't answering his phone. Is that unusual for him?"

His father's expression tightened. "Yes, it is."

She hoped she hadn't gotten him worried for no reason.

But what if there *was* a good reason to worry?

Pops grabbed his phone and began dialing.

But a moment later, he lowered the phone and frowned. "Jason's not answering for me either."

Her throat tightened. She really wanted all of this to be her imagination and paranoia.

Duke stepped closer. "I'm Duke, one of Mariella's friends and colleagues. Do you have a tracker on his phone? Maybe we could narrow down his location and check on him, just to be on the safe side."

"I do. I've never really used it before, though." Pops glanced at his phone and frowned.

"I can show you how if you'd like," Mariella offered.

Pops handed her the phone, and she tapped a few buttons. Then she showed Pops the screen where a map zeroed in on his location. "It says he's here."

She didn't know the area well enough to know where *here* was.

But Pops did. "On the other side of town, near the forest."

Mariella looked again—this time she recognized the location.

It wasn't far from her cabin.

What would Jason still be doing out there?

Had he needed some alone time to clear his head? At this hour?

That didn't make sense.

More seeds of worry planted themselves in her mind.

Pops reached for his keys on the table beside him. "I'm going to go check it out."

"If you don't mind, we'll go with you," Duke said.

"Let's go then."

Relief filled Mariella.

She wouldn't rest until she knew Jason was okay.

At that thought, she pressed her eyes closed.

Please, let him be okay.

Please.

Ten minutes later, Mariella and Duke pulled to a stop on the side of the road behind Pops' vehicle.

Sure enough, her rental was probably only a quarter mile away from the spot where Jason's phone had last pinged.

However, the only thing here was a couple other cabins rising at the end of some small gravel lanes in the distance.

Had Jason made a stop at one of them?

Mariella doubted that was the case.

A tremble captured her as she and Duke climbed from the SUV and joined Pops on the side of the road.

He still held up his phone and looked at it as if trying to make sense of the map.

"If you zoom in like this," Duke pinched the screen, "we can get some more details. These aren't always 100 percent accurate, but it should give us an idea of where the phone is."

"According to this, it looks like Jason's phone is in the woods," Mariella murmured.

What sense did that make? It was entirely too dark outside to be going into those woods.

She tried not to let those seeds of worry sprout, but it felt impossible.

"Let's check it out." Before anybody could agree or disagree, Pops headed through the woods, an urgent pace to his steps.

Duke and Mariella quickly caught up with him. Duke pulled up the flashlight on his phone to help illuminate the way.

This area was mostly uphill—rough terrain not for the inexperienced.

And Mariella was clearly inexperienced.

That didn't stop her though. She would find Jason if it was the last thing she did.

"Mariella, call his phone again," Duke said after he helped her up a particularly steep section.

She welcomed the chance to stop and catch her breath. Her hands were still trembling when she dialed Jason's number and then waited.

She wasn't sure what she expected.

But not the shrill ringtone flooding the air.

The sound was close.

Eerily close.

Pops followed the sound, tromping through the underbrush.

Then he paused and leaned down.

When he rose again, something new filled his grip.

Jason's phone.

Mariella knew without a doubt that Jason wouldn't leave this out here on his own.

Only if something had happened to him.

Those seeds of worry were definitely sprouting now. More than sprouting. They were growing at such an alarming rate that she'd nearly been knocked off her feet.

JASON AWAKENED WITH A START.

Had he been asleep?

He didn't remember going to bed.

His eyes slit open, but he only saw darkness. Only felt a cool breeze. Only heard the trickling of water in the distance and the brush of leaves.

Was he outside?

He tried to move, but his head throbbed like someone had beat it with a hammer.

At once, everything flooded back to him.

He remembered walking beside the woods on his way home when someone tackled him.

As he'd turned, something slammed into his head.

Everything had gone black.

Alarm raced through him at the memories, and he tried to sit up. To defend himself against whatever danger lingered close.

But he couldn't move. Something stopped him.

He tried again and realized his wrists and ankles were bound.

"You're finally awake," a deep voice said.

Jason blinked and turned. His head throbbed harder at the motion.

A man in a black ski mask stared at him from above.

Jason's chest tightened as apprehension rushed through him. "Who are you and what are you doing?"

Jason couldn't be certain who that man was. Crusher? Maybe.

"You need to suffer the way she suffered," the man growled.

Jason's thoughts began to spin. "Who, Hannah? I didn't have anything to do with what happened to her. I loved her. How many times do I have to tell people that?"

"No one believes you. You were jealous because she was about to run off with your friend, and you couldn't handle it." His attacker continued to stare, bitterness dripping from his words.

"Hannah was *not* about to run off with someone else."

"That's not what the rumors around town indicate. Face it. You had the motive, the means, and the opportunity. Because of you, the innocent have suffered."

More apprehension pulled taut across his muscles, and Jason fought to get the ties around his feet and arms off.

But it was no use. They were too tight.

As he stared at the masked man, the gravity of the situation hit him. This man was going to kill him, wasn't he?

That was why he'd been knocked out. Bound. Brought to the middle of nowhere, a place no one could help him.

"You need to think about what you're doing, man." Jason's voice wavered.

"Don't worry. I've thought about it long and hard. This is exactly what I want to do."

Before Jason could comprehend what was happening, the man raised his foot. His boot hit Jason's back, and he began rolling.

He kept rolling.

And rolling.

Down the steep mountainside . . . right toward the river.

To the exact area where Hannah had been found.

chapter
forty-five

TONIGHT'S EVENTS had all been unexpected.

I never thought I'd witness such excitement.

It started after I completed my ritual.

As I'd started back toward town, I'd seen him leave.

Jason Somersby.

He could be trouble. He could stand in the way of the sacrifice.

However, he hadn't with Hannah.

So maybe he wasn't as much of a threat as I feared.

Still, I'd keep an eye on him.

I moved through the woods without making a sound.

Barefoot. Just like my ancestors. That was the secret to being quiet. That and traveling light.

But as I'd moved parallel to Jason, something stopped me.

A man in the brush.

He lurked on the edge of the wilderness, watching Jason.

I'd stopped, waiting to see what he would do.

My breath had caught when I'd seen him use a rock to hit Jason in the back of the head.

Jason had fallen to the ground. Then the man—wearing a mask so I couldn't see his face—had begun dragging Jason deep into the woods.

I knew I could step in and stop whatever was about to happen.

But I didn't.

Why prevent someone else from doing my dirty work?

If Jason was out of the way, everything would be easier.

So I'd remained in place and continued to watch as the masked man hauled Jason up the mountain. I'd crept through the woods so I could see more. I'd seen the man push Jason from the edge of the mountain.

I'd heard Jason's body hit the rocky banks at the bottom with a satisfying thud.

I smiled.

Jason Somersby wasn't going to be okay.

Lucky for me.

One obstacle out of the way.

I didn't know about these other people who'd suddenly shown up and surrounded my sacrifice with what almost seemed like a protective wall. I'd find my way around them.

They wouldn't stop me.

Not when I had the power of Tlatoani behind me.

But time was running out. I could feel it in my bones. Feel it when I touched the earth. When I listened to the animals as they spoke without saying a word.

Without a sacrifice, this whole town would be destroyed.

That was why I needed to act quickly.

I had no time to waste.

The blonde was next.

She might think she was safe.

But she wasn't.

She was my sacrifice, and I wouldn't let Tlatoani down.

chapter
forty-six

EVERYTHING HAPPENED FAST.

Mariella had called the rest of the gang and told them
what was happening. Less than five minutes later, the
murder club had met Duke, Pops, and Mariella at the site
where Jason's phone had been found.

She wanted desperately to search for Jason. But Duke
and Pops asked her to talk to the police, to tell them what
had happened.

Mariella knew she was better equipped to do just that.

Ranger was a skilled tracker, so his expertise would be
helpful out there.

But Simmy, Matthew, and Mariella headed to the
station.

That was mostly because no one wanted Mariella to
be left alone—especially after she'd found the feather.

She understood.

When they got to the station, she was surprised to see

Chief Dunne sitting behind her desk. It was almost midnight.

Did this woman ever sleep? Or take time off?

It took the chief a moment to recognize Mariella, but then she nodded. "What's going on?"

"Jason is missing."

She remained stoic and unaffected at Mariella's words. "Maybe he skipped town."

"It's not like that. He was walking home from my place when he disappeared. We found his phone in the forest." Mariella fought to keep her voice—and emotions—under control. But the chief's lack of urgency sent her nerves into a frenzy.

"Maybe he threw it in the forest as he was walking away and leaving. I'm surprised, quite honestly, that he didn't leave town earlier."

Mariella shook her head, not in the mood to deal with these small-town dynamics right now. "I'm sorry about what happened to your niece. I really am. I know you guys never wanted her to be with Jason, but you need to consider for a moment the idea that Jason isn't guilty. You need to consider that he's in danger right now."

Mariella hadn't realized it until just then, but with every word she said she jammed her finger onto the chief's desk.

She wasn't usually the type to get so bossy.

But something had ignited inside her.

The chief stared at Mariella's finger as it remained positioned on the desk in front of her.

Mariella removed her hand and tucked it into her pocket. She honestly didn't want to make the chief upset. But she needed to drive home her point somehow.

"How long has he been missing?" Dunne finally asked with an icy glare.

"Probably an hour."

The chief's expression cracked as she let out an airy chuckle. "An hour? I'm sorry, but an hour is nothing."

"I know that whole 'someone has to be missing for forty-eight hours before you file a report' is a misnomer. He's in trouble. I'm telling you."

Dunne shrugged again, clearly not caring. "I'm sorry, but there's nothing I can do right now. I'm not going to awaken the search crews, not until we have more information. I will, however, put out a BOLO. I told him not to leave town."

"You can't be serious!" Mariella nearly lunged forward.

Matthew pulled her back before she did something she regretted.

"I'm telling you—someone did something to him." Mariella's voice cracked.

Chief Dunne's eyes narrowed. "Why would you think that?"

"Because, in case you haven't noticed, people in this town are constantly threatening him. They've cornered him on the street. They've treated him like trash, and no one seems to care about the whole innocent until proven guilty thing."

Chief Dunne stared at her, and Mariella prayed—yes, prayed—that her argument had worked.

Finally, Dunne rolled her shoulders back. "I'll put out that BOLO I mentioned, and I'll send one of my guys out to ask some questions. Tell me what else you know."

Mariella released a breath. At least it was *something*.

But she prayed it was enough.

As much as Mariella had wanted to go and search these dark mountains, everyone had agreed it wasn't a good idea. Even Mariella couldn't argue.

It was too risky, considering everything that had gone on.

She'd promised not to go into the woods without either Duke or Ranger.

Especially considering the dart and the feather. Before she'd left the station, Mariella had mentioned the "gift" to the chief.

That really seemed to get her attention.

Dunne said she'd send an officer over later to retrieve it.

Three hours later, at three-thirty a.m., there were still no signs of Jason. They'd tracked him as far as Talisman

Creek, which sliced down the mountainside. Then they lost his trail.

Nine people were out looking for him. Jason's dad had gathered three of his friends. Then there were Duke, Ranger, and Andi, plus the officer that Chief Dunne had sent out.

One of Jason's friends, a guy named Dustin, also showed up. He seemed nice enough and seemed to know the area. Plus, his concern for Jason seemed genuine.

Maybe not everybody in this town hated Jason as much as he thought.

And maybe now that the police chief was taking this more seriously she'd send more people out to help them.

Because Mariella was certain with every second that passed, Jason was in more and more danger.

She lingered near the forest where the phone had been found. This was the area where the rest of the group would check in. She needed to make sure no one else was hurt or needed help.

Thank goodness, Simmy was with her.

She seemed to sense whenever Mariella needed a hug, and Simmy sensed it and gave her one.

Finally, Mariella spotted someone stomping through the trees toward them.

Duke.

He paused in front of her, the expression on his face not conveying good news. "Still nothing on Jason, but we're going to keep looking."

Disappointment bit into her—and bit hard.

"Dustin did find something weird," Duke said. "There was some type of primitive site in the woods, probably only two hundred feet from your cabin."

Her breath hitched. "Wait . . . what do you mean by primitive site?"

"I mean . . . there was a doused campfire there. Scuffle marks that made it clear someone had been there recently. But there were also some rocks that had been arranged weirdly, in strange formations. There were some feathers, and it almost smelled like incense."

"That's strange."

"It really is," Duke said. "We should report it, just in case it's significant."

"If that could help us find Jason, then, yes. For sure."

"In the meantime, I'm going to keep looking for Jason." Duke nodded back toward the forest. "I just wanted to give you an update."

"I appreciate that. Let me go with you this time." Mariella wasn't sure where the words had come from— probably from a place deep in her heart. Definitely not from any logical place. "Please."

Duke stared at her another moment, that same pensive look in his eyes. "You sure you're up for this?"

She nodded. "I'm positive. I can't just sit here all night. I'll go crazy."

He turned toward Matthew and Simmy. "You guys good with staying here?"

Matthew narrowed his eyes. "I guess. But I don't like the idea of Mariella being out there."

She placed a hand on his arm. "I'll be fine. Duke will be with me. I just . . . I just need to go."

Matthew stared at her a moment before nodding. "I understand."

She released the breath she'd been holding.

Then she glanced back at Duke again.

After another brief hesitation, he pointed toward the trail. "If you're ready, then let's go."

chapter
forty-seven

MARIELLA TRIED to stay calm as she hiked through the forest with Duke. He had some type of map in his hand, and he crossed off the grids that had already been searched.

But that seed of worry had grown as tall and strong as a mighty redwood.

In her gut, she felt certain something bad had happened to Jason.

Danger had been simmering on the horizon, and it was only a matter of time before someone targeted Jason in an effort to make him pay.

The whole dynamic bothered her on so many levels.

But that was something she'd have to deal with later.

All she could think about right now was finding Jason.

As she walked, that familiar feeling hit her again.

The hairs on her arms rose.

She paused and looked around.

The forest . . . at night . . . it was dark. The underbrush was so thick.

Was someone watching her from here in the woods?

Nothing made sense to her anymore. Too much had happened, and her emotions couldn't be trusted.

She'd had that feeling multiple times since she'd arrived in Salmon-by-the-Sea.

But that feather changed everything. What if it truly did mean she was a target? That she would be next?

A shiver raced through her.

She needed to focus. Her fear would only cripple her, and she knew Duke was with her now and would protect her.

"Hey, Duke," she murmured as she hoisted herself up on another rock.

He glanced back at her, his arm reaching out as if to grab her and help.

But it wasn't physical help she needed right now.

"Yes?" He waited for her to find her footing again.

"You know in church last Sunday when the pastor talked about the power of prayer?"

Understanding rolled over his features. "I remember."

"Do you really think prayer works?" Growing up, Mariella had been taught to be self-reliant. That if she wanted something done, it was up to her to obtain it.

Her parents had told her believing in a higher power was only for the weak-minded and uneducated.

For a long time, she'd thought they were right.

But in her times of desperation, she wanted to believe there was something more to life than what was at hand. She wanted to believe there was more purpose to her existence than hedonistic pursuits. That the days she'd been given were full of purpose.

That she wasn't here on this earth by accident.

Because believing otherwise . . . it left her feeling empty.

"I've seen the power of prayer work over and over again." Duke climbed up another rock and then reached his arm out to help her. "Sometimes prayer doesn't change a situation. Sometimes the prayer will change us and how we handle that situation."

In other words, God wasn't a genie in a bottle. Mariella understood that. She understood the need for growth instead of being handed everything you desired.

Her parents had done that for her growing up. Most people thought that would be a wonderful life. The truth was, despite everything she had, a hunger still lingered inside her. She just felt like there was more to life. She needed a bigger purpose.

"Do you think if I ask God to watch out for Jason that He'll listen to me? Or do I need to have some years invested in religion before God will take me seriously?"

"Religion—or relationship, as I like to call it—isn't like a college education, Mariella. You don't have to put a certain amount of time in before there's any payoff or before you can earn the things you want. God listens to us when we come to Him just as we are."

Her life had been about working hard to get what you deserved. What if she could let go of that pressure?

Was that even really possible?

It was something to think about.

She nodded before murmuring, "Thanks."

Then she began to pray furiously.

Sometimes prayer doesn't change the situation . . . sometimes prayer will change us.

Duke's words echoed again over and over in her mind.

Please be with Jason. Protect him. I don't even know what else to ask for without sounding like a selfish child who comes to a parent only when she wants something. That's not the way I want to be.

But, God, if you're out there, I need you.

Jason needs you.

Desperately.

Mariella and Duke walked another hour without finding any signs of Jason.

Last she'd heard, Ranger had been able to track two sets of prints until they reached the creek. Then they disappeared.

That meant someone had either traveled upstream or

downstream in an effort to lose anyone following. That was what Duke had indicated, at least.

Mariella felt her hope beginning to fade.

As an eternal optimist, that realization was hard to stomach. She needed to keep believing that Jason would be okay. That they'd find him. That all of this was just an overreaction on her part.

She needed to know her prayer hadn't fallen on deaf ears.

Just then, someone shouted from somewhere in the vast wilderness.

Duke heard it too because he froze.

"Was that Ranger?" she whispered a second later.

"It sounded like him, didn't it?"

Mariella nodded but didn't dare say anything else. Instead, she waited.

A moment later, she heard, "Over here!"

She and Duke hurried between the trees.

Finally, two people appeared ahead of her.

Ranger and Andi.

Her pulse beat harder.

Especially when she saw them glancing down below.

They were at the cliffs, weren't they?

She and Duke stopped beside them, and Mariella sucked in air as she tried to catch her breath.

"What is it?" Part of her really didn't want to know.

Ranger pointed below. "I'm sorry . . . but it's Jason."

Nausea rose in her gut.

With Duke and Ranger both holding onto her, Mariella peered over the cliff.

A man lay sprawled on the rocks near the bottom.

Tears pressed against her eyelids.

Jason.

She'd heard Ranger correctly.

But was he alive?

And how would they ever get down there to check on him?

IT TOOK MORE than an hour for rescue crews to reach Jason. Then he was taken to the clinic for preliminary evaluation until a copter could arrive to take him to one of the bigger hospitals up in Anchorage.

In the meantime, Chief Dunne had promised to meet Mariella and Duke on the road near the cabin—it was the most logical location. Ranger and Andi stayed near the cliff to show authorities where he may have gone over. Ranger had found scuffle marks in the dirt.

But as soon as Mariella saw the woman pull up in her driveway in her SUV, anger rushed through her like lava spewing from a volcano.

Mariella charged up to her, unable to stop the words from gushing out. "I told you something was wrong."

Duke put a hand on her shoulder, probably to calm her down.

Too late.

Despite that, the chief's expression remained unreadable as she paused outside her vehicle.

Which only upset Mariella more.

"He could have died." Mariella clenched her fists. "We could have died looking for him. What kind of protector of this town are you?"

"Mariella . . ." Duke's voice contained warning.

"She needs to hear the truth!"

"You're right." Chief Dunne's voice still sounded too calm and nonchalant, but her eyes had softened some. "I'm sorry he was hurt. But that doesn't mean he isn't guilty."

More outrage pumped through Mariella's already white-hot blood. "You think he did this to himself?"

"At this point, I'm not sure what to think." Dunne said the words casually, like she held no responsibility in this.

Mariella stepped even closer, desperately wanting to drive home her point. "How about this? Maybe you've been so busy concentrating on Jason that the real killer has been out there the whole time, and you haven't even bothered to look. Zoe's death is on you!"

"Mariella . . ." Duke said again.

"It's okay." Mariella took a step back. "I'm done. Can we leave now?"

The chief's gaze was icy as she nodded. "I have your contact information, and I'll find you if I need you."

"What about Jason's dad?" Mariella asked. "He must have gone farther out. He's still out there searching."

"There's no cell service out there, so I'll have one of my guys wait here for him to emerge. We'll let him know."

With that, Mariella turned and began to walk back to the cabin.

Except she had no idea how to get there.

Thankfully, the rest of the gang joined her.

But no one said anything for several minutes. Certainly, they could feel her anger. She thought maybe they even understood it.

"Jason *is* alive still," Andi said. "That's good news."

"But he's in critical condition." After a moment of silence, Mariella said, "I want to see him."

"At the clinic?" Andi asked.

"Yes. He shouldn't be there alone."

"I can drive you," Ranger said.

That sounded great. She still needed time to figure some things out.

A lot of things out.

Not just about Jason but about her parents.

Or perhaps, even more pressing, who was trying to kill her.

Jason tried to open his eyes, but it hurt too much.

The slight motion made his skull streak with pain. Made his face ache—all the way to his teeth.

Instead, he closed his eyes and drew in a deep breath.

As the aroma around him filled his nostrils, he stiffened.

Where was he?

Wherever it was, it didn't smell like home or the sea.

This place was uncomfortably cold. Nauseatingly clean. And totally unfamiliar.

At once, everything rushed back to him.

He remembered being knocked out. Tied up. Pushed off that cliff.

Adrenaline surged through him, and he flung his eyes open.

Someone appeared in front of him.

He blinked.

Was that . . . Mariella?

He blinked several more times as her face came into view, a concerned expression capturing her lovely features.

She squeezed his hand. "It's okay. I'm here. You're okay."

He wanted to sit up, but he couldn't move. His body hurt too much. Had too much connected to it.

"Where am I?" His voice came out gruff and scratchy.

"You're in Salmon-by-the-Sea at the clinic. The paramedics wanted to take you up to Anchorage, but they needed to stabilize you first. Once they did, they realized your injuries weren't as bad as they feared."

He didn't stop the moan that wanted to escape as he shifted. "What injuries do I have?"

She frowned. "I should probably let the doctor talk to you . . ."

"No, I want you to tell me."

"I can tell you," another voice said.

He looked beyond Mariella and saw Pops step into the room with a cup of coffee in his hand.

He looked tired, with dark circles beneath his eyes and unkempt hair.

Outside his window, Jason noticed it was already daylight.

How long had he been here exactly?

He had so many questions.

Pops stood on the other side of his bed and set his drink on the rolling tray as he turned to Jason. "Dr. White says you're a miracle. You fell about forty feet, but you only have a concussion and a couple of bruised ribs. Unbelievably, that's it. Doc said you should be fine. You just need some time to recover."

"That's something to be thankful for, I guess."

"Dr. White is still talking about taking you to Anchorage, but I thought you'd be better off staying here," Pops said. "It's your choice."

Jason blinked, still trying to make sense of things. "How long has it been since I was found?"

"About four hours," Mariella said. "But they pumped

you with some pretty powerful pain medication in the meantime. It's no wonder everything is a blur."

"Who found me?"

"My friends and I did." Mariella's voice cracked. "But you were at the bottom of the cliff, and we couldn't reach you. It took rescuers an hour to get to you because of where you were located."

Jason's head pulsed harder. He'd almost died, hadn't he?

He squeezed Mariella's hand. "Thank you."

"When you didn't call me, I became worried. My friends and I went out to look for you. We tried to get the police involved, but . . ." Her voice cracked, and she didn't finish her statement.

Jason knew what that meant.

As far as the police were concerned, he was still an enemy.

What would it take to change that?

The real killer stepping forward to proclaim his guilt? Yet Jason would still be portrayed as the villain in the situation somehow.

That was how he felt, at least.

The thought made him feel as if a rock had been placed on his chest.

Someone knocked at the door, and he glanced over.

His gaze darkened when Chief Dunne stepped inside. "I need to ask you a few questions."

His walls went up at the sight of the woman—

someone who'd practically become an enemy over the past several years.

Now he needed to trust her? To believe she'd listen fairly to what he had to say?

That seemed as unlikely as Jason winning the Iditarod.

"I'd like Pops and Mariella to stay with me," Jason finally said.

Chief Dunne offered a stiff nod. "If that's what you're more comfortable with."

Pops and Mariella remained in the room but stepped back toward a small couch nestled against the window. Meanwhile, the chief stood in front of him with a pen and paper in hand.

Then Jason began to tell her exactly what had happened.

chapter
forty-nine

AFTER CHIEF DUNNE LEFT, Mariella stared at Jason in the hospital bed another moment.

She was so thankful he was okay. He easily could have died.

But he hadn't.

His dad cleared his throat. "Listen, Mariella, would you stay here for a few minutes while I run to get a bite to eat? Then I'll come back and take over. Would that be okay?"

"I'd be more than happy to do that."

"Can I get you a coffee while I'm out?" Pops asked. "The clinic's coffee is pretty terrible."

"From Perkatory?" Her voice lilted.

"Is there anywhere else?" He cast her a grin.

"You're my kind of person."

As soon as Mr. Somersby stepped out of the room,

Mariella pulled a chair next to Jason's bed and sat beside him.

Maybe she shouldn't, but she grasped his hand before she could overthink her actions.

She knew it was crazy. Knew the two of them didn't know each other that well. Knew they had everything working against them.

But she had strong feelings for this man. When he'd almost died, that had only compounded how she felt about him.

"You're still here for a purpose," she murmured. "Does that sound crazy? Because I can't stop thinking about it."

A smile slid across his face. "I don't think that sounds crazy at all."

The warmth and connection only lasted a moment, however. Unfortunately, Mariella had other things on her mind she wanted to talk to him about.

She'd heard what he told the police, but she wanted to ask more questions, get more details.

Her gaze locked with Jason's. "You really have no idea who did this to you?"

Jason let out a long breath. "I wish I did. But like I told the chief, his voice sounded familiar, but he wore a mask so I couldn't see his features. He didn't say anything to give away his identity. I keep thinking about it, and maybe it will hit me sometime. But not yet."

She licked her lips as she built up the courage to say

what was on her mind. "Listen, Jason . . . when we first met, you talked about guilt, and I told you I knew exactly what it felt like."

His gaze latched onto hers. "I remember."

"The truth is I made a lot of mistakes in the past. Back when I was a beauty influencer, I was bringing in a lot of money—more than I ever dreamed. A lot of really cool people were seeking me out and wanting to hang out. I got involved with the wrong crowd . . . and the wrong man."

"What happened?" He pushed himself up higher in bed.

"Let's just say I wasn't living a lifestyle I was proud of. The man I thought cared about me ended up taking some provocative pictures of me when I was passed out from drinking too much. He then posted them online for all the world to see, and he tried to get money from me to take them down."

Jason's eyebrows drew together. "That's terrible. I'm really sorry to hear that."

"It was a huge wake-up call. I gave up what I was doing, and I knew I needed to change. That's when I came to Alaska. I've been trying to reinvent myself in more ways than one since then. But I'm still trying to find my footing."

"Nothing wrong with that." His words didn't contain any judgment—only compassion.

"But there's more." Mariella hesitated a moment, the

words rolling around in her mind. "One of the reasons I came to Salmon-by-the-Sea is because I received an email saying that if I wanted answers I should come here."

"Answers about what?" He narrowed his eyes as if confused.

She licked her lips before deciding not to hold back. "Attached to the email was an article about twins who'd been kidnapped from here twenty-four years ago."

She watched as she waited for his reaction.

Jason closed his eyes as Mariella's words replayed in his mind.

Realization rolled over him. "Twenty-four years ago. Bright Armstrong. The babies . . . today they'd be the same age as you and Matthew."

Mariella nodded, feeling especially somber. "That's why I've been interested in talking to him."

"Does he know?"

"I haven't been able to bring myself to tell him my suspicions or ask him any questions about it. Honestly, the man is off-putting. Part of me wants to just walk away. But I know I can't do that until I find some answers."

"I get that."

Mariella studied him a moment, sensing an underlying emotion in his gaze. "You don't like him."

"I don't. I don't know what to tell you. I guess if I had my way, I'd tell you to stay far away from the man."

"Do you think he's trouble?"

"I think he has his hands in something dirty. I don't know exactly what, though." Jason's gaze locked with hers. "If you talk to him again, just promise me that you'll be careful."

Mariella refused to avert her gaze. "I will."

Jason wasn't sure how much to tell Mariella about Bright. Really, he didn't have that much information. Only suspicions.

But it seemed as if Bright was up to no good—and Jason didn't think that just because the man was a competitor.

Bright Armstrong was hiding something.

He was grateful Mariella had opened up. Things made more sense now. But it only made his worry grow stronger.

He studied her face, trying to read her thoughts. "So what happens if he *is* your father? What will you do then?"

Mariella shrugged, unease capturing her features. "I have no idea. No one knows about this except the person who sent me that email and now you. I haven't even told Matthew yet. I don't want to turn his whole life upside down for no reason."

"What about your parents? Do you think they actually kidnapped two innocent babies? You would think that twins being adopted would've signaled something to the authorities."

She played with a tendril of her hair, a frown tugging at her lips as she twirled the lock around her finger. "I know. Nothing really makes sense to me. My parents have always been distant. They're the type who acted like we're one big close-knit family for holidays or special events. But in everyday life, it was practically as if we didn't exist. We've always had nannies to take care of us—until we were old enough to drive ourselves, at least. Nothing really makes sense to me."

"I can imagine . . ." Jason's thoughts drifted through everything she'd told him. This would take a minute to comprehend. "I wonder who sent you that email."

"I wonder that too. Was it someone in town who did some investigating and knows what happened? Was it someone involved in the kidnapping?" She let out a deep, burdened breath. "I just don't know. Matthew might be able to trace the sender . . . but I don't want to draw him into this yet."

Jason's gaze caught with hers. "As soon as I'm out of here, if you need my help finding information or doing anything, you let me know. I'll be there."

She squeezed his hand. "Thank you."

"Of course."

They exchanged a look that said far more than words ever could.

Just then, Pops burst back into the room with coffee in his hands.

Jason's eyelids grew heavy. His pain medication must be making him tired. The feeling hit him like a brick.

"I'm going to let you get some rest, but I'll be back later." Mariella leaned toward him and pressed her lips on his forehead as she planted a gentle kiss there.

A kiss that filled Jason with waves of hope.

With one more soft smile, Mariella took the coffee from Pops and then stepped toward the door.

Jason's dad stopped her before she walked out. His voice sounded hoarse with emotion as he said, "Thank you for everything."

"It's been my honor." Mariella raised her cup. "And thank you for the coffee."

The two shared a smile.

The interaction stirred something inside Jason.

Something was changing, he realized. He only hoped it was for the good.

But life had programmed him to prepare for the fact that everything could fall apart at any moment.

And there was still the fact that Mariella was in danger . . . and a killer was out there.

AS SOON AS Mariella stepped into the lobby of the clinic, she grabbed her phone and called Duke to ask him to meet her at the clinic. She'd promised she wouldn't go anywhere alone, not with everything that had happened.

Especially not with the conch shell being blown. The ritualistic noises outside the cabin.

The feather that had been left. She remembered Ranger's words: *In some cultures, an owl feather is placed in the hands of a person who is about to die.*

That piece of evidence seemed to seal the deal as far as her being the next target.

But why so soon after Zoe?

Why kill Hannah, wait five years to kill again, and now target Mariella so quickly?

Unless . . .

Had there been other victims somewhere else in the five years since Hannah had been killed?

The chill that went down her spine made her blood freeze.

The fact that Duke had promised he and Andi would be right over made her feel marginally better.

Ranger, Simmy, and Matthew were obtaining police reports and trying to track down a couple of the cops who'd worked Hannah's case.

Mariella briefly caught a glimpse of herself in the mirror as she waited.

She looked tired. It was clear she hadn't slept all night, and it was already 8:00 a.m.

Her normally shiny hair with the big curls looked a bit dull and flat. She pulled it back into a high ponytail. The makeup she usually wore to cover any blemishes had now been wiped away.

But she didn't care.

That was a big step from her days in California.

She never wanted to go back to living life with that kind of vanity again.

Five minutes later, the doors to the clinic opened, and Duke and Andi stepped inside. Neither had changed from their jaunt through the woods. Their jeans and boots were muddy. Their hair disheveled. Their cheeks flushed with exertion.

Yet they somehow seemed like superheroes still to Mariella.

"You doing okay?" Andi paused in front of her.

Mariella nodded. "I'm better knowing that Jason is okay."

"How *is* he?" Duke glanced down the hallway to where the rooms were.

She gave them an update on his status as they walked toward the door.

Stepping outside, her eyes widened when she saw Main Street.

Some type of street festival was going on.

"Apparently, every Saturday they have a community festival where vendors set up tables and sell crafts and other items," Duke explained. "I glanced at a few things as we went past, and it seems interesting in a folksy kind of way."

"Too bad there are so many other things going on." Mariella took a sip of her coffee. "This looks like it could be a lot of fun—perfect for my travel podcast."

All kinds of people were out. Vendors sold clothes from home-based boutiques. Homemade coffee mugs. Handcrafted jewelry.

Then there was Roy from the library. He sat on a colorful rug and read a story to a group of kids sitting in a semi-circle around him.

Officer Longwood handed out plastic badges to other children passing by.

The mayor—clearly up for reelection soon—gave voters buttons with his smiling face on them.

As they reached the corner, Bianca came into view.

Mariella's first impulse was to keep going.

But the woman called to them. "I know you want your fortunes read."

Actually, Mariella didn't.

But the woman *could* be helpful.

Mariella walked toward her. "Actually, I do have a question. Any chance you're from this area?"

The woman pointed at a handwritten paper she'd displayed at the front of her table.

Questions: Five dollars.

Mariella really didn't think the sign meant *this* kind of question.

But she sighed and reached for her pocket. Unfortunately, she didn't have any cash on her.

Thankfully, Andi slipped a bill into a box wrapped in magenta-colored foil with a hand-cut slit across the top.

Instantly, Bianca's expression brightened. "What can I do for you?"

Help me find a killer.

Mariella knew better than to word it like that.

But when she thought about everything, one assumption seemed safe: the killer most likely was a man interested in the mystical. Maybe he was Native American or New Age. Mariella wasn't sure.

But sometimes, as the saying went, birds of a feather flock together.

That was why Mariella wondered if Bianca might know something helpful.

"I'm just curious, but do you have family living here?" Mariella started.

Bianca blinked as if the inquiry surprised her. "As a matter of fact, yes, I do."

"So you're from around here?" Mariella continued.

"I moved here seven years ago for a fresh start."

Seven years ago . . . . that would put Bianca and her family in the right timeline for when the last murder had occurred.

But how did she even bring up the subject without making Bianca totally shut down?

"Listen . . . I'm a travel podcaster, and I'm trying to find a variety of people in the area to interview. I try to keep everyone I talk to close to my age—that's what my listeners seem to like. Do you have a son or daughter who might be willing to talk to me?"

"Son or daughter?" She raised her eyebrows. "No, no children of my own."

Mariella's hopes sank.

"But I *do* have a nephew." Bianca grinned. "I raised him like my own, and now he's a proud member of the community."

Mariella's breath hitched. "Do you mind if I ask who he is? Maybe he'd be interested in talking to me."

Bianca practically beamed as she glanced across the street and pointed. "That's my nephew right over there."

Mariella turned and saw Officer Longwood.

She sucked in a breath.

She should have put together the resemblance earlier, but she didn't.

Her thoughts raced.

Could Longwood be responsible for this?

Mariella didn't know, but it seemed like a good possibility.

Mariella, Duke, and Andi reconvened at the town square where they'd eaten fish tacos just yesterday—though it felt like weeks had already passed. Simmy, Ranger, and Matthew were still at the cabin looking at the police reports they'd managed to get their hands on.

Mariella stared at the little town festival going on. She supposed life did continue, even in the midst of tragedy. In a way it seemed insensitive. But in another way, she couldn't blame the organizers of these events.

If life stopped every time there was hurt in someone's life, there would never be any celebrations.

But she had to wonder if there was a killer here.

Specifically, if the killer was Officer Longwood.

Could he really be involved in this somehow?

Right now, he was at the top of her list.

Andi's gaze remained on the street where Longwood continued to hand out plastic police badges. Her gaze was narrow as if her thoughts were only focused on the conversation with Bianca.

"Even if that Officer Longwood guy was involved, how are we supposed to prove it?" Andi seemed to be on the same wavelength as Mariella.

"That's a good question." Mariella stared at Longwood also. "I have no idea what the answer is. Unless we just outright ask him, which seems a little bold."

"I don't mind." Andi shrugged.

Mariella smiled. Andi was brash and daring, something Mariella admired about the woman.

One day she wanted to see Andi back in the courtroom arguing a case. She'd bet Andi was a force to be reckoned with during a trial.

As her thoughts continued to roll around inside her, someone else caught her eye.

Bright Armstrong.

He was here, but he didn't seem to be strolling about and enjoying himself. No, he was walking with purpose.

Why wasn't he out on one of those charter fishing tours that he said were booked for weeks in advance?

"You guys . . ." Mariella started. "I need to go do something."

Duke followed her gaze and bristled. "We should go with you."

"I won't go far. Give me a little space. I'll yell if I need you. I promise. But . . . I've got to do this alone. I'll explain later."

They stared at her as if she'd lost her mind. But they agreed.

She took off across the sidewalk, following Bright as he wove between two buildings.

She rushed to keep up with him, not wanting him to get out of her sight.

To her surprise, the man turned back toward another building and headed toward the docks.

She stayed behind him and paused at the corner of the building, not knowing what she would see on the other side. She didn't want to be spotted.

Then she heard voices.

Bright had come this way to meet with two other men.

She glanced back. Duke and Andi couldn't see her now.

Would they come running after her and ruin this?

Quickly, she sent them a text to let them know she was okay and would be back in a moment.

Then she ducked and slowly peered around the corner at Bright.

He was meeting with two guys, and whatever they were talking about didn't seem to be a happy subject. Their body language appeared tense, their voices tight, and their motions quick.

"We can't let anyone stop us," Bright said with a hushed whisper.

"We're not going to," one of them answered. "We're doing everything that we can."

"Don't mess this up," Bright said.

Don't mess what up? Mariella wondered. What was

going on with them? And what exactly did Jason suspect them of doing?

She had so many questions.

But right now, she waited for more information.

"We are close, and we can't let anything or anybody get in our way," Bright said. "Is that understood?"

The other men nodded.

They started to walk away.

But before they could, another sound cut through the air.

Mariella sucked in her breath.

Her phone.

It was ringing. To be more accurate, it was playing "Barbie Girl."

She'd been meaning to change that ringtone.

She shrank against the wall as she considered her options.

Mariella didn't know what those guys were up to, but she didn't want anything to do with it.

chapter
fifty-one

THE CONVERSATION JASON had with his attacker —if it could even be considered a conversation—kept replaying in his head.

Who had that man been?

You need to suffer the way she suffered.

You were jealous because she was about to run off with your friend, and you couldn't handle it.

Because of you, the innocent have suffered.

Jason swallowed hard.

Looking back, he realized the man was too small to have been Crusher.

This guy was average size and average height. But he knew the area. He also blamed Jason for what had happened to Hannah and Zoe.

That made him think that the man was someone Jason was familiar with.

The thoughts turned over in his head as he pretended to sleep.

Until a knock sounded at the door.

His eyes widened when he saw Chief Dunne step in again.

He sat up in bed, instantly more alert.

Pops was still here, sitting in the chair, drinking some coffee, and reading the local newspaper. But he folded it and put it away as the chief walked in.

"I'm here to give you an update," she started, something close to remorse in her gaze.

Remorse? Was he reading the woman right?

Probably not.

"We've caught the person who did this to you," Dunne announced.

Jason's heart beat harder. "What? When? Where? And the even bigger question. Who?"

"Someone called the station and told us that their friend confessed to shoving you over the cliff. Apparently, this person's intention was never to hurt you that much, but he got carried away. Immediately afterward, he felt immense guilt."

"But not enough guilt to call and get me the help I needed." His mood darkened even more.

The chief shrugged as if she couldn't argue with his assessment.

She drew in a deep breath before continuing. "The good news is that his friend felt differently. As soon as he found out what happened, he called us. We then went to this person's house and questioned him. He confessed, and he's now in our custody."

Jason's heart continued to thrum into his chest. "Chief, you still haven't told me who it is."

She stepped closer, and something in her eyes changed.

Was the chief beginning to believe that maybe Jason really was innocent? After all these years?

He couldn't be sure.

She pressed her lips closed as if it pained her to say whatever she needed to say. "The person we arrested was . . . Sean Whitehurst."

The breath left Jason's lungs. "*Sean* did this to me?"

The chief nodded solemnly.

Jason let out another long breath. "I knew the man hated me, that he blamed me . . . but I never thought he would take it this far."

"I know it doesn't make anything any better, but he said he wanted to teach you a lesson. Now he's torn up about it, to say the least. I don't say that to make you feel sorry for him. Because there's no justification for what he did. I just wanted to keep you aware of what was going on."

Jason's gaze locked with the chief's. "Is he the one behind Hannah and Zoe's deaths?"

The chief shook her head. "No, he's not. He was on

duty with the fire department on the night of Zoe's death and has several people who can vouch for him."

Jason let that sink in.

Sean had just wanted Jason to "get what he deserved."

The facts fit.

But they didn't bring him any closer to finding Hannah's killer.

Mariella quickly muted her phone and shoved it deep into her pocket.

Then before those men could come find her, she darted from the alley.

She glanced around and realized she wouldn't have time to make it back to the crowd without being spotted.

Mariella only saw one other option.

She ran toward her left and darted behind a wooden statue of three bears. It was a photo op for tourists, but the towering structure was just big enough to conceal her.

She pressed herself there and tried to stay still.

Then she began to pray those men didn't walk this way.

Because they could.

And if they did . . . she'd be discovered.

And cornered.

Dear Lord, me again. Are You tired of hearing from me? I still don't feel like I deserve to ask anything of You.

But if there's any way You could make me disappear right now . . .

Mariella pressed her eyes closed, and she pressed herself further into the shadows.

Should she call Duke and Andi? Maybe she should have let one of them come with her.

But then she would have to explain . . .

There just hadn't been time.

She heard steps come from the alley.

"Where did they go?" one of them asked.

"I don't know. Maybe we were hearing things. Or maybe the sound echoed over the water."

"I doubt that," the other man said.

Her lungs froze. She continued to wait, wondering what they would do.

Then she heard more footsteps. This time they came her way.

What was she going to do when they found her? What kind of excuse could she fake?

If they tried to kill her, would that be the right time to confess to Bright that she might be his daughter?

Would that make things better or worse?

She had no idea what any of those answers were.

But the footsteps came closer.

At any minute these guys were going to find her.

Then they stopped.

She heard someone say, "We don't have time for this.

Whoever it was is long gone. Probably just a tourist who got lost."

Then the men turned, and they walked in the opposite direction.

Mariella nearly melted with relief.

They hadn't found her.

But that had been close.

Too close.

chapter
fifty-two

I STOOD within the crowd and watched.

I had seen the sacrifice walking about with her friends.

She looked shaken, and after everything that happened last night, she had every reason to be.

But the worst hadn't even happened yet.

Soon enough, it would.

The gods were not satisfied with my last sacrifice.

They needed more.

I knew exactly what I needed to do. But now wasn't the time to act.

A hunter couldn't be too obvious, especially with so many people around.

But Tlatoani knew time was running out. If the sacrifice wasn't made, then the many would die instead of the one.

I couldn't let that happen.

I already felt as if I'd failed. I'd had too many missed opportunities. Other things had gotten in the way.

Now I was running out of time.

If I disappointed Tlatoani, he might decide to sacrifice me instead.

My thoughts raced.

I needed to plan my moves.

Because this no longer felt fun.

Now I felt like I was fighting a losing battle.

I'd never lost before.

My hands fisted at my sides.

I didn't plan on starting now.

chapter
fifty-three

MARIELLA HURRIED TOWARD DUKE, who waited on the street corner with a pensive expression.

"Everything okay?" Duke asked.

He must not have seen all of that. Otherwise, he'd be up in arms.

"Yes, everything is fine," she insisted. "I was just following a hunch, but it didn't pan out."

Duke's expression made it clear he didn't totally buy that.

As he shouldn't.

Before he could interrogate her more, Andi jogged up. Based on her grin, she had something to share.

"So while Duke was waiting here for you, I talked to Officer Longwood," she started, sucking air into her lungs as she tried to catch her breath.

"Wait . . . what?" Mariella's eyebrows shot up. "You did?"

Duke made a face. "Once she gets something in her head, you can't stop her."

Mariella had seen that before. "What did he say?"

"Basically, I asked him where he was the night Zoe had died."

Mariella gasped. "That was direct."

"As I expected, he got offended," Andi said. "I mean, really, who wouldn't? Am I right?"

"What did he say?" Duke asked.

"Turns out he was on an overnight fishing trip down in Homer with some friends. He said he has about five people who can verify his whereabouts."

A moment of disappointment pressed on Mariella. If that was true, then this was another dead end—another setback to finding the real culprit.

"Do you think he's telling the truth?" Mariella murmured. "That he's innocent?"

Andi blew out a long breath. "In an ideal world, we'd call those friends to confirm it. But Longwood seemed pretty sincere. I really don't think it was him, even if his aunt is kooky."

"Well, if Longwood isn't guilty, that leaves us back at square one, right?" Mariella asked.

"He did say one thing I found interesting," Andi added. "He mentioned that on the night Zoe died, the police checked Jason's phone records. His phone pinged at his cabin. His computer IP address also showed he was watching a TV show on his computer at the same time

Zoe's attack happened."

"What?" Mariella's voice rose. "So why did the police still suspect Jason?"

Andi shrugged. "Because they needed someone, and they wanted it to be him."

Anger surged through Mariella.

Then she remembered that phone call—the one that nearly gave away her presence when she'd trailed Bright.

"Speaking of which . . . someone tried to call me." She pulled out her phone and glanced at the screen.

She didn't recognize the number, but it was local. She stepped back and excused herself as she returned the call.

The clinic answered, and panic raced through her.

Had Jason taken a turn for the worse?

"I . . . I missed a call," she said, her voice shaky. "Is Jason okay? Jason Somersby?"

"I'll patch you through."

She held her breath as she waited.

Who was she being patched through to? Someone tasked with telling her bad news?

Instead, Jason's voice came over the line.

Relief swept through her.

"Hey . . . I missed your call." She tried to keep the emotion from her voice.

"I just wanted to give you an update. Dunne arrested Sean. He's the one who did this to me."

"Wait . . . what?" Mariella's voice caught.

"It's true. He wanted revenge after what happened to

Hannah, apparently. He's the one who left those pistachio shells as well as the bow and arrow at my house. He also spray-painted "Killer" on my father's boat. He wanted to incriminate me. When that didn't work, he took matters into his own hands."

"Wow . . . I'm sorry to hear that. But I'm glad he was arrested. Thank you for the update."

"Of course." Jason paused. "You doing okay?"

She swallowed hard, wondering how to answer that. "I'm fine. Absolutely fine."

"Okay . . . be careful."

"I will be." Mariella ended the call and gave her friends the update.

"I'm glad they made an arrest," Duke said. "We should probably get back to the cabin and get some rest. Last night was a long one."

"You guys can go if you want to." Mariella shook her head. "But I'm in no mood to sleep. I have too much on my mind."

"Like what?" Andi asked.

"Like finding answers." Mariella crossed her arms. "I just need to figure out how I'm going to do that."

Duke and Andi refused to leave Mariella searching on her own.

Instead, Mariella, Duke, and Andi decided to meet the

rest of the gang to figure out their next plan of action. Rather than going all the way back to the cabin, they decided to meet in town and grab something to eat from the food trucks set up for the festival.

Mariella chose fish and chips—something she'd no doubt regret later. Right now, it seemed worth it.

Everyone finally met together with their food to talk, and Mariella gave the group the update.

"I agree that it does sound like there's some type of Native American connection to this." Ranger plucked a potato chip from a small bag and held it up like a pointer. "I haven't seen a lot of indigenous people around town, other than Bianca. Is there a way we can find out more about that?"

Mariella thought about it for a moment. "I bet the librarian I talked to would have some information. He seemed like a wealth of knowledge about the area."

"Maybe you could talk to him sometime," Ranger said. "It would be one more direction we could go in."

"It is something." She tapped her fingernails on the weathered picnic table. "But I have this other idea that I want to throw out. I need you guys to listen and hear me out before you respond." She glanced at everyone at the table. "Promise?"

Andi and Simmy nodded.

Ranger shrugged.

Matthew stared.

And Duke finally said, "Okay . . ."

Mariella pressed her hand on the table as she gathered the courage to say what she needed to say. "Okay, this is going to sound like a crazy idea. But I really feel like it's the only way to nip this whole thing in the bud and figure out what's really going on here."

"Keep going," Duke said.

"I think we can all agree there's a really good chance I'm on this killer's radar, correct?"

They all nodded.

"And we can also all agree this guy has already killed two women, five years apart, and they were both staying at the Wanderlust Campground."

The group nodded again. There was no denying those facts.

"Part of me wonders why in the world he'd strike again so soon when he waited five years between his other victims." She knew she was hemming and hawing at this point, but she couldn't stop herself.

"He could be becoming more confident." Duke shrugged before taking a long sip of his water.

"Maybe," Mariella conceded. "We really don't know much about this guy, do we? Except that he leaves feathers for his victims. And maybe he's the one who makes strange noises outside his victims' homes."

"What are you getting at, Mariella?" Matthew eyed her.

She was clearly making her brother nervous.

"I think that tonight we should all stay at the campground," she finally blurted.

Mariella waited for their response.

Three seconds of silence passed—she'd counted—before everyone began talking all at once.

"Terrible idea."

"No way."

"We're not setting you up as bait."

"You can't be serious."

"Worst idea I've ever heard in my whole entire life."

That last one came from Matthew.

She looked at her brother and saw the worry in his gaze. And it was there rightfully.

"I knew you guys would object," Mariella said. "And I don't want to offer up myself as bait. Not at all. Believe me. But what if we all stay there and tell the local police what's going on? What if they stake out the woods and wait to see if this guy strikes?"

Another round of silence stretched, this one lasting six seconds.

"I don't know . . ." Duke said.

"It's still risky," Andi added.

"Terrible idea," Ranger mumbled again.

"You could get hurt," Simmy said.

"I'm not in favor of this." Matthew crossed his arms.

Mariella pounded the air with her hands, trying to tamp down their anxiety. "I promise I won't do anything stupid. We could plan all the details so this would work. I wouldn't need to put myself at risk."

Everyone still stared at her as if she was insane.

"Will you at least think about it?" Her gaze pleaded with each of them.

After a moment of hesitation, they all nodded—although still clearly reluctant.

That was a good start, at least.

But for now, she'd finish her meal. Give her idea time to settle.

Then Mariella would figure out if there was anything to do in the meantime.

chapter
fifty-four

MARIELLA GLANCED at the time and saw it was just after noon.

Even if they did decide to give the camping idea a try, they still had several hours before they'd need to go to the campground and set up. During that time, they'd also need to talk to the police about their plan. That was one of Mariella's stipulations.

Mariella remained sitting at the picnic table as she waited for everyone to finish eating. As she did, she remembered again being abducted by the Ice Fairy Killer.

She'd been terrified and certain she would die.

She never wanted to put herself in that position again.

That was why part of her felt sick to her stomach when she even suggested the idea of going to the campground.

But it was the only way she could think to draw this guy out.

They needed to catch him before anyone else was hurt or killed. So Jason could get his life back.

For the longest time, Mariella had been selfish. She knew that. But this was her opportunity to prove to everyone that she wasn't all about herself. Not that she was just doing this to prove anything. But another part of her liked the idea of doing something for others.

Doing something for Jason.

"Has anybody talked to Hannah's family yet?" Simmy's soft voice cut into the silence.

Mariella shook her head. "Not me. I assumed Jason told me anything important."

"But the family doesn't talk to Jason anymore, right?" The sun peeked out from behind the clouds, and Duke slipped on some sunglasses to shield against the brightness.

"That's right." Mariella nodded.

"It might be a good idea to talk to them. Maybe they know something that was never told to Jason." Andi shrugged. "Seems like it's worth a try."

Mariella balled up the remains of her lunch and stood. "That sounds good. But I don't think we should all go."

"What if the three of us go?" Duke suggested. "You with me and Andi."

"And what are we going to do?" Ranger's intense gaze shifted from Duke to Andi as if he didn't like being relegated to a support position.

Duke's shoulders tightened as he thought about his

response. "What if the three of you brainstorm how that idea about us camping tonight would work? What it would look like. What we need. What safety measures would need to be put in place. And if there's even a chance that the police would even consider going in on this with us."

"We can do that," Ranger muttered with a slow nod.

Matthew didn't say anything.

Mariella knew he still wasn't happy about this idea.

But no one else had any better ones right now.

Besides, if they didn't figure out something soon, Mariella might die anyway.

A rock lodged in her throat at the thought.

It had been surprisingly easy to find the address for Hannah's family online.

Even better, their house was close enough to walk to, like most things here in town.

After cleaning up their mess, Mariella, Duke, and Andi started toward Main Street.

Someone up ahead caught Mariella's eye.

Roy from the library.

He still sat at the library booth—this time on a stool instead of the colorful rug—with a storybook in hand. This seemed like the perfect opportunity to ask him a few questions.

"I recognize you." He smiled at Mariella and closed *Where the Wild Things Are.*

"I came in looking for information about that kidnapping," Mariella reminded him.

"That's right." He glanced around as if ready to make casual conversation. "Isn't this a beautiful day? Couldn't ask for better weather."

Mariella shifted from one foot to the other as she tried to form her words properly. She needed to frame her request in a nonsuspicious manner. "I was actually hoping to ask you a question. You're the only one in the area I can think of who might know the answer."

His eyes lit as if he liked that designation. "Knowledge is power. What can I do for you?"

"I'm curious about the Native American heritage of this area."

His gaze grew even brighter. "I'd be more than happy to talk to you about that. I'm tied up here for the rest of the day—I'm on the cleanup committee for the festival— but maybe tomorrow we can meet in the library to talk about it."

"Isn't the library closed on Sundays?"

"It is. But you and your friends are welcome to come. I don't mind. It's not often that people actually care about the heritage of the area. And it's truly fascinating. We're talking Russian fur traders, secret military bases, literal gold mines."

That *did* sound interesting. "I can't wait to hear about it. I appreciate your willingness to help."

He pulled a card out of his pocket and handed it to her. "Just text me, and I'll see if I can make it happen."

They thanked him and then continued on foot toward Hannah's house.

Ten minutes later, they reached her former residence.

The light-blue house looked like most of the other homes in town. Two stories, neat, and simple.

A rush of nerves hit Mariella as they arrived.

She hoped this visit proved fruitful.

But she knew it would be a hard conversation.

chapter
fifty-five

JASON LAY BACK IN BED, his thoughts turning over and over.

How could Sean do something like this to him?

Yet he knew. He'd seen firsthand what vengeance could look like.

And Jason knew he was lucky to be alive. If he had fallen at a different angle or landed in a different way, his neck could have easily broken.

He was eternally grateful that God had been watching out for him and he was still alive right now.

His thoughts turned from there to the conversation he'd had with Mariella. He was so glad she'd opened up to him. Things were finally beginning to make sense about why she was here and her reaction to Bright.

Could Bright be her father? The thought seemed absurd.

But was it?

"What are you thinking about?" Pops asked from the stiff-looking chair beside Jason's bed at the clinic.

Jason let out a long breath and wondered how much he should say. "About nothing. About everything."

"Makes sense." His father's words sounded sincere, not like he was merely trying to appease him.

Another few moments of silence fell before Jason asked, "What exactly do you know about Bright Armstrong?"

His dad's eyebrows climbed up higher. "Bright? He wasn't what I was expecting you to ask about."

"I know but . . . something about the man has been bugging me lately. I feel like he's doing something that's not on the up and up."

"I've seen him taking some boat trips at mysterious hours. Not too many charters lately either. It has been very strange."

Jason sat up more. "Anything weird about those trips —other than the hours?"

"It looked like he was hauling some kind of equipment with him, and I don't mean fishing equipment either. But it was all covered with tarps—I couldn't see what it was. Then I saw him return once—he and a couple of guys with him I didn't recognize. They were covered in dirt. I have no idea what he's been up to. But I suspect it's no good."

Jason stored that information away, hoping it would make sense at some point. Maybe once he'd recovered he could find out more information.

But right now he had bigger fish to fry, as the saying went.

"What do you know about the time his twins went missing? Did you know him back then?"

His dad let out a long breath. "I did. Back then we had worked together on a few commercial fishing boats when we were teenagers. He's a few years older than me, but we got along fine for the most part."

"Did people have any theories they threw out when the twins went missing?"

"There were all kinds of theories that were thrown out. The Russian mob. The black market. Things changed in this whole town when it happened. People were suddenly afraid."

"Did you ever talk to Bright around the time it happened?"

His dad let out a long breath as if the memories were burdening him. "We did chat a few times. And there was talk around town. You know I don't like to repeat gossip . . . but it seemed like life really hit Bright hard around that time."

"What do you mean?"

"I heard that he and his wife were having some problems. Instead of the twins making that easier, I think they only compounded the stress Bright was feeling. Twins are expensive, and the community tried to help out as much as they could. Meanwhile, Bright made some bad business decisions, and as a result he lost some of his business. He wasn't bringing in a very steady income, and his wife couldn't really work with caring for the twins. I heard that they were fighting and that Bright was trying to convince her to move to the Lower 48 because maybe they would have more job opportunities down there. But she didn't want to go."

"But then the twins were kidnapped . . ."

"That broke his wife's heart. She fell into a depression. On top of that, she ended up dying of a heart attack only a couple years later."

"And Bright never remarried."

"He never remarried. Said there'd never be any other woman like his wife."

"That does give me a different perspective on him, I guess. But I still think the man is rude, and I still suspect he could be up to something."

"You're not the only one. Gerald and the rest of the boys think there's something going on with him also. But it's none of our business. Hopefully, Bright will get everything worked out. He has a history of making bad decisions. I'd hoped with age he would put that behind him." Pops shrugged. "But who knows?"

That was right. Who knew? But what did that mean

for Mariella? If Bright really was her biological dad, what would that mean for her and her future?

Jason had no idea.

He wished he could think of a way to ease any pain she might feel about the situation. Any pain she might experience in the future because of Bright.

But the situation was out of his hands.

Jason could only pray for the best.

A woman answered the door at Hannah's house.

She was probably in her mid-fifties, but it was hard to tell because somehow she seemed older. Her spirit seemed heavy, like she'd experienced too much pain. Still, she was a pretty woman with light-brown hair that curled inward near her ears, a sharp jawline, and a gentle profile.

She stared at them skeptically. "Can I help you?"

Duke plastered on a gentle smile. "We are so sorry to interrupt, but we're true crime podcasters, and we're hoping to find out some information about your daughter's death. I apologize for putting you on the spot like this by stopping by without invitation. But we couldn't find a phone number, and there was no other way we knew to go about it."

Her eyes scanned each of them. "True crime podcasters? And you want to cover her story *now*? Where were you five years ago?"

"In our defense, we only started the podcast four months ago," Mariella said.

The woman eyed her another moment, her gaze narrowing. "Do I know you?"

Mariella shook her head. "No ma'am. We've never met."

She continued to stare. "Are you the girl who's been hanging out with Jason Somersby?"

Mariella wanted to deny it. Not because she was ashamed, but because she wasn't sure what kind of road-block this would present.

Finally, she nodded. "I am."

Mariella waited for the door to slam. For this conversation to be over.

Instead, the woman opened the door wider. "My name's Grace. You have fifteen minutes. Then my husband will be back from the hardware store. So we'll need to make this quick."

Mariella's pulse raced. She hadn't seen that coming. But she was thankful the woman hadn't sent them away.

She seated them on the couch in the simple but clean living room, and then she sat on a seat across from them. She didn't bother to offer them food or drink, which was fine. They needed to make the most of their time here.

"What do you want to know?" Grace folded her hands in her lap.

Duke shifted before jumping right in. "We don't believe that Jason is guilty."

Grace's gaze fell. "I don't either. I don't say that often in front of my husband because he's so convinced that Jason is responsible. Honestly, he just wants someone to blame."

"I'm sure that would be easy to do," Mariella murmured.

"Sometimes it's easier to stay angry than it is to be sad." Wisdom gently rounded out her words.

No truer words had ever been spoken.

"But Hannah loved Jason," Grace continued. "I really thought the two of them would get married and give me grandkids. But then . . ." Her voice trailed.

"Do you have any suspicions about who might be guilty?" Andi asked.

Grace shook her head. "Believe me, I've thought about it. The only conclusion I've come to is that it was some random person passing through town. But now that it's happened again . . . I just don't know."

"Let's say it wasn't random." Andi's voice remained easy and calm. "Was anything off in the days before Hannah died?"

Grace thought about it a moment. "She was in town for the summer. She seemed really happy to be home. She liked going to college up in Anchorage, but she missed Jason. I know she even thought a couple times about quitting and just coming back down here and doing college online. But we encouraged her to get her education in person. I thought it was important. She and Jason were truly well suited for each other."

"So there was nothing strange about her behavior?" Duke clarified.

Grace nibbled on her lip for a moment. "There's one thing that she told me that I can't get out of my mind. The day before she died, she came back from the grocery store, and she wasn't quite acting like herself. She told me she was spooked."

Mariella straightened. "Did she say why?"

"She said she felt as if someone was watching her. She said it was probably just her mind playing tricks on her. Said that when she looked around, there was nobody."

Mariella's throat tightened. That was the exact same feeling that she'd had.

"The next morning when we went to get coffee, she said the same thing. That she couldn't shake the feeling. But I looked all around where we were standing on the sidewalk, and I didn't see anybody either. It was all very strange. Up in Anchorage, she had had a stalker for a while, so she tended to be on edge about stuff like that."

"Could her stalker be guilty?" Mariella asked, wondering why his name hadn't come up before.

Grace shook her head. "No, it can't be him. He actually became obsessed with another girl after Hannah. The other girl . . . well, she ended up shooting him to death."

Mariella's eyes widened. That hadn't been what she expected to hear.

At least they could rule him out, she supposed.

But Mariella couldn't shake the fact Hannah had felt as if she was being watched in the days before she died.

Just like Zoe.

And just like Mariella.

chapter
fifty-six

WHEN THEY GOT BACK to the cabin, Mariella was surprised to see Chief Dunne there speaking with Matthew, Simmy, and Ranger.

The chief stood to address Mariella. "I stopped by to see how you're doing. As usual, I got so much more. You always have a lot going on around you. Lots of . . . *excitement.*"

"Any updates?" Mariella rushed.

"I'm sure you heard about Sean."

She nodded. "I did. Anything else? What about that ceremonial site? Did you have a chance to investigate?"

"We did, but so far it's inconclusive. It does seem as if there was some kind of Native American ritual taking place there. However, that's not illegal."

"It's not, but it could be a clue," Mariella insisted. "What else can you tell us?"

The chief let out a sigh, closed her eyes, and then ran a hand over her face.

Maybe Mariella shouldn't be so eager. But how could she not be? Time was of the essence right now.

"We did find a substance on the end of the dart you found in the woods," Dunne said.

"What?" Mariella's eyes widened. "What kind?"

"We just got the results back. It's Turbina corymbosa."

"What's that?" Mariella asked.

"It's a plant, not native to this area. But it can cause people to hallucinate."

Her throat tightened. When she'd felt as if she might crawl out of her skin, that was why. Maybe that was the reason she felt like the earth wanted to swallow her, like the rocks were moving, and the trees mocking her.

"We're doing some additional tests on Zoe to see if that was in her system also," Dunne continued. "Hannah . . . well, that would be more complicated since she's been buried for so long."

"I see." Mariella drew in a deep breath. "That's good news."

"It's going to take a while to get those results, so don't get too excited." Dunne took a step toward the door.

"Wait . . . I had an idea on how we might be able to catch this guy," Mariella rushed.

The chief frowned. "Your friends told me, and I think it's too risky."

"That's because it is," Matthew said, a wry tone to his voice.

"I don't want to use you as bait," Chief Dunne said.

"I'm already a target. I'm not sure the situation will make it any more dangerous for me. In fact, I might be safer this way. At least you'd be there to catch him, and he'd be behind bars and not running lose threatening me."

"It screams bad idea," the chief continued.

Andi stepped forward. "What about if I make myself look like Mariella?"

Mariella gasped at her words. "What? You would do that?"

"Another bad idea," Duke muttered. "How does that help anything? You'll just be a target instead of Mariella."

"I know I'm not trained law enforcement," Andi said the words carefully. "But I think I can handle myself."

Duke pressed his lips together in a grimace as if he wasn't so sure about that.

"Why would you think you can handle yourself?" Dunne stared at Andi.

"Because I'm a lawyer by trade, and I did my own investigations for my cases. I've learned to keep a cool head in tense situations."

"And I haven't . . ." Mariella added with a frown.

She couldn't deny that was the truth.

There was a good chance she'd panic—especially after what happened with the Ice Fairy Killer. She was still dealing with trauma from that.

"I'm shorter than Mariella, but at night someone shouldn't be able to tell." Andi studied Mariella. "I could wear a wig with curly blonde hair."

"I have some old extensions we could use." Mariella shrugged, unsure if she should pursue this line of thought or not. "I found them in one of the compartments of my suitcase. They've been there a while, but they still looked pretty good."

Andi nodded as if they were talking about something as simple as attending a wedding. "We could use those."

They both turned to the chief and waited for her reaction.

The woman said nothing for a few minutes. Then she frowned and said, "If we do this, we're going to need to set some rules in place."

Mariella's breath caught. "What kind of rules are you thinking about?"

"There's no straying from our plan, for starters. You and your friends are always together. You don't venture out on your own to do anything. You don't try to be the hero."

"Of course."

Chief Dunne stared at her another moment. "We'll have more to talk about, and we need to be careful not to be seen together. We don't want it to seem as if we're planning this."

"Of course not," Mariella said.

But her breath hitched.

When she'd suggested it, she felt certain no one would go for it.

But now it sounded as if her plan might work.

That filled her with both hope and fear.

She just hoped no one got hurt on her account.

While the rest of the group gathered the camping equipment, Andi drove Mariella back to the clinic to see Jason.

Mariella had promised Jason she'd stop by again, and she wanted to be true to her word.

But she didn't want to tell him what they were doing either. She knew Jason wouldn't like the idea, and she didn't want to do anything to hinder his recovery.

If she told him about the plan, he might worry. That was the last thing she wanted.

In the meantime, the whole group had agreed that they'd try to appear as if they were going camping simply to have some fun. Since they were podcasters, she hoped that plan would work. Otherwise, it would seem too much like a setup. For that reason, they needed to make sure they had plenty of photo ops to place on social media. They might even need to record some snippets in order to make everything look real.

She never considered herself an actress, but today she would have to be.

Andi waited in the lobby while Mariella wandered down toward Jason's room.

As soon as she walked in, his dad stood and said he needed to stretch his legs.

Then Mariella took her place by Jason's bed, thankful for the privacy.

She studied him a moment.

Some of the color had returned to his skin, and he did look better. She was thankful for that.

He grabbed her hand this time. The act felt totally natural.

"How are you feeling?" She continued to study his face.

"I feel surprisingly good, all things considered," he said. "I tried to talk the doctor into letting me go home tonight, but he said no. Said he wanted to monitor my concussion just a little bit longer."

"That's probably a good idea."

"What have you been up to?"

Her mind raced through everything that had happened today. How much did she tell him? She needed to be careful.

She finally told Jason about seeing Bright and following him then seeing him talking to those two men.

Jason's gaze darkened as if he knew there was more to the story.

"What aren't you telling me?" she asked.

"I didn't want to say anything earlier, just because I have no proof. But I suspect that Bright's up to something. Maybe something illegal."

He told her about the black package on the small boat. About following those men as they climbed up toward the old fort.

"What do you think it means?" she asked.

"I'm not sure. I had plans of trying to go back to see if I could figure anything out, but I haven't had the chance yet."

"Maybe it's better if you don't. You should tell the police instead."

He gave her a look. "You know all about my track record with the police. I have no hope they'll take me seriously."

She frowned but didn't argue.

They chatted a few more minutes, but Mariella knew she didn't have much time. She had stuff to get ready for camping.

"Listen, I need to let you get some rest. But I'll check on you first thing in the morning, okay?"

He cast her a soft grin. "I look forward to it."

As Mariella stared at him, she couldn't help but wonder . . . what if she didn't see him in the morning?

What if this maniac did manage to grab her?

And what if tomorrow morning was something she wouldn't ever see?

Two hours later, the Artic Circle Murder Club was at the campground.

Mariella's nerves continued to rattle through her bones. This had bad idea written all over it. Even she couldn't argue with that fact.

But at least they'd gone about this the right way. Cops would be monitoring the woods. Dunne had decided to call in the state police as backup, and those officers would also assist. If anybody tried to grab Andi, they'd be arrested.

Then maybe this killer's reign of terror would finally come to an end.

That was Mariella's hope.

The murder club had gotten the camping equipment from a rental company in town. They'd also run to the grocery store to buy some things for the campfire.

Thankfully, Ranger seemed to know exactly what he was doing. In no time, they'd gotten two tents set up, sleeping bags laid out, and a bonfire ready to go.

The three women would stay together in one tent, and the guys would stay together in the other. But they were side by side.

Even though it was still daylight outside, it was close to dinnertime. But an hour ago, clouds had covered the sun. At least it wasn't raining.

In other circumstances, Mariella might look forward to this camping experience. The fresh air and beautiful scenery were definitely something to be admired.

But it was hard to enjoy anything when a killer lurked out there.

"This was the exact site where Zoe was staying," Mariella murmured as she stood outside and glanced around, a chill washing over her.

"We need to collect some kindling before it gets dark," Duke said. "But we stay together, and we don't wander far from the campsite. If you can't see the tent or the campground then you've gone too far."

Ranger, Matthew, and Mariella were teamed together.

They stepped into the woods at the edge of the campground. She wasn't sure exactly what she was looking for, other than broken branches already on the ground.

Yet her mind was somewhere else.

She couldn't stop imagining the killer being out here. Watching Hannah and Zoe. Planning his next move.

She shivered.

No doubt, search parties had already trampled all over this area, covering any clues.

Still, it would be good to get a feel for the area.

As they walked, she grabbed some dried sticks and bundled them in her arms.

In front of her, Matthew paused and pointed to the ground. "You guys, check this out."

They all paused, but Mariella didn't have any clue what he was pointing at. It appeared to be dirt and leaves.

Ranger squatted on the ground to study it more closely. Then he let out his signature grunt.

"What am I missing?" Mariella hated how confused she felt.

"Look at these three marks right here." Ranger pointed to each of them.

Mariella saw the little indentations on the ground. But what were they?

"How are those significant?" she asked.

"It looks like someone set up a tripod," Matthew said. He glanced back to the forest at the campground. "If so, they'd have a perfect view of Zoe's campsite."

Mariella followed his gaze and saw he was correct.

A shiver rushed through her.

Was that what had happened? Had the killer taken pictures of Zoe before killing her?

Or were these marks from a reporter or film crew who'd come to take some B-roll video footage of the area?

She wasn't sure.

But she stored the information in the back of her mind.

She glanced at Matthew and knew he had a theory brewing.

He stared up at the sky, and she followed his gaze. An opening in the tree branches stretched above them, where overhead the gray skies peeked through.

She still had no idea what her brother was thinking, but she'd give him time to sort his thoughts.

She pushed down her eagerness to hear his theory.

Besides, she had enough other things on her mind to keep her thoughts occupied.

Things like staying alive.

JASON HADN'T DIED.

I'd heard the news.

It wasn't until then that I'd realized how happy I'd been when I thought he was dead and out of my way.

Tlatoani had not told me to sacrifice Jason. But deep inside, I knew the man was trouble.

I knew if anyone could stop me from making my sacrifice, it was him.

He was at the clinic now. That should hinder him from doing anything.

But from what I'd heard, he was making a surprisingly speedy recovery.

That meant he could still be trouble.

As I sat on one of the benches in town, I thought everything through.

I needed to figure out how to handle this.

I'd heard rumors that the sacrifice and her friends were

going to go camping. From the scuttlebutt in town, it was for the podcast.

Yes, the podcast.

She did a true crime podcast, apparently, and the group thought it would be interesting to record from the very area where those two girls had gone missing.

Clever.

Or stupid, depending on how you looked at it.

My mind raced through my options.

What would my ancestors do in this situation? What would they do if they'd been hunting prey for such a long time only to be intercepted?

I knew.

They would get rid of the thing that intercepted them.

Because Tlatoani only wanted one.

He only wanted the blonde.

As if in response to that thought, I placed my hand on the wooden bench beneath me, and I felt it tremble.

Trembles were so much a part of Alaska that most people barely noticed them, especially when they felt as faint as this one.

But I knew there was more to it.

People could trust all those machines and technology all they wanted.

But nothing was greater than intuition.

The earth was rumbling, and if I didn't feed it, it would destroy me.

I reached in my pocket.

I had another feather there.

I needed to set this near Jason.

It would be the beginning of my ritual.

When I had the chance, I'd leave this for him to find.

It was my way of marking my territory.

Would I do away with him first? Or the blonde?

I wasn't sure. But Tlatoani would lead and guide me.

Whatever needed to happen, it needed to happen tonight.

I ran my finger along the edge of the feather, feeling its softness as my mind raced.

chapter
fifty-eight

JASON COULDN'T IGNORE the feeling of worry swelling in his gut. Yet he couldn't place it either.

Someone was targeting Mariella. And she was putting on a good front—probably for his sake—but that didn't mean she wasn't in danger.

That killer was still out there.

Would this guy wait another five years to strike?

It was hard to say whether or not that was his pattern or if it had simply taken him that long to build up his courage to strike again.

Or was there more to his timing than people realized?

Jason's thoughts raced.

Was there anything happening here in town five years ago?

His mind raced back in time.

He recalled that right after Hannah's death, tourism

had dried up for a few months for the remainder of the summer.

He remembered that one of the glaciers near the bay had a big chunk fall off, and reporters had come to talk and interview people about it as well as climate change.

A dead whale had washed ashore.

None of those things seemed significant.

There had been an earthquake later that summer. Jason couldn't remember exactly how it registered on the Richter scale, but he thought it was a three or four. Enough that everyone around had felt it, but not serious enough to cause any damage.

Not like the earthquake back in Anchorage in 1964.

But an earthquake seemed like something odd to base a murder on.

At that thought, Jason glanced outside at the rapidly falling darkness.

He sucked in a breath when he saw a man outside his window . . . a man wearing some type of Native American mask.

The killer . . . was he here?

Jason braced himself for whatever might play out next.

At the campground, Mariella and her friends sat around the bonfire and cooked hotdogs. They had a microphone and camera capturing the moment and their thoughts for the podcast. She might actually use some of the interviews.

But right now, social media was the last thing on her mind.

Thinking about it seemed irreverent considering everything else that was going on.

Matthew had already told everyone about the tripod marks, but he still seemed distracted, as if he had other things on his mind.

Finally, he announced, "I have a hunch. But I need the internet in order to prove it."

Duke and Ranger glanced at each other.

Finally, Ranger stood. "I'll drive you closer to town if you think it's important. You should be able to get a signal not far from here."

"I wouldn't ask unless it was important. And I think it might be."

Ranger stood, and Matthew followed.

A few minutes later, they climbed into Duke's SUV.

Then it was just Andi, Simmy, Duke, and Mariella.

The crackling of the fire somehow soothed her soul.

But she wondered how Jason was doing. She wanted to talk to him again. To see him again.

However, if he knew she was out here he'd only worry, and worry could hamper his recovery. Mariella didn't want that to happen.

"This wasn't the case I saw us taking on next," Andi said during a lull in the conversation.

"Me either," Mariella admitted as she stared at the dancing yellow and orange flames in front of her. "We're supposed to meet next week to talk about that."

"Sometimes life has other ideas."

She glanced around the circle. "I'm really honored all of you came here to help me. Thank you."

Honestly, she'd thought she had friends back in California. But none of them had been true friends. In her gut, she knew the group around her was different.

"We've always got your back," Duke told her.

Gratitude spread through her. Mariella knew he meant the words.

Yet that gratitude was quickly replaced with worry.

Now they had to live through the night in order to continue putting that sentiment into practice.

chapter
fifty-nine

TWENTY MINUTES LATER, Ranger and Matthew returned.

But this time, instead of Matthew seeming distracted, his eyes were bright, as if he had something to share.

"I have a theory." He joined them at the campfire, and all their attention was on him.

"Please share," Duke said.

"Those tripod marks . . . we assumed they are from a camera, right?" he started.

"That's right," Andi said. "It makes the most sense."

"I had a different idea I wanted to explore. You see, right above where those tripod marks were there was an opening in the tree canopy, which allowed a view of the sky."

"Someone was taking pictures of the sky?" Mariella tried to follow his line of reasoning.

"Actually, I believe those marks were left by a telescope."

Mariella continued to listen, unsure where Matthew was going with this or if it was significant.

"You think the *killer* was using a telescope?" Duke questioned.

"I'm not even sure if the killer left those marks or not. But I still think the telescope angle could be significant." He pushed his glasses up higher, his words coming out faster with excitement. "Get this. It turns out that on the night Zoe was killed, there was a meteor shower in this area. A big one. In fact, there hasn't been one so intense in—"

"In five years," Andi finished. "Am I right?"

He nodded. "Exactly."

Her thoughts raced. "Wait . . . did that same meteor shower happen when Hannah was killed?"

"Not the same one, but there was one," Matthew said.

"You think this killer is listening to the stars and this meteor shower is somehow signaling when he needs to kill?" Duke clarified.

"I think it's a good possibility, especially when you mix it with everything else that we know about this guy."

"I think he could be onto something," Ranger said.

"If that's the case, then shouldn't Mariella be safe for another five years or however long it takes for this meteor shower to come back around again?" Andi asked.

"You might think," Matthew said. "Meteor showers

don't exactly run on a schedule. It's not like Haley's comet where you can assume it's going to be here every seventy-five years or so. Meteor showers can be predictable, but they can also be random."

"What are you getting at?" Mariella said.

"I'm saying there's supposed to be another meteor shower tonight. A decent sized one."

Mariella felt the blood drain from her face.

Would this killer see that as a sign that tonight was the night he should strike?

Suddenly, it felt like the stakes had risen even more.

At eleven o'clock, the gang escaped to their own tents. Before lying down, Mariella had helped Andi add the extensions to her hair. They'd exchanged sweatshirts—and now Andi looked pretty in pink.

But it wasn't time for Andi to leave the tent yet.

As they passed time, Mariella lay in her sleeping bag, nestled between Simmy and Andi. She tried to get comfortable, but the ground felt hard beneath her. She tried to put her high-maintenance days behind her, but some moments were more difficult than others.

Her heart pounded with anticipation.

Would their plan work?

She didn't know. The idea had been risky.

Right now, fear pulsed through her.

Fear because she was in the wilderness with only a nylon tent for protection. Fear because nature sounded so alive around her that it felt threatening. Fear because the cooling air felt like a stark reminder of how unforgiving this place was.

Her heart continued to thrust into her chest at an unnerving pace.

The police were outside hidden in the woods and keeping an eye on the situation, she reminded herself. That did make her feel better. As did the fact that her friends were with her.

But she was still on edge.

"My ex-husband used to love to go camping." Simmy's quiet voice cut through the silence.

Mariella's attention suddenly snapped from the danger they were in to Simmy.

It wasn't often her friend talked about herself, and Mariella hadn't even realized Simmy had an ex-husband.

Andi turned over, resting her head on her hand. "Did you go camping with him?"

"I did. I thought it was a lot of fun back then—back before . . ." Her voice trailed.

Mariella waited for her to finish, but she didn't.

Whatever had happened . . . Simmy sounded hollow.

Mariella had never heard her friend sound like that before, and she hated it.

Silence stretched for a moment.

Then a stick snapped in the distance.

Her breath caught.

Was it an animal? A police officer? Maybe one of the guys had gotten up to go to the bathroom.

She had no idea.

But she wondered if this was the start of an eventful evening.

For now, she needed to wait.

Andi and Simmy must have heard it too. Andi reached over and grabbed Mariella's wrist, squeezing tight as if to reassure her.

"This is it," Andi whispered.

Mariella knew what she meant. This was when Andi would step outside and pretend to be Mariella.

At once, the situation seemed even riskier.

Like a terrible idea—just as everyone had told her earlier.

They should pull the plug.

But Mariella feared it was too late.

She could hardly breathe as she waited to find out what would happen.

Andi unzipped the tent and stepped out. She would make it seem as if she was walking to the bathroom.

But sitting in this tent unable to know what was happening out there made Mariella feel like a nervous wreck.

Simmy seemed to sense her nerves and wrapped an arm around her.

"It's going to be okay," her friend assured her.

She had such a calming way about her.

Mariella wished she had just a touch of that.

She squeezed her eyes shut, praying yet again.

Please be with her. Don't let her be hurt.

And help us to catch this guy. Please. Before he hurts anybody else.

She heard her heart beating faster as soon as she whispered a silent Amen.

Though there were windows on the tent, they had all decided it was better for them to remain zipped closed. The last thing they needed was for the killer to see inside as Andi and Mariella switched places.

Blood rushed through Mariella's veins, causing her heart to beat more quickly.

Maybe everything would go as planned.

This guy would emerge.

He would be arrested.

Andi would be okay.

And then what?

Would Mariella stay in town and question Bright?

Would she head back to Fairbanks and try to resume her life as normal? Pretend like none of this had happened?

And how would she leave Jason behind? They weren't officially together. Yet the thought of not seeing him again made her heart twist with regret.

Footsteps sounded outside and pulled her from her thoughts.

Then a rush of footsteps followed.

"Police!" someone yelled.

More footsteps sounded.

More yells.

More commotion.

A tent—no doubt Duke's, Ranger's, and Matthew's—unzipped.

Mariella and Simmy clung to each other.

They'd been given strict instructions not to leave this tent until one of the guys got them.

But right now, the anticipation was killing her.

Was Andi okay?

That was all she could think about.

chapter
sixty

MARIELLA COULD HARDLY BREATHE AS she waited to find out what was happening out there.

She and Simmy continued to cling to one another.

Finally, footsteps came toward their tent.

Her throat tightened.

What if it was the killer? What if he managed to take out everyone, and now he was coming for her?

She didn't think that was the case, but her imagination ran wild. She needed to expect the worst. Be prepared to defend herself.

Then she heard, "It's me. Duke. You can come out."

Relief flooded her.

Quickly, she climbed from her sleeping bag, unzipped the tent, then she and Simmy hurried out.

Her gaze darted to Andi, and Mariella let out a quick puff of air.

Good. She was okay.

Her friend's safety had been her number one concern.

Then her gaze went to the huddle of police officers in the distance.

They had a man in custody, but it was dark, and Mariella couldn't see his face.

Had they really caught this guy? Had their plan worked?

It almost felt too good to be true.

Mariella stepped closer, anxious to see the culprit behind all this.

Who was it? Officer Longwood? One of Bright's men?

A vaguely familiar voice rang through the air, animated and loud. "I don't know what you're doing. I wasn't doing anything wrong."

"We're going to need to take you in for questioning," Chief Dunne said.

A flashlight popped on, and the beam hit the man's face.

Mariella sucked in a breath.

Jason's friend Dustin. The one who'd helped them look for Jason last night.

Had he been the one behind this the whole time? Had he let his friend take the fall for it?

Her head spun as questions raced through her mind.

But Mariella was having trouble making sense of all of it.

Why in the world would Dustin do this?

"I'm not the one behind this!" Dustin exclaimed as he sneered at the cops surrounding him.

Mariella remained on the edge of the group, listening with rapt attention to everything he said.

She desperately wanted to know what the man was thinking . . . because she couldn't fathom why he would set up his friend.

Had he also been in love with Hannah? Had he met Zoe?

Was this about love? Power? Money?

Those were the usual motives for murder.

But there were other reasons as well. Mariella had done her research into the subject matter for the podcast.

Some serial killers murdered out of hedonistic motives. Others were visionary, while still others were mission oriented.

But Dustin . . . why?

As they stood there, Matthew was on one side of her and Simmy on the other. They stood close enough that she could feel their body heat, and she appreciated the warmth. The air felt surprisingly cool around her—or was it the gravity of the situation that made her shiver?

Either way, she was grateful to have people surrounding her.

"Tell us what you're doing in the woods." Chief Dunne stared at Dustin, her eyes hard and unyielding.

"I wanted to see if this psycho came back. *That's* what I was doing out here."

The chief crossed her arms. "You came out here to see if you could catch the killer? Since when have you wanted to be the town hero?"

Dustin's scowl deepened. "Look, my best friend almost died last night because of everything that's happened here in this town. He's been an outcast for years, and it's not fair. It's not right. Jason deserves so much better. So I thought if I could get a glimpse of this guy then maybe I could—"

"Be the hero and take him down?" the chief finished with an eyeroll.

"No." Dustin sliced his hand through the air. "That's not what I'd do. I would have reported the guy once I knew his identity."

Duke crossed his arms. "Why did you think this guy would strike again tonight?"

Dustin shrugged. "I didn't know. In fact, I've come out here a couple of times since it happened to see if I could find anything. I know I'm not an official investigator or anything, but I do know these woods. Since this guy has struck here before, I thought there was a good chance he might come back to look for more victims. That's the truth—no matter how you want to spin it."

Chief Dunne glanced at the state police officer holding onto Dustin, who shrugged.

"I checked the woods, looking to see if he brought

anything with him," the officer said. "It's dark, but I didn't find anything."

"Something like a bow and arrow?" Dustin asked. "I don't even own one."

The chief still appeared unconvinced. "You're not under arrest, but we're going to have to take you to the station to be questioned."

"Yeah, whatever. But I wasn't about to kill anybody. You set Jason up to take the fall for Hannah's death. I'm not gonna let you set me up to take the fall for this."

"We didn't set him up to take the fall for anything." Exasperation entered Chief Dunne's voice for the first time.

Usually, she was so even-keeled. But she was beginning to crack, Mariella realized.

"You've always thought he was guilty," Dustin shot back.

Something glimmered in the chief's eyes. "Maybe I was wrong."

"Well, your wrong assumption has made Jason's life miserable for the past five years. So I hope you can live with yourself knowing that."

The chief narrowed her gaze. After staring at Dustin another moment, she nodded behind her. "Take him to the car so we can take him to the station."

Mariella believed what Dustin said. She didn't think he was the killer.

But the truth was, if he wasn't the killer and the real

killer had been thinking about striking tonight, this whole ordeal may have just scared him away.

Which meant this whole camping trip was for nothing.

Which also meant that this killer would still be out there and looking for his next victim.

Maybe for Mariella.

She frowned and glanced around again.

What if the killer was in the woods right now watching them?

The thought made her want to crawl out of her skin.

chapter
sixty-one

OFFICER LONGWOOD WALKED BACK inside the clinic holding a wooden mask in his hand.

Jason's heart pounded into his rib cage as he waited. "Well?"

"Someone left the mask on a stick near your window." Longwood held it up.

"What?" His voice rose with surprise.

Longwood frowned and nodded. "I guess they wanted to send a message."

Jason and his dad exchanged a glance.

"Does that mask mean anything to you?" Longwood asked.

With gloved hands, Longwood turned so Jason could get a better look.

Jason shook his head. "Looks Native American, I'd guess. And new, like someone made it recently. I don't know of anyone around here who makes these. I can check with Roy at the library. Maybe he knows of someone."

Roy was somewhat of an unofficial town historian.

"Why would someone leave that mask here?" Jason murmured.

"They left this also." Longwood pulled a plastic bag from his pocket.

A feather was inside.

Jason's breath caught.

"You're right. Someone is trying to send a message—a message that I'm still a target." Jason rubbed his jaw, not liking the tightness in his gut.

A storm was definitely brewing, and the worst of it seemed to be closing in by the minute.

"I don't like this," Pops muttered.

"I've been worried about Mariella," Jason told Longwood. "Do you know if Dunne has someone keeping an eye on her?"

A strange look passed through Longwood's eyes. "She does."

"She hasn't been answering her phone."

He shrugged. "Maybe she's out of range."

Jason narrowed his eyes as he observed Longwood. Why was he acting shifty? There was more to this.

"What aren't you saying?" Jason asked. "You know something I don't."

Longwood swallowed hard, his Adam's apple bobbing up and down. "She's safe . . ."

"Longwood . . ."

He scowled. "If you must know, Mariella is at the campground."

"What?" His voice rose.

Longwood glanced around before shushing him. "We have people there. She's fine."

"Why would Mariella go there?" Jason had to use every ounce of his self-control to keep his voice calm.

When Longwood didn't say anything, the truth hit Jason. "Is she trying to lure the killer out?"

Longwood motioned again for Jason to keep his voice low. "We've got the situation under control."

Jason tugged at his IV, suddenly feeling like a prisoner here at this clinic. "I doubt that."

"You should stay here." Longwood placed a hand over Jason's wrist, stopping him from pulling out the IV catheter. "It's safer this way."

"I suppose I'd have an alibi if I'm here all night." The words tasted bitter as they left his lips.

"Jason—we've got this."

He stared at Longwood a moment before shaking his head. He had no confidence in that.

But if he tore out of here and somehow made it to the campground, he might blow their entire operation.

Maybe that was what he *should* do.

Because the whole thing was a terrible idea.

A decent-sized crowd had formed at the campground to watch Dustin being taken away.

Even though it was one a.m., no one seemed to care. In fact, everyone seemed on edge.

Including Mariella.

She turned to Duke and the rest of the gang. "What now? I feel like this opportunity has been ruined."

Duke scrubbed a hand over his jaw. "I don't know. This isn't the outcome I hoped for, and our whole plan is now down the drain."

"I guess now we pack up and go back to the cabin." Andi shrugged.

"I don't know that we should do that," Duke said. "We're already here. We didn't get much sleep last night. We could finish out the night and then pack up in the morning."

"That makes the most sense to me," Ranger said.

But as they turned to go back to their tents, the ground trembled beneath them.

Mariella grabbed Andi's arm as fear raced through her.

This wasn't a small tremor like they'd felt earlier.

Rocks tumbled down the mountainside. Trees cracked. The earth groaned.

Panic filled the air as everyone realized what was going on.

Was this really an earthquake?

As if in response, the tremors deepened as the world around her shattered.

chapter
sixty-two

A SENSE of panic filled the air.

Mariella looked for somewhere to take shelter. But there was nowhere. Out here, everything was exposed.

As another rumble filled the air, a woman across from Mariella fell. She began to slide downhill.

Duke, Andi, and Ranger rushed to help her.

Mariella stood back, unsure what she could do.

She hated feeling so helpless.

But panic ripped through her.

As more rocks tumbled into her legs, she moved farther away. But there was nowhere to escape.

Suddenly, a tree crashed.

A man standing nearby disappeared beneath the branches.

Simmy and Matthew darted toward the man.

But Mariella remained frozen with fear.

Disaster struck everyone around them.

Oh, God . . . what's happening right now?

Mariella tried to take a deep breath to calm herself.

But as soon as she closed her eyes, something stung her neck.

A bug?

As she reached for the area, she felt something there.

She plucked the object from her neck and studied it a moment.

A dart.

She froze as realization rolled over her.

At once, her thoughts went haywire.

The man . . . the killer . . . he *was* here.

And he wasn't going to let a natural disaster stop him from enacting his plan.

Mariella was going to die.

She was certain of it.

After Longwood left, Jason took a moment to compose himself.

But as he turned to Pops, he felt the earth rumbling around him.

A tremor?

This one was stronger than usual.

"Pops—I need to go find Mariella," he stated, even as the room shook.

Surprisingly, his dad didn't argue. "I understand."

He'd probably known Jason would go with or without his help.

Jason still had a concussion and needed to be careful. His ribs were also wrapped and still tender.

But he could ignore that for a little while.

Right now, he just needed to see Mariella with his own eyes.

He managed to check himself out of the clinic in record time and hop into Pops' truck.

The ground continued to rumble as if angered.

As they drove away from town to the campground, the trees on either side of the road swayed.

The truck rattled.

"Pops . . ." Jason grabbed onto the dash.

"I think it's a heavy tremor." His father's jaw tightened.

"Feels like more than a heavy tremor to me."

Jason halfway expected Pops to stop or to turn around.

Instead, his dad pressed the accelerator.

Just as they pulled into the campground, something crashed behind them.

A tree.

Everyone at the campground was now trapped.

If Mariella was here, then she was in more than one kind of danger.

As Pops threw his truck into Park, Jason shoved his door open and climbed out.

The ground shook violently beneath him.

He'd never felt anything like this before.

It was unnerving, to say the least.

This was definitely more than one of the small tremors they sometimes felt.

This just might be one of the big ones that all Alaskans dreaded and feared.

"What now?" Pops met him on his side of the truck.

Jason glanced around. Saw people running in panic.

"This way." Jason nodded toward the sites where tents were set up.

If Mariella was here, he needed to see her with his own eyes and know she was okay.

He hurried by the campsites until he finally spotted Duke and Andi standing near a woman who lay on the ground holding her leg.

He paused beside them and glanced around. "You guys . . . where's Mariella?"

Duke looked up in surprise before nodding toward a tent. "She was right over there."

When Jason looked in that direction, he didn't see Mariella anywhere.

"Simmy, Matthew—where's Mariella?" Duke called.

Jason looked over and saw those two helping a man who was halfway buried beneath a fallen tree.

"She was just with us." Matthew rose, his voice tightening with concern.

Panic raced through Jason. "Mariella?"

No one responded.

He called again.

Still no answer.

Worst-case scenarios began to pummel him.

What if he was too late?

chapter
sixty-three

SOMEONE HAD GRABBED MARIELLA.

Pulled her into the wilderness.

It was a man. Wearing a mask. A terrifying wooden mask with a hook nose and painted markings that made him look evil.

Or was she imagining that also?

Right now, she had no idea what was real and what wasn't.

The earthquake . . . it had been real.

Right?

The trauma at the campground had also been real.

And she was pretty sure the dart really had embedded into her skin.

Stranger . . . the rest of the man looked normal. Jeans and a black T-shirt. Boots.

Only the mask was different.

It made him seem like he was just an everyday guy who liked to tap into primeval ways.

As the man dragged her, the forest seemed to close in. It was as if the earth was collapsing around her and trying to trap her inside, to swallow her in its depths.

But that wasn't possible . . . was it?

Nothing seemed certain anymore.

Mariella only knew she had to get away from the man in the mask.

The man's grip on her tightened. "If only my first sacrifice had worked, we wouldn't be here right now."

Sacrifice?

Was that what she was?

A sacrifice?

Terror ripped through her at the thought.

Jason ignored the trembling earth around him as he darted to the edge of the dark woods. All he could think about was Mariella.

What if that madman had somehow grabbed her?

He cupped his hands around his mouth before yelling, "Mariella!"

There was no answer except the rumble of the earth around him.

When he glanced down, he saw the grass had been trampled. A scuffle of footprints had been left.

One smaller set and one larger one.

His heart raced.

Had Mariella left those? Right before a madman grabbed her?

He had to go find her. With every second that passed, this madman would get farther away with her.

Jason took a step toward the woods when the ache in his ribs caused him to stop. To clutch his side. To try to suck in a deep breath.

He couldn't.

Someone grabbed his shoulder.

"You're in no shape to do a rescue," Pops said.

"I can't let that man kill her like he killed Hannah." Jason's voice cracked as he said the words.

Pops stared at him a moment before nodding. "You're right. You can't. You're going to need a team to go with you."

"Where am I going to find a team?"

Just then, Duke stepped forward, along with the brute of the man who'd cornered him outside Mariella's place. Jason thought his name was Ranger.

"We'll go with you," Duke said.

Chief Dunne stepped into the conversation, a stern look in her gaze. "You guys don't know what you're getting yourself into."

"Unfortunately, we do," Duke said. "But we have no other choice."

chapter
sixty-four

MARIELLA JERKED AWAY from the man holding onto her.

At least she tried to.

But it didn't work.

He held tight.

Her head spun as she looked at him. As she tried to figure out who he could be. He spoke in a weird voice, one that was almost cartoonlike.

And his mask . . . sweat spread across her skin at the sight of it.

Was that what the man wanted? For her to be afraid?

Because he'd succeeded.

The drug the dart had been laced with—Mariella couldn't remember what the chief had called it—made her head spin. Made everything feel overblown and bigger around her.

Including the way the earth shook.

Including her terror.

This forest was no place for people to be during an earthquake. Things broke apart around her. Big things—trees, mountains, the very ground.

"I should have sacrificed you earlier," the man said. "Then we wouldn't have to go through this."

"Sacrificing me won't do anything," Mariella said. "It won't stop the earth from shaking."

She knew trying to rationalize with this man would probably do no good.

He was clearly delusional.

But Mariella had to try anyway. She couldn't just sit here and let him do whatever he wanted. Not when her life was on the line.

"What are you going to do with me?" She stared at him as she waited for his response.

"I'm going to sacrifice you."

"You don't have to do this." She needed to keep him talking as long as possible. "Why me?"

"Tlatoani sent me signs that confirmed his wishes. I must do this now or there will be no hope. This whole area will be destroyed."

Tlatoani? The whole area would be destroyed? What was he talking about?

Just then, the earth moved all around her again, and Mariella stumbled.

So did her abductor.

His grip slipped.

Run!

Despite how everything spun around her, she drew herself to her feet.

Then Mariella took off across the vast quaking wilderness.

Before Jason and his team set out, the chief's radio crackled. The way her voice rose indicated something had happened. A new development.

He paused, hoping for an update. A *positive* update.

When she put her radio back on her belt, she turned toward them. "That was Micah Moeller. He's with the US Geological Survey, and he's been in town the past few days."

"Is he the man who was wandering the woods with a map?" Duke asked.

"Wandering the woods with a map?" Jason repeated. What was he talking about? There was obviously something he was missing.

"Long story," Duke muttered.

"He very well could be that person," Dunne said. "He believes this earthquake could have been caused by human interference. That's what Micah believes happened here, that someone has been disturbing the ground around the glacier."

"Disturbing?" Jason repeated. "You mean like digging?"

Chief Dunne's gaze narrowed in on him. "Digging but with equipment that could shake up the ground. What do you know?"

He ran a hand over his face. "You need to check out Bright Armstrong. I'm not saying that because he's our biggest competition in the charter fishing world. He and some other guys have been up to something. They've been going up to Caines Head and acting suspiciously. I wonder if they discovered something up there."

"You didn't tell us this earlier?"

Jason shrugged. "I had no proof of any crimes, and you wouldn't have listened to me anyway."

She opened her mouth as if to argue, but then shut it again. "I'll see what I can find out—as soon as I make sure everyone here in town is safe."

"A tree fell over and blocked the entrance to the campground so you're going to have some trouble getting out of here."

"I heard. We've had reports of damage already, but no casualties. Let's pray it stays that way."

Jason turned to the people around him. "We don't have much time. We need to get going. We need to find Mariella."

With one last glance at the chief, they took off into the wilderness.

The ground had been shaken too much for them to follow any tracks. Still, they knew the basic area where Mariella was standing when she was last seen. So they headed in that direction.

Thankfully, the quaking around them stopped. But trees were down, and rocks had shifted.

This would be difficult, and Jason prayed he was up for it. His body still hurt. But in the long run, it would hurt him even more if he didn't do everything in his power to help Mariella.

As he searched the woods, calling Mariella's name, his mind flashed back to when Hannah had disappeared.

Though he hadn't realized she was gone until the morning, the moment he'd known that her whereabouts were unaccounted for, he had begun searching these woods. He feared maybe she had wandered off and gotten lost.

Those minutes—which felt like hours—had been agonizing.

He'd searched the first day to no avail.

Then he'd searched every day after that, barely sleeping. Even as people thought he was guilty. Even when he was bone-tired. Even when he wanted to give up.

If he hadn't been taken in for an interrogation . . . maybe he could have saved her.

No. It had already been too late.

He'd replayed the what-ifs a thousand times.

Hannah would have already been dead by then. The killer had murdered her that night.

The heaviness of grief pressed into him.

Jason couldn't give up.

He had to keep looking.

He wouldn't stop until he found Mariella.

MARIELLA RAN THROUGH THE FOREST. Through the darkness.

Trees seemed to reach out and grab her. Rocks rolled in front of her, intent on making her fall. Even the dirt seemed to come alive and try to consume her.

No, it's all a mind game. It's the drug he gave you. Push through it!

She sprinted forward. But where were those cliffs?

It was so dark out here. She had no light. Even if she did, it would be too risky to turn it on.

She wanted to glance behind her. To see how close this man was.

But that would only slow her down.

She had to move!

"You won't win," the man muttered behind her, his voice sounding almost like a goblin now—an out-of-breath goblin.

A goblin?

Was that her imagination again? A hallucination?

Mariella didn't want to find out.

An arrow brushed the edge of her hair and embedded in a tree beside her.

She sucked in a breath.

Was this how it would end? With an arrow through her chest?

No, Mariella. Keep moving.

Then she heard something crack in front of her.

She didn't slow. She couldn't.

But as she looked up, she saw a tree crashing toward her.

Mariella dove out of the way.

She hit the ground, the impact stealing her breath.

The tree missed her—but only by mere inches. The smaller branches brushed her leg. Maybe even cut her skin.

She wasn't sure.

Right now, she didn't care.

She had to get up. Had to run.

She only cared about escaping.

But her depth perception was off. She couldn't tell where exactly she was.

Had the tree hit the man?

Would she be that lucky?

Probably not.

Oh, God . . . what am I going to do? Can You just make me disappear?

I need You. I need You so badly right now.

Would her request fall on deaf ears?

She had no idea.

But she wanted to believe that wasn't the case.

She wanted to believe there was more to this life.

More to *her* life.

She continued to race forward.

Until the trees fell away, and nothing stood before her but a stark emptiness.

She came to an abrupt stop.

As she glanced down, her head spun.

The cliff.

She'd reached the cliff.

She started to turn. To scramble along the rocky edge to safety.

Then she realized that not only was she at the cliff, but she must have run onto a ledge.

She needed to go back in the direction she'd come. To keep running.

Before she could reach solid ground, someone stepped from the shadows.

The masked man.

He stood there, holding a bow and arrow in his hands.

Grinning behind the mask.

She didn't know how she knew. She couldn't see his face.

But she *knew*.

Beneath that mask he was smiling at his fortunate turn of events.

Now no matter which way she stepped, her death loomed close and taunted her.

JASON and the team moved quickly, knowing there was no time to waste.

They fanned out to search more ground but stayed within eyesight of each other.

They needed to stay quiet too.

If this guy knew they were coming, that might make him act more quickly. That wasn't what they wanted.

They had to find Mariella first.

The element of surprise might be their best bet.

Jason held his side as more pain shot through him.

He could recover later. That was what he kept telling himself.

For now, he continued up the mountain.

The darkness concealed much of the damage from the tremors, but the landscape had changed. It was broken and uneven—unstable even.

He heard voices ahead and froze.

Someone was talking. But his voice almost sounded ghostly.

He shivered.

Who was that?

The rest of the team heard it also. They slowed and quieted.

Then Jason began to creep forward.

Finally, a man wearing a Native American mask—just like the one left at the clinic—came into view. He held a bow and arrow in his hands.

It was him. The killer.

As his gaze shifted, he spotted Mariella.

She stood there looking terrified.

Near the edge of the cliff.

She was on a ledge.

One wrong move and she would go over.

They would need to proceed very carefully.

Because they couldn't risk something happening to Mariella.

Mariella stared at the man. "Who are you?"

She wasn't sure why she thought if she kept him talking that it might help the situation.

Maybe she was just delaying her death.

That delay caused more and more fear to swell in her until her throat nearly felt as if it was closed.

As hard as she tried, she couldn't get a deep breath. Her arms trembled—and not from the cold either.

"Tlatoani chose you as the sacrifice. I don't know why he does the things he does. I'm just his humble servant, and I do what he asks for the sake of the town. I'm the protector, though no one in the area would understand that. They don't understand how many disasters have been averted because of my actions. It is better that way. Tlatoani told me that himself."

"Do I know you?" Mariella stared at him still, wanting to step back.

Wanting to run.

But she didn't dare.

She was trapped.

"It's not important who I am."

She stared at that mask, fear trickling down her spine.

She needed to try a different tactic, she realized.

She knew that she'd have to tap into her acting skills tonight. But she never thought it would be in this way.

She stared at the man. "I'm going to die anyway. Why not show me? I want to know who's protecting this beautiful area. You deserve recognition."

He paused a moment before saying, "That's right. I *do*. But I fear no one will understand me."

"Try me. I can appreciate these things. It's why I came here."

"Yes, you are inquisitive."

Wait . . . did that mean Mariella had talked to this man before?

She tried to make sense of things. To keep him talking. To buy some time.

"Before I'm sacrificed, I need to know who you are as the Chosen One. It will help me feel more at peace with my place in all of this. You understand that, don't you? I need to understand . . . just like you need to be understood."

Finally, he reached for the mask.

Slipped it off.

She nearly stumbled backward.

The face Mariella saw staring back at her was the last one she'd expected to see.

JASON STARED AT THE MAN, his pulse racing out of control.

Was that . . . Roy? From the library?

He was the one behind all of this?

Why? Why would he do this?

He glanced at Duke on one side and Pops on the other. Ranger seemed to have disappear into the shadows.

Without saying a word, they all silently agreed to stay where they were.

Especially since Roy had a bow and arrow in hand.

"I had no idea," Mariella said, her voice trembling.

"No one does."

"I still don't understand." She wobbled as she stood close to the ledge. "You don't even appear to be Native American."

Had Roy given her that drug again? The one he laced some kind of dart with?

Because she looked unstable. Her eyes looked glazed.

But somehow she managed to hold herself together.

Jason prayed that would remain the case.

"My mother married a man from Mexico. He taught me the importance of the Aztecs, the natives of this continent."

"He really had an effect on you." Mariella was keeping him talking.

Good.

Because timing was going to be everything right now.

"He was a brilliant man who taught me to be at one with nature. He changed my life."

"Why did you come here instead of staying wherever you grew up?"

"I wanted to see the world. To learn from other civilizations. Tlatoani guided me. He led me here and told me this was where I could do the most good."

"The most good being . . . sacrificing others?"

"It was the only way to protect the land. Human sacrifice. You may say it's barbaric, but the military uses the technique all the time. People die so more can be saved. Sometimes, it's just the way it has to be."

Jason felt a chill creep down his spine. This guy really believed what he was saying.

He thought these murders were noble. That some unseen god was directing his actions.

Sure, Jason believed in God. Maybe some people thought he was crazy for doing so.

But this was different.

"Now I need to finish what I started." Roy shifted.

He dipped his chin slightly. Notched an arrow and drew it back.

At that close range, Mariella didn't stand a chance.

Mariella saw Roy pull back the bowstring.

The ground might have stopped shaking.

But the world still wobbled around her.

That drug he'd given her put her at an extreme disadvantage.

One wrong step could send her toppling.

She had to try to stay focused. To keep her wits, despite her spinning thoughts.

Roy aimed the arrow at her heart.

She knew these were her last moments.

If I had had more time, I would have done better.

I'm sorry for those I've let down.

God, I'm sorry for letting You down.

She braced herself, waiting to feel the pain.

As soon as she did, she'd fall back.

If the arrow didn't kill her, the fall would.

But just then, a movement in the woods caught her eye.

Someone emerged from the shadows.

Was that . . . ?

Mariella sucked in a breath. "Jason?"

Roy turned slightly, looking over his shoulder. "I knew you were going to be trouble. Tlatoani warned me. I tried to get you out of the way. It appears I might be too late. The purge has begun."

Just then the ground rumbled yet again.

Mariella thought the growling earth was real, at least.

She braced herself, unsure if she could keep her balance and remain upright.

Roy shifted, and the arrow released, just missing her.

"Mariella!" Jason ran toward her. Grabbed her arm.

Yanked her away from the ledge.

Away from Roy.

The two of them collided and tumbled back into the trees.

Duke, Ranger, and Pops surrounded them in a protective shield.

As she glanced up, the cliff let out a war cry before eroding.

The ground beneath Roy crumbled.

He dropped out of sight.

He was gone . . .

She froze as shock washed over her.

Could this be over?

They all remained frozen as if waiting to see if anything else would happen.

It didn't.

In fact, an eerie quiet seemed to settle over the area.

Almost as if nature was signaling that it was all over.

At once, reality hit her.

The arrow missed its mark.

She was alive.

Roy had tried to sacrifice her. But the tremors threw him off-balance.

Then the abyss swallowed him, a victim of his own darkness.

"Did he hurt you?" Jason asked.

He hovered on top of her, shielding her from any more harm.

Even with his injured ribs.

Her heart drummed quicker at the realization.

She stared up at him, nearly breathless. "You came for me."

"Of course I did." He cradled the side of her face with his hand. "Are you okay?"

She nodded. "Now I am."

Their gazes caught. The next instant, he pressed his lips into hers.

Fire rushed through her.

The motion was quick—but enough to make her feel like she was soaring.

Just as quickly, Duke, Ranger, and Pops moved in. They helped both of them to their feet.

"You sure you're okay?" Duke studied her face.

Mariella nodded. "I'm fine. Thanks to all of you."

Duke paced toward the cliff and carefully peered over.

Then he walked back to them. "I don't see him anywhere. I don't think there's any way he survived."

Jason wrapped an arm around her shoulders. "Let's get you back to the chief and tell her what happened. But I'm pretty sure she has her hands full right now with everything that happened in town."

Mariella leaned into Jason, grateful for his presence.

That could have turned out so much differently.

So much differently.

chapter
sixty-eight

SUNDAY NIGHT, everyone gathered at Jason's house.

They'd been invited over to try some of his father's smoked salmon.

As soon as Mariella had set foot on the property, she'd smelled the smoky aroma and her stomach rumbled.

She couldn't wait to sink her teeth in.

"I'm going to go see if Mr. Somersby needs help," Simmy said.

"I'll go with you," Ranger said.

"Let's go say hello, then we can practice some of those self-defense moves we talked about," Duke told Matthew.

"Sounds good to me." Matthew shrugged.

Andi grinned as she glanced around. "And I'm going to make myself scarce also. But sometime soon we need to chat about our next case. Steven Calderson is anxious to talk to us."

Steven was on death row for a crime he claimed he didn't commit. And he wanted their help.

The whole gang needed to sit down and figure out what they were going to do.

But they wouldn't do that now.

Right now, it was time to celebrate.

Then she saw Jason standing on the wooden porch.

He walked toward her, a slight limp to his steps. But that was probably because of the pain in his ribs.

A lot had happened since the earthquake. Thankfully, there were no casualties other than Roy. A few houses had been damaged and were currently being assessed.

But it could have been much worse.

So much worse.

Everything was a blur.

Rescuers had retrieved Roy's body. Confirmed he was dead.

Chief Dunne had sent officers to Roy's place where they'd discovered a greenhouse where he was growing Turbina corymbosa. He also had numerous bows and arrows, dozens of masks, feathers, blow guns, darts, and other pieces of evidence that pointed to his fixation with the Aztecs.

The chief had confirmed that his stepfather was indeed from Mexico and believed to have Aztecan roots. That was where his fascination had begun. They'd been able to track down Roy's mother, who'd filled in some parts.

Before Roy's stepfather died, he'd passed the torch. He'd told Roy it was his job to guard the land.

The loss had been devastating to Roy—and he'd taken the anointment seriously.

Very seriously.

It had only grown from there.

The man was a naturalist. He'd learned how to study nature and animals in order to sense when tragedies might strike.

He'd indeed known by watching the animals that something would happen.

From the sounds of it, he'd truly believed that if he'd been able to sacrifice Mariella that the town would have been spared.

His intentions might have been honorable. But his methods were sick and twisted.

And the different voices he'd used . . . they all made sense now. The man was a natural storyteller. Mariella had heard him talking to children at the town festival.

She just hadn't put it together in time.

As soon as Jason reached Mariella, he paused in front of her.

Everyone else seemed to quickly disappear to give them a moment.

A moment was just what she wanted.

Because she'd had no time with Jason since all of this happened.

It had been a rush of being questioned and examined and assessing the earthquake damage.

"I'm so glad you're okay," Jason said.

She squeezed his forearm. "And I'm so glad that you're okay. In case I haven't said it yet, thank you for coming for me."

"I'm only sorry you got wrapped up in the whole mess."

"I'm hoping since the real killer has been discovered, the town will realize how unfair they've been to you."

Jason nodded slowly. "Me too. My father got his boat slip back, so that's a good start."

"His boat slip?"

He explained what had happened.

The injustice of it all made her heart hurt.

They stared at each other, and there was so much more that Mariella wanted to say. She just didn't know where to start.

Before she could speak, she heard a vehicle coming down the road.

She tensed, halfway expecting to see more trouble show up, even though she knew Roy was dead.

Instead, it was Chief Dunne.

She had someone with her.

Bright.

He stepped out of the car and slowly approached her as if uncertain how she would respond. Guilt marred his features, making his shoulders look drawn and his expression pinched.

He paused in front of her. "I was hoping to find you here."

Jason stepped back. "I can go."

Mariella grabbed his hand. "No. Stay. Please."

Jason let out a breath as if relieved at her response.

"I heard you were looking for me." Bright shifted awkwardly in front of her.

"And I heard you were arrested."

"I told the chief I'd talk—but only if I could see you first." He studied her face, something swirling in his gaze. "You were asking me . . . if I knew about the missing twins. Are you my daughter? You . . . you look like the spitting image of Phyllis. I don't know why I didn't see it sooner."

"That's what I've been trying to figure out. What happened on the day the twins disappeared? What was your involvement in it?" Bright being involved was the only conclusion she'd been able to draw.

He ran a hand over his face, his features strained. "It's a long story. But I got myself into quite a bit of debt, and I became desperate. I'm not proud of my actions."

"We were never kidnapped, were we?" she asked. "You sold us."

He hung his head as shame seemed to capture every motion. "They promised me you would be put with a good family."

"But you never checked to see if that was true?" More disgust rose inside her.

He shook his head. "I couldn't bring myself to do so."

"I can't believe you'd put your wife—my mother—through that kind of heartache."

"It wasn't something I'd planned to do. Not at first. If I could go back . . ." He ran a hand over his face again.

"I'd like to have a blood test done," Mariella stated, keeping her voice neutral. She didn't want to sound as if she was promising anything—a future relationship or even that he'd get a Christmas card.

A blood test would merely be a formality.

A final answer.

Bright nodded. "I can do that."

"But it's going to be really hard to get to know you—if we choose to do that—when you're in jail."

Bright shook his head again, more agony flooding into his gaze. "I never wanted any of this. Someone on one of my charter fishing tours told me about some gold up in the mountains. I thought maybe if I just had a little more money that everything would be okay. My sorrows would disappear. So I went up there, and I actually found it. But it was buried deep in the ground. I got some guys I met to help me in return for part of the profit. I never imagined it would lead to this."

She'd heard he was facing federal charges since the property officially belonged to the government. Things weren't looking good for his future, but he'd done it to himself.

"Tell me this . . . did my parents know that Matthew and I were abducted or sold on the black market or whatever you want to call it?" Mariella held her breath as she waited for his answer.

Bright shook his head. "They had no idea. As far as they're concerned it was a clean adoption."

But Mariella wondered if that was true. Her parents were smart. Had they ever suspected there was more to it? Or had they simply turned the other way and hoped for the best?

That was something Mariella would have to work out later.

At that moment, Chief Dunne rolled down her window. "It's time."

Bright nodded and glanced at Mariella one more time. "I'm sorry." Then he looked at Jason. "I'm sorry to you too. My actions have hurt a lot of people."

Neither Mariella nor Jason said anything.

What else was there to say?

But she did have to wonder . . . who had sent her that message leading her here?

There was only one person that came to mind.

Alpine.

She had a feeling he'd never admit it. But something about him made her think that he liked to toy with people.

That he liked to flex his power in subtle ways.

Or maybe even that he wanted something to happen to her that would lead her into his arms. What if she was the one thing he wanted that he couldn't have?

Was any of that true?

Mariella really had no idea. She was sure if she asked him he'd deny it.

But the theory still lingered in her mind.

Right now, she needed to figure out a way to let Matthew know about this gut-wrenching update on their past. She glanced back at him and saw him with Duke learning some self-defense moves in the backyard.

He glanced at her in curiosity, and she plastered on a smile, trying to let him know everything was okay.

For a little while longer.

Then she knew his whole world would be shattered.

She didn't look forward to being the one to break the news.

She would wait until today was over.

It had already been so much.

For now, she and Jason needed to get back to the rest of the gang.

Chief Dunne did a U-turn on the narrow road and then pulled to a stop near them. With her window still rolled down, and her gaze on Jason, she said, "I know this doesn't mean much, but I'm sorry. I was convinced . . ." Her voice cracked as she tried to find the words.

"I'm sorry too," Jason said.

The two of them looked at each other another moment. Finally, Chief Dunne nodded and put her window back up before pulling away.

It was a start, at least. But it would take a long time to repair the damage that had been done.

Mariella let out a long breath. She needed to talk to the rest of the gang and figure out if they were still going to be able to meet the next weekend to talk about their regularly scheduled podcast.

There was still so much to work out.

Right now, she glanced up at Jason. "It sounds like I may need to come back to town as I try to sort through everything with Bright."

"I understand how difficult that might be for you. But on the positive side, I would love to see you as often as possible."

She grinned. "I would love to see you also."

He stepped closer, his gaze softening. "Thank you for standing by me. That really means a lot."

"Of course." She raised her head toward him. "We all deserve the benefit of the doubt."

A grin stretched across his lips. "Yes, we all do. Thanks for reminding me of that."

The next moment, he leaned down and gently brushed his lips against hers.

His kiss held the promise of many more.

But not now.

For now, he took her hand and led her back to the

house.

"I can't wait for you to try this smoked salmon," he murmured. "It's out of this world."

Her lips tugged up in a smile. "It sounds like the perfect highlight for my travel podcast on Salmon-by-the-Sea."

~~~

Thank you so much for reading *The Dead of Night*. If you enjoyed this book, please consider leaving a review.

Coming next: *Leave the Lights On*.
~~~

you also may enjoy:

fog lake suspense

Edge of Peril

When evil descends like fog on a mountain community, no one feels safe. After hearing about a string of murders in a Smoky Mountain town, journalist Harper Jennings realizes a startling truth. She knows who may be responsible—the same person who tried to kill her three years ago. Now Harper must convince the cops to believe her before the killer strikes again. Sheriff Luke Wilder returned to his hometown, determined to keep the promise he made to his dying father. The sleepy tourist area with a tragic past hadn't seen a murder in decades—until now. Keeping the community safe seems impossible as darkness edges closer, threatening to consume everything in its path. As The Watcher grows desperate, Harper and Luke must work together in order to defeat him. But the peril around them escalates, making it clear the killer will stop at nothing to get what he wants.

Margin of Error

Some secrets have deadly consequences. Brynlee Parker thought her biggest challenge would be hiking to Dead Man's Bluff and fulfilling her dad's last wishes. She never thought she'd witness two men being viciously murdered while on a mountainous trail. Even worse, the deadly predator is now hunting her. Boone Wilder wants nothing to do with Dead Man's Bluff, not after his wife died there. But he can't seem to mind his own business when a mysterious out-of-towner burst into his camp store in a frenzied panic. Something—or someone—deadly is out there. The killer's hunger for blood seems to be growing at a brutal pace. Can Brynlee and Boone figure out who's behind these murders? Or will the hurts and secrets from their past not allow for even a margin of error?

Brink of Danger

Ansley Wilder has always lived life on the wild side, using thrills to numb the pain from her past and escape her mistakes. But a near-death experience two years ago changed everything. When another incident nearly claims her life, she turns her thrill-seeking ways into a fight for survival. Ryan Philips left Fog Lake to chase adventure far from home. Now he's returned as the new fire chief in town, but the slower paced life he seeks is nowhere to be found. Not only is a wildfire blazing out of control, but a malicious killer known as "The Woodsman" is enacting crimes that appear accidental. Plus, there seems to be a strange connection with these incidents and his best friend's little sister, Ansley Wilder. As a killer watches their every move and the forest fire threatens to destroy their scenic town, both Ryan and Ansley hover on the brink of danger. One wrong move could send them tumbling over the edge . . . permanently.

Line of Duty

Jaxon Wilder didn't plan on returning home to Fog Lake, Tennessee, following his tour of duty in Iraq. But after a gut-wrenching failure during his stint in the Army, he now faces a new challenge: his family. Abby Brennan always did her best to be the good girl and to live by the rules. When a wrong decision changes her entire life, she tries to hide from the world. However, a madman known as the Executioner is determined to find her and enact his own brand of justice. When Jaxon and Abby are thrown together in the killer's crosshairs, they're forced to depend on one another to survive. Will Jaxon's sense of duty be enough to help keep Abby safe? Or will deadly secrets lead to the penalty of death?

Legacy of Lies

The justice system failed her family—and so did her hometown. Madison Colson knows deep down that her father—a convicted serial killer—is innocent. But believing it and proving it are two entirely different things.

Unable to help her father, Madison has spent most of her adult life overcompensating by helping others. When her aunt dies unexpectantly, duty calls her back to Fog Lake, Tennessee, a beautiful but painful place she'd rather forget. Terrifying events begin to unfold once she arrives, unleashing her worst nightmares. The Good Samaritan Killer—or a copycat—is back, and now Madison Colson is his target. FBI Special Agent Shane Townsend is determined to stop the deadly rampage that has sent the tightknit community into a frenzy. But he needs to earn Madison's trust first. The task feels impossible, especially considering his father is the one who put her dad in prison. With the whole town on edge and pointing fingers, tension escalates out of control. Madison and Shane must sort the facts from the lies—and fight for a legacy of truth—before The Good Samaritan Killer has the final say.

Secrets of Shame

A killer has a promise to keep . . . Attorney Isaac Colson only wants to put his tumultuous past in Fog Lake behind him and return to his life in Memphis. But when an ominous text threatens that he must come back or there will be deadly consequences, he knows he can't take any chances. Rebecca Moreno has only ever loved one man—her high school sweetheart, Isaac Colson. But when his dad went to prison for murder, Rebecca's father forbade them from seeing each other again. Years later,

Isaac is back in town and old feelings are stirring. But Rebecca is harboring a secret that could change everything. When The Good Samaritan Killer strikes again, guilt pummels her. She has to tell Isaac the truth. But as events unfold, she has more to lose than ever. Isaac and Rebecca must find answers—their lives depend on it. But everyone seems to have secrets, each that forms an obstacle to finding the truth . . . and to staying alive.

Refuge of Redemption

Home is a place of refuge—unless it's a killer's playground. For years, Bear Colson has been known as the serial killer's son. But now, someone else is behind bars for the crimes his father was accused of committing. Bear wants to believe hope for a brighter future is in sight, but he has reason to suspect more than one killer was involved. Forensic photographer Piper Stephens' career crashed and burned when she trusted the wrong man. Now, after discovering an alarming secret about the infamous Good Samaritan Killer, she sets out to find both answers and redemption. But things go awry when her assistant becomes the next victim. As fear batters Fog Lake residents once again, Bear and Piper join forces to track down the truth. But the killer is determined to remain in the shadows—and he'll destroy anyone who stands in his way.

about the author

USA Today has called Christy Barritt's books "scary, funny, passionate, and quirky."

Christy writes both mystery and romantic suspense novels that are clean with underlying messages of faith. Her books have sold more than four million copies and have won the Daphne du Maurier Award for Excellence in Suspense and Mystery, have been twice nominated for the Romantic Times Reviewers' Choice Award, and have finaled for both a Carol Award and Foreword Magazine's Book of the Year.

She is married to her Prince Charming, a man who thinks she's hilarious—but only when she's not trying to be. Christy is a self-proclaimed klutz, an avid music lover who's known for spontaneously bursting into song, and a road trip aficionado.

When she's not working or spending time with her family, she enjoys singing, playing the guitar, and exploring small, unsuspecting towns where people have no idea how accident-prone she is.

Find Christy online at:
www.christybarritt.com
www.facebook.com/christybarritt
www.twitter.com/cbarritt

Sign up for Christy's newsletter to get information on all of her latest releases here: **www.christybarritt.com/newsletter-sign-up/**

 facebook.com/AuthorChristyBarritt
 x.com/christybarritt
 instagram.com/cebarritt